W9-BYL-536

[Outtakes from a Marriage]

Also by Ann Leary

. . .

An Innocent, a Broad

Outtakes [from a] Marriage

[a novel]

Ann Leary

Shaye Areheart Books
NEW YORK

This is a work of fiction. Names, characters, places, and incidents either are the product of the author's imagination or are used fictitiously. Any resemblance to actual persons, living or dead, events, or locales is entirely coincidental.

Published in the United States by Shaye Areheart Books, an imprint of the Crown Publishing Group, a division of Random House, Inc., New York.
www.crownpublishing.com

Shaye Areheart Books with colophon is a registered trademark of Random House, Inc.

Library of Congress Cataloging-in-Publication Data
Leary, Ann.
Outtakes from a marriage: a novel / Ann Leary. —1st ed.
p. cm.
1. Actors' spouses—Fiction. 2. Adultery—Fiction. 3. Upper East Side (New York, N.Y.)—Fiction. 4. Domestic fiction. I. Title.
PS3612.E238O98 2008
813'.6—dc22 2007046004

ISBN 978-0-307-40587-6

Printed in the United States of America

Design by Lynne Amft

10 9 8 7 6 5 4 3 2 1

First Edition

For Devin, with love

[Outtakes from a Marriage]

First of all, he's a Joe.

Dad warned me about this. A different kind of dad might have said, upon first meeting his daughter's fiancé, something along the lines of, "Seems like a nice enough fellow." Or, "What does he do for work?" My dad chatted with us for a few moments that April morning in 1987 when we drove all the way up to the Cape to give him the happy news, then he pulled me aside to offer an urgent, intervention-minded critique. "He's a Joe if I ever saw one," he grumbled, squinting off at some indiscernible point down his dead-end, crushed-shell road. You could tell it pained him to have to say it. He stroked his thick nose with the crook of his finger in an effort to conceal his words.

"He's a real Joe," he emphasized again, wincing slightly, and just like most Neds are thoughtful and Jakes tend to be sly, Davids smart and Jacks funny, Joes, according to Dad, are a handful.

He's a Joe and he's a Leo, he's part Italian and, if that weren't enough, he's starring in a television show. A Joe with his own show is a lethal combination. I see that now, of course, but back then, when I was still in the blinking, gushing, smitten stage of our relationship, I wasn't alarmed or annoyed by Dad's dire admonition, his superstitious "nameology," as my brother Neil used to call it. I was thrilled. *He's a Joe!* I told myself. *I've got myself a real Joe!* And he didn't have a show then, and nobody but Dad gave a shit what his name was, and truth be told, I didn't find him much of a handful at all until many years later, when he was almost out of my grasp.

Now Dad has more or less lost touch with reality. He lives at the VA hospital in Bedford, Mass. He's got Alzheimer's with a little wet brain thrown in. But even though he usually forgets who the kids and I are, he always remembers Joe.

"Joe Ferraro," he says when he catches a glimpse of him on the TV at the VA home, where he's known to his nurses not as Ralph Manning, but as Joseph Ferraro's father-in-law.

"A real Joe, the son of a bitch," my father says. And he knows one when he sees one.

[one]

Joseph Ferraro."

The two words rose above the restaurant din from one of the tables behind me, rose up and out of the dull white drone of late-night chatter and the chink of fork upon china and the distant half-drowned tracks of a forgotten Hindi-jazz CD. Had they been any other two words, they might have become part of the ambient clamor that surrounds each table at Pastis like a protective garment, allowing its occupants to speak of love or desire or deals or just to leisurely gossip, as Karen Metzger and I had been doing for the past five minutes. It was Wednesday night at Pastis, we were celebrating Joe's Golden Globe nomination with the Metzgers, and the guys had gone outside for a smoke.

"This is amazing, Julia, you have to try it," Karen said. She was hacking away at a mound of hard hazelnut ice cream. "Here. Try it," she said, tapping the plate with the tip of her spoon. Then she carved out one more little bite for herself.

"I just saw him, he's standing outside smoking. Right outside the door." It was the same man's voice behind me, eager and disbelieving.

"I know. We saw that guy, but we don't think it's him. He looks too small." This was a girl. A tipsy girl. And young, that was clear. She divided the word *small* into two syllables and then dropped the second syllable an octave, just the way my daughter, Ruby, and her friends did when they spoke to one another.

"Everybody looks smaller in real life," said the guy. "Ever seen Tom Cruise? Guy's a dwarf. Ever seen Al Pacino, Sean Penn? Pygmies!"

I shot Karen a look of startled amusement but she hadn't heard him. She was shaving tawny ice-cream crescents onto her spoon and reexamining, in a tone that was rising with shrill indignation, the "perfect storm" that had swept her husband Brian's just-released film to the bottom of the box-office charts, where it clung, battered by reviewers, looking for a dignified and timely route to next season's DVD releases.

"The studio was out to lunch on this one," Karen said. "And Sophie Wilkes just can't act. A director can only do so much."

"I don't know, I think she's all right," I said. "Everybody liked her in that movie about the teacher. Didn't she win the Oscar?"

"That was a fluke. She's awful. Why aren't you eating this?" Karen pushed the ice-cream plate to my side of the table and then she stared at it, wistfully.

"Go ahead," I said. "I like it when it's a little melted." I slid the plate back to her. "Can I use your phone?" My phone was in my purse, dead.

Karen took one last swipe at the ice cream and then she plunged her arm up to her elbow into the oversized Balenciaga tote that hung from the back of her chair. She probed the depths of that two-thousand-dollar handbag, biting her lip and staring straight ahead, and I was reminded of a young English veterinarian I had recently seen on a television show, struggling to extract an unborn calf from the womb of its desperate mother.

"I can use Joe's phone when he comes back," I offered.

Karen frowned for a moment, thrusting her arm slightly deeper, and I could see the bulge of her knuckles as they rolled along the supple leather walls of the bag. There was the muffled tumbling of keys and coins and then she extracted the phone triumphantly.

"And I told Brian not to cast Gregory Mason. He's just too gay. Nobody believes him when he plays a romantic lead." Karen held the phone at arm's length and squinted at the screen. Then she handed it to me.

"Greg Mason's gay?"

"Julia . . . yes. Everybody knows this."

"Wait. I know somebody who dated him. A girl."

"Nonetheless. Giant fag."

"No . . ." I said, laughing helplessly, but Karen interrupted me. "When they were shooting the scenes in Thailand, Greg had a parade of local working boys wandering in and out of his trailer every day. Ask Brian!" she said when I gave her a look. "And listen to this. We invited him out to Southampton one weekend and he brought tasteful gifts for me, the kids . . . even the dog." Karen was whispering now because Joe and Brian were heading back to the table.

"What straight man is *that* thoughtful?" she murmured as I began to punch out my phone number.

"Well, I hear Tim Robbins is thoughtful. . . ."

"Julia . . . Gregory Mason brought an Hermès collar for Waffles."

My thumb gleefully hit the last four numbers. An Hermès collar for poor old Waffles!

The Nextel recording prompted me to enter my security code, and as I tapped it in, I watched Brian and Joe make their way through the crowded room. I recall, now, that Joe wore his "Yes, it's me" expression—a shy half-smile, his gaze fixed just above the nudges and hungry glances that carried him along like a gentle wave. From behind me the man said, "I toldja! Joe Ferraro," and then Joe Ferraro himself, grinning broadly now, slid into the chair beside me.

"Jesus Christ, we could hear you girls cackling all the way outside."

"I love it," said Karen. "We *were* cackling, Julia, like a pair of witches."

"A pair of well-toned witches," said Brian.

"I prefer sorceress," I said, kissing Joe on the lips. "Somehow it sounds so much more attractive than witch."

"They both sound evil. And sexy," said Joe. "Who are you calling?"

"My voice mail. I just want to see if Ruby or Catalina called. . . ." I stopped talking then because the first message was playing.

"Hi, babe," said a woman's voice.

Who? The voice was Southern, I knew that at once. Just from those two words I knew.

"Thanks for the message. I can't believe you had to ask if I'm happy, baby, you know I am. Where are you, Joey?"

Who?

I leaned away from Joe and he raised an eyebrow. "Everything all right?"

I nodded slowly, listening.

"I want to see you, babe."

"Is it Catalina?" Joe asked, and I nodded again, still listening.

Joe turned to Karen and Brian. "You know, the first night Catalina babysat for us we thought she stole Ruby?"

"I'm horny as a motherfucker," said my mysterious confessor.

My face burned. I felt waves of what must have been blood and adrenaline surging across my chest, shooting upward and then pounding against the top of my head. I was vaguely aware that Joe had launched into his "how we thought Catalina stole Ruby" anecdote. It's one of his favorites.

"We never left Ruby with a sitter before that night because we were completely broke," Joe began, and he shot me a little smile as he always did when recalling something from the days when we couldn't eat at places like this, couldn't afford cell phones or babysitters, couldn't really even afford a baby—though we had gone ahead and had one, anyway.

". . . and Julia was out of her mind with anxiety about leaving her."

It's true. In those days, we either stayed home or took Ruby out with us. But when she was almost a year old, Joe got his first starring role in an off-Broadway show and I wanted to go to opening night. So I asked Carlos, our super, if he knew any experienced babysitters.

"Somebody honest and reliable and caring" is what I told Carlos, but what I was thinking was, *Somebody who won't smack the baby, or steal the baby, or hurl the baby against the wall in a crack-induced frenzy.* Carlos recommended his sister Catalina, who looked nice enough when she arrived. She was a short, middle-aged woman with an enormous bosom and a warm, shy smile. Her English wasn't great then, and this is the part of the story where Joe likes to announce that although I had boasted for years about speaking conversational Spanish, it turned out only to be true if the conversation is limited to greeting words. After saying *hola* and *cómo estás,* Catalina and I just stood there grinning nervously at each other.

"Miss, where is the baby?" Catalina finally asked, and then she laughed with delight when she saw Ruby smiling up at us from her high chair behind me. For some reason I had been blocking her from Catalina's view with my body.

"¡Que linda!" she exclaimed, clapping her hands and winking at Ruby, and Ruby laughed and clapped her hands along with Catalina. She *is* linda, I thought to myself. How can we go out and leave our beautiful, *linda* daughter here with a complete stranger? But we did leave her there. We left her laughing and clapping with Catalina, and although I tried to get Ruby's attention as we walked out the door, she didn't seem to notice we were leaving.

"I like that the babysitter is older," I said to Joe in what I hoped was a breezy, casual tone on the way down in the elevator. I was clutching the handrail and forcing myself to breathe. *She's not a stranger. She's Carlos's sister.*

"She seems nice," said Joe. And then he stepped right up behind me and pulled me close, his arms traversing my chest and his face buried deep in the curve of my neck. "I'm really, really fuckin' nervous," he whispered into my hair, and I said, shakily, "I know. Me too."

Joe stiffened then and said, "I mean I'm nervous about the show."

"I know," I lied. "Me too."

After the show, there was a cast party at a bar on Bleecker Street, and I walked over with Joe's agent, Simon. Joe arrived a little later with the cast and it was a great party. A grown-up party! I hadn't been out at night in ages, and now here I was with people who talked about things like auditioning and making art and finding a drummer for their band. Nobody talked about weaning and Ferberizing babies, everybody raved about Joe's performance, and I was having the time of my life. Within minutes I was doing things I hadn't done in ages—flirting, smoking, drinking—and it was a good hour before I told Joe that I wanted to call Catalina and check on the baby.

"I'll call," said Joe, and he found a pay phone in the back. I watched him dial the number, and then the man next to me started talking about Joe. It was somebody from the *New York Times.* The *Times*! I introduced Joe when he returned, and after he talked to the writer for a minute, he turned to me and said, "We have to go."

"Everything all right?" I asked, and Joe said, "Sure," but when we went outside and got into a cab, he told me that nobody had answered the phone when he called. He had called twice. No answer.

"Now, don't freak out," Joe said. "I'm sure they're fine."

I was bent over, jackknifed, hugging my knees, breathing in . . . and out.

"Maybe they went out for a walk," Joe said, and I considered this. I thought about Catalina putting Ruby in her stroller. I imagined Catalina and Ruby riding the elevator down to the lobby and then casually strolling outside, where Catalina would place baby Ruby in a van driven by men wearing masks. I thought about Ruby crying for me as they drove across the Triborough Bridge to . . . who knew where . . . dark, wretched baby-selling lands . . . Ruby and Catalina and the men wearing masks.

Breathing in . . . and . . . out.

But Catalina didn't sell Ruby! When we threw open the door of our apartment, we found Catalina sitting happily on the couch watching Spanish television. Ruby was asleep in her crib. I had unplugged the phone that afternoon while Ruby and I napped and had forgotten to plug it back in. We all laughed with relief over the confusion and Catalina told me about a home remedy she thought I should try for Ruby's cough. Something to do with honey and milk and warm, weak tea that she had used for her own children when they were babies in Nicaragua. Now I thought about Catalina as we sat there crowded around that cluttered table at Pastis, Karen and Brian and Joe and me. I thought about how I had wanted to climb into Catalina's lap that night thirteen years ago, how I had wanted to climb into her lap and be cradled in her plump arms like a baby. In my ear was *horny* this and *motherfucker* that.

This girl is young, I thought. *Just listen to the mouth on her.*

If I had charged my phone the night before that dinner with the Metzgers—if I had made it a habit to *just plug it in each night,* as Joe had repeatedly advised me, I might never have heard her breathy sex talk, that fresh, foul purr that poured into my ear like contaminated runoff. And who knows, I might have gone on forever like that. Unaware. But I hadn't charged my phone. Instead, I left it in that old red nylon bag—that ugly old red bag that hung from the back of Sammy's stroller. Just left it there, turned on, until the wallpaper photograph of Joe's smiling face on the screen slowly faded to black.

For the record, I didn't mean to dial Joe's number that night. It was an accident, I don't care what Joe says. It was out of habit—I called Joe a lot, and I rarely dialed my own number. And our cell phone numbers are almost identical. Mine ends with 8804 and his ends with 8803, but it wasn't until that night at Pastis that I discovered we both had the same code to access our messages. The PIN number is what it's called, and 7829 was the number we had used for our ATM cards ever since Ruby was born.

It was RUBY on any keypad.

7829.

It was our daughter's first name, but in numerical form it had become the sentinel for most of the other things we held dear—our wealth, our safety, our privacy. It was my AOL password and my PayPal code, and as Joe's success grew, it was how we accessed our online mutual funds and individual investment accounts. When we bought our beach house, it became the code for the alarm system. Once Sammy was born, I had tried to use his name, 72669, for other codes—it seemed like the fair, impartial thing to do—but I could never remember when to use each child's name, so I used 7829 for everything. I typed it in as my code when Joe's assistant, Catherine, gave me my new cell phone, and apparently that's what Joe typed into his phone, too.

I borrowed Karen's phone again before we left the restaurant. I went to the ladies' room and I dialed Joe's number. I held on to the sink, punched in 7829, and there she was.

"Hi, babe, thanks for the message. I can't believe you had to ask if I'm happy, baby, you know I am. . . ."

Half an hour later, I stood in our kitchen, in the dark. Joe was taking a shower and I tapped out the code one more time.

7829.

My thumb knew exactly where the numbers were. I didn't have to look.

"I'm horny as a motherfucker. . . . I just thought you should know that, baby."

That lilting, sultry voice. Southern, that's for sure. And the mouth on her.

Then, the crisp, automated female voice. My familiar Nextel friend: *"To repeat this message, press eleven."*

11.

"Hi, babe, thanks for the message. I can't believe you had to ask if I'm happy, baby, you know I am. . . ."

"Julia," Joe called from the bedroom, "are you coming to bed or what?"

"Shhh! Joe! You'll wake the kids! I'll be there in a minute."

"To repeat this message, press eleven."

11.

"Hi, babe, thanks for the message. I can't believe you had to ask if I'm happy, baby, you know I am. . . ."

It was 1:33. The digits on the microwave clock emitted a miniature aura—a pale emerald haze that seemed to hang in the air in the dark. The refrigerator hummed lazily and every few seconds the freezer tumbled ice. From the street below came the sound of two raised voices, one singing in a hollow, drunken tone, the other inexplicably yelling, "Hey! . . . Hey!"

"I'm horny as a motherfucker. . . ." said the voice in my ear.

"Hey!" cried the voice from the street. "HEY!"

The Golden Globe nominations had been announced live, on national television, two weeks before our dinner with the Metzgers. The announcement was scheduled for eight-thirty, during the morning news shows, which was the same time that our son, Sammy, was supposed to be at preschool. It was the last day of school before the holidays, and at first I had considered sending Sammy to school with Catalina. Then I decided to take him myself—I wanted to be distracted from the excruciating suspense of it all. This wasn't the first time there was a lot of hype surrounding Joe and his show. The year before, I woke up early and waited three hours for the announcements. All the critics had insisted that Joe deserved it, that he was guaranteed a nomination. Although Joe went off to the gym, so as not to "jinx" himself, I had watched the morning news with a sense of impending glory, the phone on my lap, ready to dial Joe the second his name was called out. I watched the new 007 guy and America's Sweetheart read off the list of nominees, and when they skipped Joe altogether, I honestly thought they had made a mistake. I sat there and watched for several minutes before the network switched back to the regular broadcast and then I made the unhappy call to Joe, but he already knew. He had been running in front of the TV. I imagined his shoulders sagging with disappointment and his feet slowing down on the rushing treadmill when they announced the other nominees, and I wondered if he was carried backward, just for a moment, before he was able to regain his stride. A week later, on Christmas morning, Ruby presented Joe with a Golden Globe award she had made out of papier-mâché, carefully replicating the trophy from a photo she found on Wikipedia. She had painted a bronze-colored plaque on the Styrofoam base and etched in the words "Best Performer in the Role of Father." Joe had displayed it proudly on a bookshelf, where it remained for several months, but at some point it ended up in a toy box (four-year-old Sammy sometimes used it as a sword), and that was the last I saw of it.

This year I had opted for a different tack. Joe wanted to watch the announcements live, and I decided I'd rather be told the news, so we planned to meet for breakfast afterward. I was looking at my menu when he arrived at our favorite neighborhood spot. I wasn't really reading it, just using it as a diverting focal point, and when I glanced up, there he was, a Yankees cap pulled down low over his eyes, moving between tables, ducking around waitresses and waiters.

Christmastime . . . is here, chimed the child-chorus from the recording of *A Charlie Brown Christmas* that the diner had been playing every day for the past week.

A man seated at a nearby table called out, "Hey, Joey Ferraro! How's it goin'?" and Joe nodded at him. "It's going great, man, thanks."

Then he sat down beside me and glanced up from under the brim of his cap, grinning.

"Oh . . . my . . . God," I said slowly, reacting to his grin with my own. I bit my lip, searching his eyes cautiously, but I knew.

"I got it."

"I knew you would!" I cried, and Joe grabbed the seat of my chair and pulled it right up next to his. He kissed me, and when he let me go, I was blinking back tears and laughing.

"I wish I saw them announce it," I said. "I should have had Catalina take Sammy to school. Who else was nominated?"

"I need a coffee. Where's the waitress? I'm starving," said Joe, as if it were just another day, but then he placed his palms down on the table and pushed his shoulders back, causing his chair to tilt up onto its hind legs, and he grinned at the ceiling for a moment. He rocked forward a few seconds later, letting the chair slam back onto all fours, and he beat the table like a bongo drum. "I'm fucking starving."

We ordered our breakfast from Zara, the waitress who had been serving us breakfast for years, and Joe told me about turning on the *Today* show just seconds before his nomination was announced.

"I thought I missed it, but I turned it on and the category they were announcing was for Best Actor, TV Drama. I was the first name they read. Joseph Ferraro. *The Squad*."

"When do we go to L.A.?" I asked.

"I think the show is on January 22. It's a Sunday. We'll probably go out Friday."

"The twenty-second is Dad's birthday," I said. "You know I like to take the kids up to see Dad on his birthday."

"So go see him the weekend after," Joe said. "He won't know the difference."

"Yeah," I said. And it really wouldn't make any difference to Dad. He thought Gerald Ford was the president and that I was married to an astronaut. He told me that the last time I visited, told me how proud he was. I had asked one of the nurses if I should try to correct him when he was confused like that, and she just shrugged and said, "Nah, what's the point? It's easier on everyone if you just go along. Act as if."

By the time Zara brought our eggs, Joe had shut off the ringer on his phone, but it continued to vibrate nonstop, and he would look at the caller ID each time and tell me who was calling without answering. "That's Scott." "It's somebody from the UK." "It must be Frank." "Mom." He smiled each time he checked. "By the way," he said, popping his last crust of toast into his mouth, "Brian Metzger called right after the nominations. He just wrapped that sci-fi movie. They want to have dinner."

"After Christmas," I said, and then I said, "I'm really proud of you, baby."

He nodded, grinning broadly, drumming the table with his palms like a teenager.

[two]

Joe was asleep by the time I finally put the phone down that night. He lay naked on his side with one of his hands, strangely palsied and twisted-looking, curled up under his chin. His dark brown hair fell over his eyes, his mouth hung slightly open, and I realized for the first time that Joe looks quite simian when he sleeps. The lower half of his body had stretched out onto my half of the bed and the wrath inspired by his trespassing genitals and limbs took me by surprise. *Get your disgusting ape legs off my side of the bed,* I thought. I sat down and drove my thumb into Joe's hamstring, and when he mumbled in protest, I said, softly, "Move over, Joe. There's no room."

Somehow I slept. I had closed my eyes and thought, *I'll never get to sleep tonight, never,* and then it was six o'clock the next morning and I discovered that Sammy had crawled into bed beside me sometime during the night. Joe was gone—he'd had a five o'clock call—and now Sammy lay sprawled out, belly up, in his place. Sammy's blond hair formed a feathery halo around his head, and his arms were thrown out to either side as if he had landed there after a long backward free fall. I wrapped my body around my son—a classic Sam (Dad never met one who couldn't look you in the eye)—and the smell of his sweet, damp hair and his freshly laundered pajamas filled me with an aching sense of longing and regret. My youngest, my last child, was no longer a baby. I would never again hold my own sleeping newborn against my shoulder or feel the weighty, sensual anticipation of milk-heavy breasts. My children were getting older—someday they would leave. I was forty, my life was half over, and my husband had found somebody new.

"He's gonna grow up to be a serial killer, you know."

Ruby, our fourteen-year-old, was standing in the doorway in an oversized T-shirt, frowning at the sight of Sammy lying asleep in my bed.

"Good morning, Ruby." I sighed.

"Mom, you have to stop letting him come into your bed every night or he'll develop a narcissistic personality disorder and end up going on a killing spree when he's older."

"Really?" I whispered, carefully climbing out of bed. "Well, you slept in our bed almost every night until you were at least Sammy's age, and you don't seem to be too terribly deranged."

"Um . . . Mom? Could you please stop telling me that? It's really damaging for me to have to visualize myself in the same bed with you and Dad."

"I'll damage you!" I said, and I aimed a fake karate kick at her. I was forcing a laugh now, trying to be fun, but Ruby just scooted out of the way, exhaling a weighty grunt of disapproval.

"Mom! You almost kicked Sammy!"

Ruby considers Sammy as much her child as Joe's and mine, and she spends a great deal of time worrying about, and second-guessing, our behavior toward him. She seems to view herself as some sort of buffer, a human firewall that will, ideally, protect Sammy from the reckless parenting that she feels she has had to endure all these years. She goes to a progressive school that offers a course in psychology to eighth graders, and ever since she started taking the class, she has been telling us how just about everything we do is "damaging" or "undermining" or "demoralizing" to her or to Sammy.

When people first meet our family they often comment on the age discrepancy between our two children. "Decided to start all over again, huh?" they'll ask, as if suddenly, after ten years, we decided it was time to produce another child. It's taken for granted that Sammy is an afterthought. That we almost forgot to have a second baby. In fact, we didn't forget. In fact, after Ruby, there were three other pregnancies and three miscarriages and then, finally, there was Sammy, whom we didn't really trust or believe in until I held him in my arms, all slimy, breathing, squalling seven pounds of him, delivered so quickly that we almost didn't make it to the delivery room. "What a lucky mom," Dr. Rajaman said as he casually slid him onto my belly. "Such a short labor!"

And it's true; we felt blessed and just dripping with luck that day at Lenox Hill Hospital. I still remember the way Joe wiped his teary eyes with the palm of his trembling hand when the nurse handed over Sammy, now all clean and swaddled, that round pink face peering seriously up at him. The nurse was giddy and distracted in Joe's presence, and when he thanked her for her help, she giggled and sputtered, "No problem . . . Mr. . . . Ferraro!" Because Joe was famous by the time Sammy was born. It was the end of his first season starring in *The Squad,* NBC's breakout number one show, and for the first time in his career, people called out to him wherever he went and pleaded for autographs when all he wanted to do, he loved to complain to his friends, was buy a pack of cigarettes or take Ruby to the movies.

He had been only a little bit famous when Ruby was born. He

was mostly doing commercials then and was at the level of fractional fame where people would just stare at him, or sometimes waiters and cashiers would say, "Hey, you're that guy!" But usually they wouldn't really know which guy they were talking about. It wasn't until Ruby was in kindergarten and he was doing more supporting roles that people started greeting him like a semiforgotten friend.

"Hey, you're the guy who kidnapped Julia Roberts and then had your ass kicked by Nicolas Cage, man. You're, uhh . . . ," a kid would shout at Joe as we walked by. Joe would smile and nod and then the kid would call out, "Hey, really, who are you, man?" This usually wiped the smile right off Joe's face. You know what really annoyed Joe in those days? The way that many people felt entitled, because of his familiar face, to openly chastise him for his career decisions, as if he could afford back then to not take any job that came his way. Typically, we'd be sitting in a restaurant and a Wall Street–type guy would approach us, smiling apologetically. "My buddies and I know we know you, but we're trying to figure out who you are."

"Is that right?" Joe would mutter.

"Yeah! You're in the movies, right?"

"Right."

"I knew it! What movies have I seen you in?"

Early in his career, when Joe was still wildly flattered at being identified at all, he would actually participate in this type of exchange. He'd begin by listing his favorite film credit, *A Simple Mind,* in which he'd costarred with Ralph Fiennes.

"Is that the one where Ralph Fiennes played the retard?"

"Yeah, I was his teacher!"

"Nope, missed that one. What else have you been in?"

Joe would then begin to painstakingly recite his résumé until he'd finally come across something that the Wall Street guy had seen. This would, inevitably, be the most embarrassing film of Joe's career.

"That's it!" the guy would shout. "*Fraternity of Brothers!* I saw that one! Hey, man, no offense, but that movie was a piece of shit."

"Thank you. Well, nice to meet you."

"He played the psychotic white guy in that Eddie Murphy frat house movie!" the guy would shout over to his friends at the bar. "Hey," he'd then say to Joe, "come over to the bar and meet my buddies. They're big fans, too."

"Actually, we're just leaving."

"Oh, I get it, you think you're too important to meet a few regular guys, don't you?"

At which point we'd pay our bill and leave, but the answer was yes. Yes he did.

"Mom?"

Ruby had pulled the sheet up over Sammy's chubby legs and we were tiptoeing out of the room.

"Yeah?"

"Some lady called last night for Daddy."

"Who?"

"I don't know. She didn't leave her name."

Okay, I told myself, *just take it easy.* Then I said, "What did she sound like? Did she have an accent? What time did she call?"

"I don't know. I think it was someone from the show."

"You do? Why? What'd she sound like?"

"*Mom!* What's the big deal? The only people who call Dad on that line are usually people from the show."

"Okay. Okay." *Change the subject.* "What do you want for breakfast?" I chirped.

The phone. The phone.

"I'm just gonna have a muffin."

Ruby is a vegan, which is, in my mind, just a glamorous way of saying that she hates food. Born a picky eater, she has never liked anything but juice and sweets, but it wasn't until my friend Alison began proselytizing to us all about the poisonous mucus in cow's milk and the antibiotics in meat that any hopes I had of someday feeding Ruby protein were dashed. Early in Ruby's vegan career, Joe and I would have to listen to her gag dramatically at the sight of "that disgusting ground flesh" in the refrigerator. Or, just as we were about to tuck into a delicious steak, we would be treated to seven-year-old Ruby's musings about how our colons were going to cope with "all that animal tissue." Joe finally put his foot down and forbade Ruby to comment on anybody's food but her own, ever, which Ruby has more or less adhered to, limiting her commentary to nonverbal grimaces and retching noises.

Now Ruby picked at her spelt muffin and I tried to focus on her, tried not to stare at the phone that rested on the charger on the counter behind her, recovering from last night's exhaustive overuse. The desire to snatch it up and smuggle it into the bathroom to check Joe's voice mail was almost unbearable. *Had he heard his filthy girlfriend's message? Was she his girlfriend, or could she just be an irksome stalker? But how would she have his number if she was a stalker?*

"Zoe and I want to go out for pizza tonight with some other kids," Ruby was saying. I nodded.

And why did it sound like she was returning his call?

"It's freezing out and we want to take a cab from her house, so can I borrow some money?"

Mmm-hmm, I thought. *Who does he know from the South? She sounded like she was from Texas or Louisiana . . . maybe Georgia?*

"Mom?"

Who the hell was it?

"MOM!"

"What?"

"Jeez, it's no wonder I have intimacy issues."

"Ruby. C'mon. That's really enough. How can a fourteen-year-old have intimacy issues?"

"By having parents who don't pay attention to her," said Ruby.

"I'm sorry. I heard you. How much do you need?" I fumbled in my bag for my wallet.

"Well, I just realized that you owe me ten for babysitting the other night, and if you loan me another ten, that should be enough. Actually, I'll deduct the extra ten from the money you owe me for the two weeks' allowance you forgot to pay me last summer and that time I babysat on a Saturday and you never paid me, so you'll only owe me forty after you give me the twenty."

Ruby has perfected this impenetrable flimflam routine to a science. In normal commerce, when a sum is paid out to another party in the form of a loan, that party is expected to pay back the initial sum, usually with interest. The *borrower* is beholden to the *lender.* Somehow, in our family, this whole tradition has been turned on its head, and whenever I think I'm loaning money to Ruby, the amount of the "loan" ends up being just a drop in the gigantic bucket of debt that I apparently owe her, the detailed account of which she always has at her fingertips.

"Wait a minute," I said, determined not to be made into a chump this time, "you keep talking about that Saturday and I keep paying you for it."

"No, you just keep saying you paid me," said Ruby. "You paid me for the time I bought lunch for Allie and me with my own money because you told us to go out to lunch since you hadn't been to the store, but you never paid me for that Saturday babysitting, and now that I think of it, you never paid me back for the time I paid for my MetroCard with my own money."

"Well, it seems to me that if you're riding the bus with your own body, you should pay for it with your own money."

I knew my error as soon as the words escaped my mouth. Ruby had both barrels loaded for this one.

"Oh, so *now* I have to pay for my own MetroCard? I only use it for transportation to and from school, and my allowance barely covers the cost of one. I'm *sorry* that the school *you chose* is on the other side of town! Nobody I know has to pay for their own MetroCard, but apparently *this* family can't afford for me to take public transportation to school. The next thing I know, you'll have me working as an escort to pay for my tuition!"

"All right, all right. Stop being so dramatic. Daddy and I just want you to understand the value of money, but I don't want to get into a big thing about it this morning. How much do you need for this afternoon?"

"Just the forty."

"Okay," I said, handing her the money with relief.

"Thanks, Mom," said Ruby, kissing me swiftly on my cheek. "Now you only owe me fifty. But tomorrow's Friday, which is allowance day, so you owe me another twenty, but you can pay me later!" Ruby grabbed her backpack, and before the door had closed behind her, I had already dialed Joe's number.

"Hello?"

It was Joe. It hadn't occurred to me that he would now be answering his phone, and I was struck mute.

"Hello?"

I hung up. A moment later the phone rang. I let it ring twice before I answered.

"Hi, honey," I said.

"Hey," Joe said. "Did you just call?"

"Yeah, sorry. I had another call coming in and I thought I was putting you on hold. . . ."

"Oh. What's up?"

"Hmm?"

"Why did you call me?"

"Just wanted to see how your morning is going."

"Oh. Well, it's going good."

"Great!"

"By the way, you gotta call Catherine about getting a dress. Get her on that right away, it's only two weeks from now. . . ."

"Okay. Are we still going to Susanna's party tomorrow night?"

"Yeah, of course. Why?"

"I think I'll buy something to wear, that's all."

"Okay, she told me it's casual. Just a small birthday party. Casual. She said it more than once."

"I know, you've told me more than once."

"I gotta go."

"Okay, bye, hon."

I placed the phone back on the charger. I heard a toilet flush from the other end of the apartment, which meant that Sammy was up. Sure enough, he wandered into the kitchen a moment later.

"Hi, baby," I said.

"Hi, Mommy."

Sammy was smiling up at me with his sleepy, flirty, flushed morning face, which on an ordinary day might have caused me to scoop him up in my arms and cover his face and tummy with kisses.

Instead, I was trying to calculate the exact time that it would take for Joe to go from the makeup trailer to the set. He would have to turn the phone off while he was on set, which is when I would be able to check his messages.

"Mommy, I want pancakes!"

He might have already turned off his phone as soon as he hung up with me. Then again . . .

"Mommy, *pancakes*?"

"Sure, sweetie, Catalina will be here any minute now and she'll make you pancakes." Breakfast was really the only meal I was responsible for anymore, and I was increasingly passing that responsibility on to Catalina.

"Will Catalina take me to school?"

"Uh-huh," I said, smiling enthusiastically. "You know how much Catalina loves to take you to school!"

"I don't want Catalina to take me to school! I want *you* to take me to school!"

"I know, but . . ." I had, of late, also passed on the responsibility of school drop-off to Catalina. I felt guilty. Plus, I realized I needed to get out of the house. "Okay," I said. "I'll take you."

I pulled a carton of orange juice out of the fridge and looked at the clock. It was 7:46. Joe would have to be on the set by now.

"Here's a nice glass of juice. I don't know where Catalina is. Hey, how about a little *SpongeBob*?"

"Yeah!" said Sammy, thrilled that the no-TV-in-the-morning rule had somehow been circumvented. The two of us raced into the family room and I inserted Sammy's favorite DVD into the machine. After handing him the juice, I spun on my heel and flew back to the kitchen. I was like a woman possessed—it took me two attempts to hit the numbers right before it started ringing. *Please don't answer, please don't answer,* I prayed, and my heart soared at the sound of the Nextel recording informing me that the subscriber I was trying to reach was not available. I hastily punched in the access code and just then Catalina walked into the kitchen, all pink-cheeked and out of breath.

"Sorry I'm so late, I—"

I turned so that Catalina could see that I was on the phone, and she mouthed, "Sorry, sorry, sorry," and scurried into the other room, looking for Sammy.

"You have no new or saved messages."

Okay, now I felt that I was getting someplace. Now I had some answers. Joe had heard and erased the message. I had saved the message each time I played it, so now I knew that Joe had heard the message and erased it.

He hadn't saved the message.

Which meant . . . what?

It meant nothing, I realized. Why would he save a message like that? If she were a stalker, he would be annoyed, and if she were a girlfriend, he would feel guilty (one would hope). But here comes the weird part: I felt oddly disappointed that the message had disappeared. She was gone and I was left with only the memory of her crude communiqué, and I wanted more. I wanted more access to the mysteriousness of it all, more clues. I pushed the hang-up button and instantly the phone rang, which caused me to startle and drop the handset onto the floor, where it came apart, sending the batteries rolling across the marble tiles.

"Julia?" Catalina called from the back hall.

"Yeah, it's okay, Catalina, I just dropped the phone."

The batteries had sought refuge under the refrigerator, so I rattled around in my cluttered cabinets for some fresh ones, which I eventually found and jammed, shakily, into the handset. As soon as the second one was laid to rest, the phone rang again and this time I answered it.

"Hey, what's going on?" It was Joe.

"Nothing," I said, trying to sound bored.

"Well, my phone rang, and when I saw it was you, I tried to answer but I got a weird busy signal. . . ."

"Really?"

"Yeah, and when I tried to call back, it rang once and then I was cut off."

"I know. I dropped the phone when I tried to answer it."

"Well, what is it?"

"I just wanted to know if you felt like chicken tonight."

"I guess so. You know I might be working late, right?"

"No . . . I thought since you had the early call this morning . . ."

"Yeah, but we're shooting a stunt sequence that's kind of time consuming, and my stunt double isn't working out so great, so we have to bring another guy in. . . ."

"Okay, just let me know when you have a better idea what time you'll be home," I said briskly, but when we hung up I thought, *Working late, my ass.*

Working late, my big, fat ass.

[three]

The Multicultural Montessori School is located in a brownstone exactly two blocks from our apartment. If you were to read their glossy admissions brochure, you might decide that the Multicultural Montessori School—or "Multi," as many devoted parents refer to it—is the right place for your preschooler because it offers "an enriching, noncompetitive whole learning environment for the whole child." Or you might be interested in the fact that Multi's literacy program allows a child to explore "a whole language approach to literacy development." Or you might, like Joe and me, decide that it's the perfect preschool for your child, solely based on its whole convenient location, a mere two blocks from home.

The summer before Sammy turned three, I was in the playground with Karen Metzger and her friend Abby, when Abby asked where Sammy was going to go to preschool in the fall. "I don't know," I said. "I like the looks of that little Montessori school on Eighty-fourth Street. I think I might want to send him there."

Karen and Abby just stared at me.

"What?" I asked.

"Are you talking about the Multicultural Montessori School?" said Karen.

"Yeah, that's it."

"Have you applied?" Abby asked.

"Not yet," I said. "I guess I should."

Abby and Karen stared at each other for a moment and then they both burst out laughing.

"Julia," Karen said, "everybody applied to preschools last fall. Multi is one of the hardest schools to get into in Manhattan. You actually have to call on the morning after Labor Day—I'm talking about last year—in order to get them to send you an application. It takes all day to get through. How could you not know this?"

"I guess I didn't know it was that . . . organized. It's just a nursery school, for Christ's sake."

Now Karen's amused look had turned into one of deep concern.

"Julia, Multi is a feeder school. Everybody wants their kid to get into that school so that they can get him into the best kindergarten possible. Didn't you go through this with Ruby?"

"No," I said, and I explained that when Ruby was of preschool age we were on location, first in London, next in Nevada, and then we rented a house in Los Angeles while Joe worked on the first season of a sitcom that was never picked up for a second season. Ruby and I went to various Mommy and Me classes, but I never enrolled her in an actual school until we were back in Manhattan, and by that time she was old enough for kindergarten.

"Nobody made a big deal about Ruby not having attended preschool when we applied to Walton," I told Abby and Karen, "and she got in, no problem." I couldn't help feeling slightly defensive about the whole thing. Karen had always presented herself as the expert on all things related to parenting, which really irked me because she was the mother of five-year-old twins. I was the one with fourteen years' experience. So why did I feel like a perpetual novice?

The first time I pushed Ruby in her stroller, not long after she was born, I remember feeling like a giant child playing house. Playing "mommy." I felt that everybody I passed could see by my awkwardness—my crouched posture, my death-grip on the handles and frantic deer-in-the-headlights stare—that I was a student driver. With achingly stiff arms, I inched the strange vehicle along the sidewalks of Broadway while the other NASCAR-level moms whipped past me pushing a double stroller with one hand and balancing an iced latte and a cell phone in the other. Somehow Karen skipped the whole intro-level, beginner-parenting stage. By the time she pushed out her twins at age forty-two, she knew everything she and everybody else needed to know about parenting and was happy to gently bring me up to speed.

"Jules, Ruby was reading chapter books when you applied to kindergarten for her. Sammy, obviously, isn't quite as . . . advanced." I followed Karen's gaze to where Sammy teetered precariously near the top of the climbing apparatus. He waved his hands mockingly at a child on the ground below him and shouted, repeatedly, "Nana-nana-poo-poo!"

I watched him. There really wasn't much I could say.

"Okay, okay," Karen said, "I think we can make this work in your favor. You have to put some sort of show-business spin on it. Make an appointment to meet with Elaine Mayhew—she's the head of the school—and kind of act as if you've been doing the same thing with Sammy. You know, running all over the world while your husband makes movies and TV shows. Honestly, most of the parents in these schools are lawyers and investment bankers and the schools love to have their little celebrities. It creates diversity! These schools are always bragging about how diverse they are."

This, I came to learn, was an understatement.

I followed Karen's advice and insisted that Joe attend the admissions interview with Sammy and me, and when we arrived for our appointment, the three of us followed a very pretty young teacher named Amber into a small, cluttered classroom.

Sammy, we learned that day, doesn't interview terribly well. His responses to all of Amber's carefully phrased questions, such as "Do you want to draw for me, Sammy? Let's draw together!" were lines from movies he had watched repeatedly with Ruby and her friends. Lines like "Oh, be-have" and "Do I make you randy?" delivered in what we had, until that moment, considered a brilliant attempt at a Cockney accent. He also did his rapper impersonation, grabbing his crotch and saying, "Yo, yo, yo," in a deep, throaty little voice. Then, apparently desperate—all the material that had worked so well at home was falling flat here—he resorted to his old standby: poop jokes.

"Do you see the truck in the picture, Sammy? What color is the truck?"

"Poop colored."

"Hmm . . . Well, it's actually orange, which isn't quite the color of—"

"Poop!"

"Sammy . . ." Joe scolded.

"That's okay," said the teacher. "This kind of talk is age-appropriate. I bet this is left over from our potty-training days."

"Well, actually, he's not—" Joe began, and I interrupted, "We're still . . . working out a few kinks."

Sammy had never actually used the potty at that point in time.

"Don't worry," said Amber. "School doesn't start for another six weeks. Of course, you know that he must be using the toilet by the time school starts."

"Of course," I said.

At this point, having been quite cheerful all morning, Sammy was getting tired. He started to whine.

"I wanna go home. Want Catalina."

"That's fine, Sammy, we're all finished," said Amber. "I know that Elaine wanted to have a quick word with you before you left. Let me see if I can find her."

"WANT CATALINA!"

Amber forced a smile in Sammy's direction, then scurried out the door in search of Elaine Mayhew.

"You know what?" Joe said. "I'm gonna take him home. You stay here and meet whoever it is you're supposed to meet."

"Elaine Mayhew," I hissed. "The head of school! You can't leave now. She wants to meet you. This is important!" I was becoming completely unwound. For some reason I hadn't anticipated anything but wonderful behavior on Sammy's part, and now that he had totally flubbed his interview, I was beginning to panic. What if we never did get him into a preschool? How would we explain to grammar-school admissions directors the fact that even though we lived in New York, Sammy hadn't attended preschool? And if he didn't go to preschool, his social skills, with a little help from Ruby and her friends, were likely to deteriorate even further, and then what?

"You meet with her. He's too tired to make a good impression now, anyway," said Joe, and I could see he was right. Sammy was butting his head against Joe's thigh. I kissed them both good-bye and sat myself down in a tiny chair to await Elaine Mayhew.

And I waited.

It was a good thirty minutes before Elaine finally marched into the room. She was a tall, lean, masculine woman whose manic energy caused me to sink down into the Lilliputian chair until my knees nearly covered my ears.

"I've been behind schedule all day," she said with such an accusatory tone that I almost apologized to her. Later I would come to understand that Elaine doesn't waste her valuable time with frivolous greeting words such as "Hello, how are you?" and "Nice to see you."

"I'm the head of ISAAGNY, as you probably know, and *New York* magazine is doing a feature on independent schools, so I had to talk to the writer."

"ISAAGNY?"

"Independent School Admission Association of Greater New York. I'm the chairman. Well, I'm sorry your son and husband couldn't wait, but it's probably just as well. A lot of parents, especially the dads, get nervous meeting me for the first time. They believe all the playground banter about me."

Playground banter is not something Joe would be privy to, but I just smiled up at Elaine.

"I think the other Multi parents will tell you that I'm totally approachable. Yes, I'm busy promoting my book, and the school, of course, but I take an interest in all of the families."

Now I felt as if I was missing something. Apparently Elaine Mayhew was a very big deal. I looked around the classroom in despair. When we had first walked in, the space had seemed small and cluttered. I knew from reading the school's brochure that twenty-two children were assigned to each classroom and I had wondered how they all fit into such squalid, confined quarters. But now that I sat here, at a child's level, enjoying a private audience with Elaine Mayhew herself, I saw that the space was rich in stimulating and mind-broadening . . . stuff. I didn't really know what all the stuff was—there seemed to be an overabundance of blocks—but I knew that the industrious young geniuses who were allowed entry to this exclusive enclave of the best and the brightest would know exactly what to do with them. I was suddenly stricken with the heart-racing conviction that I would get Sammy into this school . . . or die.

"I've heard so much about your great auction!" I blurted out. I *was* privy to playground banter myself and knew that Elaine Mayhew took great pride in the fact that her school's auction outgrossed those of the other Upper West Side schools by tens of thousands of dollars.

"Yes, our auction is always a big success."

Elaine picked up a long red wooden rod from the table in front of me and began tapping her palm with it thoughtfully.

"My husband . . . Joe. He's . . . Joseph Ferraro. I don't know if you've heard of him. He's an . . . actor."

"Yes, Amber was telling me. I never watch television myself," Elaine said, placing the rod next to a group of other red rods that were scattered about on a broad, squat table next to her. They were all different lengths and she fussed with them for a moment, placing them side by side, making them line up in descending lengths. The tilt of her head and the precision of her movements led me to understand that this sequencing had some kind of significance that was beyond the intellectual grasp of the average person, so I gazed at the rods with her, nodding and smiling in what I hoped was a thoughtful and comprehending manner.

"Oh, I know, neither do I. We don't like the kids to watch it . . . too much, either. Anyway, Joe is on this show. On NBC.

And I know that he donated a set visit to the Robin Hood Foundation recently. I'm sure he'd give something like that to the school."

"Oh?" Elaine said, putting the last rod in its place. She had simply lined them up, side by side, longest to shortest, but she glanced at me and then back at her completed task as if to say, *There it all is,* and a bright future instantly unfolded for Sammy in my mind. I saw my son standing next to this very table, his underpants dry but his vocabulary just dripping with complex and expressive wordage. I saw him placing the rods next to one another as Elaine had done, and as each rod took its proper place, his mind and his soul expanded. This grouping of objects and their proper sequencing would unravel the mysteries of mathematics and logic and reasoning. He would learn to add and then to multiply. He would become organized and responsible and he would, like Elaine, take pride in his tasks, no matter how small.

"One of the producers of *Sex and the City* had a child here a few years ago," Elaine said. "They used to donate a walk-on part. That's always an exciting item."

"Oh, I can see that it would be." Then, without thinking, I gushed, "What about a speaking part? That might be a fun item! A speaking part on *The Squad*!"

Three weeks later Sammy received his acceptance letter to the Multicultural Montessori School. And one week after I sent in our deposit, I received an auction item donation form. When I sent it back with a lengthy explanation about why the producers of *The Squad* no longer gave out speaking parts (union rules, previous problems with other charities) and offered a set visit instead, I received a gracious thank-you note from one of the auction organizers. But I knew Elaine was miffed, because there were very few bids on it that year at the auction. A parent whose husband's status as a billionaire had earned them the privilege of being seated at Elaine's table told me that Elaine had sniped, "This is New York, not Peoria! Who would pay money to walk around a television set all day?"

School starts at eight-thirty at Multi, and Sammy and I, true to form, left our building at eight-forty that Thursday morning after the dinner with the Metzgers. Sammy's teacher was "concerned" about tardiness. She told me that she had noticed a certain "fragility" when some children arrived at the classroom setting later than the others. It took them longer to begin to focus on their "work." To me, the kids looked no more or less fragile at eight-thirty than they did at nine o'clock. "They're four-year-olds," my one Multi friend, Jennifer Weiss, always scoffed. "Give me a break."

When we turned onto the school block, Sammy wriggled his hand from my grasp and ran for the building's front door.

"Wait, Sammy," I called, breaking into a little jog. Ruby had always hated leaving me to go to school when she was young. Separation anxiety, her teacher had called it. "Totally normal," she had said as I peeled my weeping daughter from my knees every morning. Sammy was different. He liked to separate.

"Wait, Sammy," I called again, but the wind was blowing and Sammy had his hat pulled tight down over his ears. "Wait," I said, my eyes inexplicably filling with tears. I watched my son run up the steps to the brick-faced schoolhouse. "Wait, Sammy," I called, one last time, trotting after him, but I was calling into the wind and he was already gone.

[four]

Just calm down," said Beth. "I think you might be making a big deal about nothing."

Beth and I were sitting at a window table in Starbucks where the morning sun was streaming fierce and blinding through the grimy plate-glass window. We both wore sunglasses and sat facing out toward Broadway. I didn't think I was making a big deal. It didn't even look like I had been crying. Beth didn't even know I had been crying.

Beth wore a gray wool skirt, skinny black boots, and a long black trench coat that would have looked frumpy and staid on me but made her look like she was going off to snub Humphrey Bogart someplace. I wore sweats and those hideous, shapeless tan winter boots that were trendy several years ago. "Fug Boots" Beth called them. Even when supermodels wore those boots, Beth wouldn't have been caught dead in them. "They look like they were designed to be worn on paws, not feet," she had scoffed the first time she saw me wearing mine. Today, though, she wasn't looking at my clothes.

She was staring out the window, shaking her head slowly, trying to sort it all out in her mind.

"Start over. Tell me everything," she said. "Tell me everything again."

"All right, but first promise you won't say anything to Alison."

"I already said I wouldn't."

"Promise, though."

"I promise. Now tell me everything about the message from the beginning."

"Well, it began with the thing about her being happy. She said, 'Of course I'm happy, you know I am,' like he had asked her if she was happy."

"So what do you think she could be so happy about?"

"Who knows. Maybe it's the first time they've talked since his nomination. He's been with us almost nonstop over the holidays. Maybe it's the first time he got a chance to ask her if she was happy that he was nominated."

"But why would he ask her if she was happy about *his* nomination?"

I peered over my sunglasses at Beth. She had known Joe for twenty years. She was always the one who felt compelled to say to him, in response to some egomaniacal statement or other, "Everything isn't about *you,* Joe." How could she doubt the obvious now? He had called his girlfriend, his filthy-mouthed girlfriend, to ask if she was happy that he had received the recognition he felt he so richly deserved. He hadn't asked *me* if I was happy, but then again, I guess he knew I was happy when I bounded into bed with him after the diner that morning. Recalling the tryst now, I realized that I had behaved like a senseless but affable puppy that morning, all wagging tail and lolling tongue, while Joe had assumed something resembling the manner of a dutifully indulgent master.

"I just think we're not leaving room for all the possibilities," Beth said. "Maybe he was asking her if she was happy about something that was going on in her life that had nothing to do with him. What did she say next?"

"She asked him where he was—as if they had plans to meet or something."

"Again, Julia, you're making assumptions here. Lots of people want to know where everybody is all the time. She might just be nosy."

"Beth . . ."

"Or who knows, maybe he was invited to something that she was also invited to and she expected to see him there. It doesn't mean that they had made a plan."

"She kept calling him babe. And baby."

"Sometimes 'babe' is just an expression. You know who talks like that? My friend Liz who works for Virgin Records. She calls everybody babe."

"Okay, well, she wanted him to know how horny she was. 'I'm horny as a . . . motherfucker' is what she said. I mean, who talks like that? She sounded like a nineteen-year-old porn star."

Beth was nodding slowly. She was thinking. This part was hard to explain away, but I knew she was going to try. Beth considers herself the ultimate authority on just about everything, and now that I had asked her to help me with this problem, she was in her glory. Sitting with her now, I realized I hadn't seen much of Beth since I'd had Sammy. Our lives had become at odds, as people's lives do. Beth was a television producer. I was a mom. She booked guests for Anderson Cooper, spent her days looking for hard-hitting news stories and rarely left the studio for dinner and drinks before eleven. I tended to my children, sort of, and was usually in bed before she finished work.

"She might be just a friend from the set. She might talk to him all the time about how lonely she is."

"Please."

"Okay, you tell me who *you* think it is." Beth pushed herself away from the table and turned to me, crossing her arms slowly. It's difficult for Beth to have to listen to other people's mediocre ideas, but she knew how upset I was, and she was indulging me.

"I don't know, but I'm pretty sure she works on the show. He doesn't have time to meet anyone else, for one thing. And . . ."

"And what?"

"And the show was also nominated. Best Drama Series. So it's possible that he called her to ask if she was happy about the show being nominated, you know, because she works on the show."

"That makes sense," Beth said. "I didn't know the show was also nominated. That explains everything." She slapped her palms on the table and smiled, talking faster. "He probably called everybody in the cast and crew to congratulate them. Maybe she was just calling him back to say, 'Yes, I'm happy.' And then threw in the business about how horny she was as a funny aside. She might be some fat, ugly friend of Joe's from the set who bellyaches all the time about how she never has sex."

"Beth, you had to hear the tone of her voice. It was sex talk."

"All I'm saying is this: You really don't know what's going on. Why don't you tell Joe that you heard the message and ask him to explain it?"

"I don't know. . . ."

Beth turned and faced me again. "I think you don't want to ask him because you know he'll lie."

This is the thing that kills me about Beth. Her own romantic life is a mess, but when it comes to analyzing other people's problems, she's always uncannily on the ball. This is a woman who arrived home one night last year to find her then-husband, Walt, a hedge-fund manager, passed out drunk, wearing her bra and panties, and, most egregiously, her Manolo Blahniks. Now she was suddenly Carl Jung.

"I don't *know* he'll lie . . ." I began, but the fact was that Joe, like most talented actors, was highly skilled in the art of lying. He made lying look easy. There was no fumbling over words or reddening of the skin, no visible "tell" that I could ever interpret. Joe made things true just by saying them, and this usually worked in his favor both on camera and off. Over the years, he had told many fibs to the press—just little things like why he didn't take a particular role (fib: turned it down; fact: wasn't offered it)—and to me (fib: the cast and crew were shooting until dawn; fact: the cast and crew were out drinking until dawn). To my knowledge he had never deceived me about being with another woman, but now I realized that the key words here were *to my knowledge.* Suddenly my scope seemed rather narrow and my gullibility quite vast, and to yield my only advantage to Joe by revealing what little I knew seemed naive at best. I knew what he wanted me to know and now I knew what he didn't want me to know. And I wanted to know more.

"I feel like I'd be a fool to let him know I'm onto him before I get more . . . proof. It'd be too easy for him to cover his tracks."

"Okay, Columbo. Do what you have to do."

We both turned to gaze out the window. The brightness of the midwinter sun revealed broad streaks formed by a hasty window cleaner's squeegee, and we looked out through this abstract glaze at the people rushing past.

"Have you called Dr. Boyfriend?" Beth asked.

Okay, this is a little complicated. Beth calls my former shrink

Dr. Boyfriend. At one point I thought I was in love with him, but it wasn't real. He told me so.

"I stopped going to him last summer," I said. "You knew that."

"I know, but you're in a crisis now. You could call him. You really need to talk to somebody, and if you go back to him, you won't have to do so much filling in, you know . . . of the gaps. He already knows your whole deal."

"Right," I said, unconvinced.

"Listen, Julia . . . I'm sorry but I have to go. I'm late for a meeting."

"Wait, do you think my ass looks fat?" I asked as we got up to leave. I know it sounds trivial now, in the whole scheme of things, but Beth is my only friend on the East Coast who I could ask that question, and I didn't see her very often.

"C'mon! Your ass isn't any fatter today than it was the last time I saw you."

This stopped me in my tracks, causing Beth to slam into me and spill the remains of her latte all over the front of her coat.

"So you mean my ass *is* fat? That it was fat the last time you saw me and is just as fat today?"

"Shit, Julia." Beth gave me a little shove and stomped over to the counter to grab a napkin. "Your ass is not fat!" she called to me. "You just feel fat because . . . you know, the phone call and everything."

It wasn't my imagination. People seated near me actually looked at my ass. A man at the counter did a double take, and then he bounded over.

"Hey! Mrs. F!" he said, offering an outstretched hand. "Mike! Mike Giammati! We met last year at a Knicks game! My girlfriend and I were talking to you and Joey at halftime!"

"Um . . ." I said, my eyes fixed on Beth, who was still dabbing madly at her coat.

"Remember us? We're from the Bronx, too, prob'ly from the same block as Joey. I think he grew up just down the street from me."

I wanted to say, "Sure, I remember you. You and the five thousand other Italians who introduce themselves to us every year. All from the Bronx, all thinking they grew up next to Joe." Somehow a rough Bronx *Mean Streets* persona had formed over the last several years and attached itself to Joe, leading people from the Bronx to tell their friends that they remember Joe when he was a kid, that they grew up on the same block, dated the same girls, went to the same schools. Joe's name, his dark good looks, and his well-publicized Italian lineage (he's played a mob guy in three different films) leads people to assume that he's at least half Italian, when actually he has very little Italian blood left on his father's side. His mother is Swedish/Irish. The fact that he was born in the Bronx makes people think that he grew up there, when truthfully, the Ferraro family moved out of their attractive home in the upscale Riverdale section of the Bronx when Joe was three years old, and Joe grew up in the artsy, liberal suburb of Nyack. When journalists asked Joe what part of the Bronx he was from, he would make vague references to Arthur Avenue and the old neighborhood where his family had come from—and it was true, his grandparents had once lived in the Bronx's Little Italy neighborhood—but his own parents were aging, overeducated hippies, ex-teachers who were now retired in Florida.

Once we were outside, Beth hugged me and said into my ear, "Look, call Dr. Boyfriend."

"All right," I said. "I will."

"Where are you going now?"

"I'm getting my hair colored."

Beth squinted up at my roots. "Good plan. Just don't do anything impulsive or anything. And don't call his voice mail again."

"Okay," I said. I started across Eighty-sixth Street, and when I was almost on the other side, Beth yelled, "And your ass is not fat!" Then she burst out laughing and disappeared down the subway stairs. I speed-dialed her.

"Yeah?" she answered, still laughing.

"Don't say anything to Alison!"

I hung up and started down Broadway using the fast, determined stride that I could only use at times like this, when I was without kids. When Sammy was with me, our pace was usually a mad dash down the block (me frantically chasing him) with periodic abrupt halts to stare at a dead bird or at a child eating candy, and then back into sprint mode. Ruby, on the other hand, always liked to walk slowly, daydreaming, the way I always had as a child.

Dillydallying was what my mother used to call it. Mom was a Caroline.

"Out of their friggin' minds, all of 'em," my dad said once, when we saw Caroline Kennedy on TV making a speech.

"The Kennedys?" I had asked.

"Carolines. Nut jobs, all of 'em."

"Oh," I had said, but no matter how hard I tried, I could never get anything more out of him about our Caroline, specifically. My memories of her are limited and precious in number and all from the dwarfed perspective of a child.

"No more dillydallying, now!" our Caroline used to call back to Neil and me as she strode purposefully forward, young, and usually barefoot, in her sleeveless cotton summer "shifts."

As a New York mother, I am always trying to herd my children in front of me where I can see them, but as I recall, my mother always led the way whenever we went anywhere, and it was up to us not to lose her. I remember the backs of my mother's bare heels more than anything else about her. She hated wearing shoes in the summer. When my dad was stationed in Annapolis teaching at the Naval Academy, she used to take us swimming in the Chesapeake Bay every afternoon when the weather was nice. She would park up the road from the beach in the warm first days of spring and then she would stride along the rough road, barefoot, carrying our towels and toys, always looking forward toward the beach. Never back.

Neil and I, anxious, foot-sore stragglers, limped along the coarse, searing-hot blacktop, watching her slim, tanned legs carry her farther and farther ahead of us, and occasionally I'd call out, "Mommy! My feet hurt. Wait up!"

"C'mon, it's good for you kids to start walking barefoot now—you need to toughen your feet up for the summer," she would call back, jollying us along. And our feet did toughen up. By midsummer, we could have skipped across a bed of nails, so tough were our little soles, and it wasn't until I was in my twenties that I learned that it is actually undesirable to have feet that are as impenetrable as hooves. I tried explaining all this to Ruby once, when we were sitting in a nail salon having mother-and-daughter pedicures. Ruby had asked if my mother and I ever had beauty days together.

"My mother never had a pedicure in her life," I told her, thinking of my mother's tanned feet. The bottoms of her heels were hard and made a clicking sound when they met the backs of her sandals, but the skin under her graceful arches was tender and soft.

"Gross!" Ruby had said.

My mother died long before Ruby was born. She was killed in a car accident when I was eight. We have plenty of pictures of her, but to Ruby she's just a woman frozen in random events of another time. The hopelessly young bride dancing with my father in his naval officer's uniform on their wedding day. The pretty mother smiling down at my brother in his christening gown. The blond flower child in a maternity dress and a floppy hat, sunburned and freckled, waving from the front seat of a yellow Beetle convertible, a cigarette scissored between the very tips of her middle and index fingers. She always held her cigarettes that way, at the very tips of her long, slim fingers.

Later, Neil and I would fight over who had to ride in the back of that VW, because the floorboards had rotted out there and you had to ride with your feet tucked up beneath you. I told Ruby once about how my mother and Neil and I sang "rounds" while she drove. I liked to start. I was the youngest and would begin with "Row, row, row your boat . . . ," and Neil would chime in with "Row, row, row your boat" just when I began the next stanza, and finally my mother would join in and we'd all sing as loud as we could, each on our own musical path, winding in and out of one another until we'd fade out, one at a time, with my mother trilling "Merrily, merrily, merrily, merrily, life is but a dream," like an abandoned songbird, all alone at the end.

When I arrived at Jonathan's salon, his assistant, Lexi, parked me at his station.

"He'll be right with you," she said.

And there I was. The mirror, in all its steely honesty, laid it out for me as plain as day: I wasn't getting any younger, and it wasn't just the lighting. I had recently become aware that my jawline was softening almost imperceptibly, probably something nobody else would notice, but I knew it was a precursor to the heavy jowls that were evident in the photographs of my ancestors—my grandmother, my aunts, and especially my father. When I tilted my head up to sharpen the angle of my jaw, I saw two blond hairs firmly planted beneath my chin. The actual hair on my head was limp and lifeless that morning, and a thin strip of my natural hair color—a color I can only describe as something between dirty blond and filthy gray—bordered my part on each side. I ran my fingers through my hair, trying to disorganize the roots a little. I pursed my lips and opened my eyes wide. I sighed, looked around for Jonathan, and then gazed back at myself.

The mirror arose from a thin metal shelf, upon which lay pointy steel scissors and hair clips and a jar filled with a blue antiseptic solution and combs. On the other side of the mirror, a woman sat facing me, but I could only see her legs and feet, expensive black slingbacks, and crossed tanned ankles.

". . . and it was in move-in condition," the woman was saying to her stylist. "We did a quick paint job—all white. Everything white. I'm into that whole Scandinavian-chic thing. The floors are bleached almost white."

"White, eh?" replied the stylist, a cute Scottish guy named Frank. I recognized his voice. He had worked with Jonathan for years.

"I know. Everybody tells me I'm insane with three kids and all that white. But everybody takes their shoes off when they come into my apartment now. Everybody. My mother-in-law told me I was rude and I told her, rude or not, I spent fourteen thousand dollars on those floors."

There was a pause, then: "She has bunions. I guess she doesn't want anyone to see them."

Another pause. "So now I'm all done! We're all moved in!"

"Sounds nice," said Frank. "I was thinking of doing the same thing to my floors. But we're just renting. Did you have to remodel the kitchen?"

"No! I loved what the people before us had done." A pause. "Of course, we had to have the whole place de-vibed."

"You did? I think my friend did that. . . ."

"Yeah, well, the people we bought the place from, they were going through the messiest divorce. It's one of the reasons it took so long for us to close. And they were in a nasty custody dispute—allegations of adultery and child molestation. It was just so . . . toxic! So we got this priest to come in and sprinkle holy water all over the place."

"I thought you were Jewish."

"Yeah, I am."

"Is your husband Catholic?"

"No. Jewish. My friend suggested we do it and we thought, Why not. Actually, I don't even think the priest was Catholic. Maybe . . . Episcopalian?"

"Cool!"

I thought about the vibes in our apartment. We had bad ones now. A strong and dark undercurrent pulled treacherously at our household, at all its members. My heart began racing and I felt it coming on, the waves of adrenaline, the fear surges—anxiety attacks that I had been experiencing on and off ever since becoming a mother—and as I reached into my purse for my phone, I thought of Catalina reaching for her rosary beads.

"Why didn't you tell me you're such good friends with Cillian Murphy?" Jonathan shrilled, planting himself between the mirror and me.

"I'm not friends with Cillian Murphy," I said. I dropped the phone back into the murky depths of my bag.

"How come I saw a picture of you sitting next to him at a restaurant? I think it was in *Vanity Fair*?"

"Oh. That wasn't a restaurant. It was a fund-raiser. Big Brothers or something. Joe and I were just seated at his table. It was months ago—last spring."

"I just saw the issue the other day! C'mon, what was he like?"

"He seemed nice."

"I *love* him. He's got my abs. The abs I want."

"On yourself or somebody else? Listen, I think I should try blonder. . . ."

"Myself *and* somebody else. Why can't *I* meet Cillian Murphy? All you have to do is introduce him to me. He's gay, right?"

"How should I know?"

Jonathan turned now to admire the profile of his abs in the mirror.

"You sat next to him at dinner, didn't you? Did he flirt with you?"

"Well, no, but he's probably ten years younger than me, so I don't think that's a very good indication."

"Did he flirt with Joe?"

"He didn't flirt with anyone. He was very nice."

Jonathan had to go mix the hair color and when he returned he had a small plastic bowl that he held just above my head. He frowned into the bowl, stirring its contents in a sweeping, scraping motion with a small brush, glancing up now and then to view the busy activity in the salon. A tall young woman walked quickly past, her head sprouting foil, and Jonathan nudged my knee with his.

"That's so sad," Jonathan whispered, glancing up at the woman. Then he resumed his stirring.

"What?"

"That's my poor client who just finished sitting for her color. She's had it really bad."

I didn't want to hear about somebody else's problems, especially now, but before I could interject, he continued, his voice low, his highlight brush dipping in and out of the pungent gold cream. "She was engaged. To a rich investment banker. Really rich. Goldman Sachs guy. She bought the dress, sent out the invites, booked the Rainbow Room. Deposit and everything . . ."

"And he left her standing at the altar," I guessed.

Jonathan paused for dramatic effect, the highlight brush erect. "He killed himself."

"Oh my God . . . how?"

"Jumped!"

"From a bridge?"

"From her fourteenth-story apartment!"

"No!" I tried to get a glimpse of the woman's face, but she was at a sink with her head tilted away from me.

"Right. After. They. Finished. Making. Love." Jonathan tapped the air with his brush after each word and then shook his head sadly. "I mean, how do you go on?"

"Right after?"

"Right after."

"Like the minute the . . . deed was finished? Or after she fell asleep? Or what?"

"Julia, I don't know! I didn't ask! But I think she was asleep."

"Wow," I said. And then I was silent. Jonathan began painting on my highlights, and covering them with foil, humming away.

Jonathan was one of my first friends in New York. He knew Joe and me long before Joe became famous. In fact, Julian, Jonathan's boyfriend and business partner, loves to brag that he remembers the days when Joe Ferraro's checks used to bounce regularly. In return, I remind him that I knew him and Jonathan when their salon was a dingy hole-in-the-wall on Columbus Avenue. Now they have a large salon on Madison, a huge salon in SoHo, and a product line sold in those hair-supply stores in malls all over the country.

I was aching to tell Jonathan about Joe's phone message. Jonathan has a unique vantage point from which to observe the female condition, and he has consoled me and countless others many times over the years. Difficulties conceiving, unrequited crushes, unfaithful lovers, pregnancies, births—these are the things Jonathan's clients fret or rejoice about while sitting, facing their own mirrored images, and they find him to be a sympathetic, if somewhat overly opinionated, counselor. As a result, Jonathan has become an expert on love, loss, and the female reproductive system, and I have, more than once, consulted him before calling a doctor. "It's normal for your periods to be getting heavier now," Jonathan told me once when I complained. "You're approaching perimenopause." Another time, after I'd felt what I thought was a lump in my breast, Jonathan asked, anxiously, "Is it soft or hard? Painful or not?" When I told him sort of soft and painful, he visibly relaxed. "It's just a cyst or something. Breast cancer lumps don't hurt." Of course, I went in for the mammogram anyway, but he was right, it was nothing. Now I wished I could tap into his mother lode of knowledge about cheating husbands and spying wives, but I realized that while I didn't mind if Jonathan blabbed about my rather bland gynecological travails, it wouldn't do to have him whispering about Joe and Julia Ferraro. And asking Jonathan to keep it to himself would have been like asking him not to breathe.

"I'm going to the Golden Globes," I said suddenly. Here was something I didn't mind having repeated. "Joe was nominated!"

"Oh my God. I forgot! Julian told me yesterday morning. That's fantastic! So, who are you wearing?"

"I don't know."

"Honey, it's soon, isn't it?"

"It's the twenty-second."

"You have to call my friend Monica. She works for Vera Wang. And my client Sharon Bronson works for Calvin Klein. She's the one who outfits celebrities for events. I'll get Julian to get you their numbers. What about your hair?"

"I don't know. I guess the network will send somebody over to do hair and makeup. I'll just get a blow-dry." I've worn my hair in the same style since Ruby was a baby. Shaggy layers. Not long, not short. Easy.

"You have to let me give you hair extensions. It'll be gorgeous on you. We'll book it today and I can do them next week."

"Extensions? I don't think so. . . ."

"No, Julia, listen to me. Everybody your age and older in Hollywood has extensions. Everybody you see with long hair. Mariska and Julia and Sharon Stone and—"

"Sharon Stone," I said. "Please!"

"Julia, this haircut is cute, but it says one thing. It says . . . Mom."

Sold.

[five]

I had told Catalina that I would pick up Sammy after school that afternoon, so I had the cab drop me off on the corner of Eighty-fourth and Broadway. Then I walked a block west to the double-wide town house that heralds the letters MMS from a rainbow-colored flag waving piously above the front door.

The Multicultural Montessori School had been called the Riverside Montessori School until sometime in the mid-eighties, when Elaine Mayhew took it over. Elaine is a white, upper-middle-class woman who grew up in Short Hills, New Jersey, received her master's in education at Columbia, and has been married and divorced twice. Elaine hates her type, and if her clone had a child she wanted to get into Multi, that child would almost certainly be rejected. The ideal child at Multi would be a Rwandan adoptee raised by a pair of biracial, trilingual lesbians. Every holiday at Multi is marked by an angry passage penned by Elaine in her monthly Parents' Memo, outlining why the particular holiday is hurtful and exclusionary and thus, while of course families are free to practice the rites surrounding the holiday in the privacy of their own homes, there would be no school celebration. The October memo reminded us that our children would not be allowed to wear costumes on Halloween because the holiday's origins may be found in rituals of pagan Christianity. Celebrating Thanksgiving? Why not celebrate all forms of genocide? Instead, suggested Elaine in her November Parents' Memo, consider inviting a Native American neighbor over for a meal in the spirit of atonement. (I imagined a mad scramble by all three hundred Multi families to locate the one Native American family on the Upper West Side. What a coup it would be to have one's child say he hosted an atonement dinner!) The winter holidays would obviously not be acknowledged at Multi, and Elaine would appreciate it if parents would keep in mind, while considering holiday decorations, that "not all of your child's playdates understand your traditions. Trees, stockings, and candles can be confusing, alienating, and hurtful to children who don't share these idolatries with their own families." I knew better than to expect a Valentine from Sammy—everybody knows it was *Saint* Valentine—but I still held out hope for a Mother's Day card that first year. What could it hurt to have the kids scrawl out a card for their mom? Maybe a little handprint pressed into a slab of clay? It could hurt plenty, explained Elaine in her April memo, if, for example you are being raised by two dads.

It was clear, after that first year at Multi, that in Elaine's mind, the ideal world would be inhabited by people who all looked different and were multiculturally diverse on the outside, but inside were in intellectual and spiritual lockstep with one another. Every speech Elaine gave was peppered with language about "celebrating difference," but celebrating different religions or holidays was not tolerated. I tried tossing this out once or twice at cocktail parties where there were other Multi parents, but it was usually met with an appalled silence, or worse, robotic statements like, "We're glad our children are growing up in a time of greater sensitivity about differences."

As I approached the school, I noticed the usual group of predominantly white, upper-middle-class "difference-aware" parents standing and talking among themselves. This group was slightly outnumbered by the brown-skinned, working-class group of caregivers who were "difference aware" enough to keep themselves slightly set apart from the parents. The kids hadn't been let out yet, so I slowed my pace considerably. A year and a half of picking up Sammy at school had created an actual anxiety condition that only presented itself when I was surrounded by other Multi parents, and sometime that past fall I had gotten into the habit of having Catalina drop off and pick up Sammy each day, so I was working to change that.

I was almost at the school's front steps when I saw the three mothers I dreaded most—Bunny Northrop, Vicki Walker, and Judy Green—standing slightly apart from the group of other parents. They stood to the side and surveyed the rest of the adults with a sense of casual superiority, like three lionesses surveying a flock of useless birds. Occasionally Bunny or Vicki or Judy would swing her freshly coiffed head toward the others and whisper something with a sly smile and the other two would return the smile and nod. I hastily fumbled about in my purse for my phone, a prop I often used at pickup time, but before I could press it to my ear, Bunny cried out, "Julia!"

I smiled and waved. The three waved back and motioned me toward them.

"Three days in a row!" said Judy. "This is getting to be a habit!"

"Is Catalina okay?" asked Bunny earnestly.

"Yes," I said, forcibly turning up the corners of my mouth. "Why?"

"Oh . . . no reason! It's just nice to see you, that's all."

These three took great pride in the fact that despite their full-time nannies—Bunny had a cook and housekeeper as well—they made it a point to drop off *and* pick up their children from school each day. Most of the working moms just did drop-off.

"Gregory is so relieved to see me when he gets out of school," Vicki told me once. "I feel sorry for the little ones who have a nanny pick them up every day."

"I suppose you'd feel even more sorry if the parents left their jobs to pick up their kids, got fired, and could no longer send them here or feed them," I ventured, to which Vicki replied, "Oh no, I didn't mean the working parents. I just meant the parents who stay home and send the nanny. Kids know the difference." The funny thing is, I used to be a lot like Bunny, Vicki, and Judy. When Ruby was little, I harshly judged parents whom I felt were negligent, based on the lack of quality time I thought they spent with their children. I didn't have a nanny, so I picked Ruby up every day. Now that we had Catalina working full time, she loved to pick up Sammy, so it seemed easiest to let her do it. Now that I thought about it, I'd love to be Catalina at pickup time. Bunny, Vicki, and Judy didn't talk to nannies.

"Did you get my message?" asked Judy.

"Umm . . . I don't think so." I actually had not checked my own voice mail since the night before when I started checking Joe's. "Were you calling about a playdate?"

"I wish," said Judy, rolling her eyes. Vicki and Bunny smiled at her sympathetically.

"Actually, I have the unfortunate honor of chairing the auction again this year. Elaine knows we live in the same building, so she's asked me to ask Joe if he'd be willing to be the auctioneer this time. But since I don't really know Joe, I was wondering if you would ask him. . . ."

"Or persuade him!" said Bunny.

"Or beg him," laughed Judy. "Really, I do hate to have to ask you."

"No problem, I'll ask him," I said, knowing that it would save everybody's time if I just said no now. Joe would never stand up in front of a bunch of parents in a school auditorium auctioning off trips to Paris and Nantucket. He had told me so last year when they asked. "I'm shooting that night," he had said to them, but he said to me, "I'd rather be sodomized with a burning poker."

"Thank you, Julia, you know I can't stand doing this. It just comes with the job. . . ."

"Chairing the auction, that's such a lot of work," I said, because Bunny, Vicki, and Judy liked to be told how hard they worked. They considered themselves the best kind of working mothers: the stay-at-home kind. They were kick-ass, hardworking, career stay-at-home moms who rarely stayed at home. Their mornings were devoted to dropping off their children at their various schools, a task that was rarely delegated to the nanny, not only because they considered school drop-off time "quality" time with their children, but also because it was prime time for viewing and judging the other mothers and their children. Bunny, Vicki, and Judy were concerned about all children, not just their own, so they kept tabs on who looked hung over ("Poor Libby Myer. I wonder who puts the kids to bed while she's out drinking with clients all night?") and who was having trouble coping ("Two under three and working full time as a litigation lawyer—no wonder Claire looks so . . . old. I hope she's not sick. For the kids' sake"). The remainder of the school day was devoted to meetings of various school, playground, co-op, and condo committees, and their afternoons were spent monitoring their own and all the working mothers' children and nannies at the playgrounds. At night, they poured themselves a generous glass of wine while the nanny got the children ready for bed and another after the nanny went home. Bunny, Vicki, and Judy had husbands who worked in finance. They rarely saw them.

I had always viewed these women as ridiculous but harmless sanctimommies, but now I felt a sense of guarded rage toward them. "You don't *do* anything," I wanted to say to them. "Chairing the auction isn't a real job! How can you justify having a full-time nanny when you don't *do* anything?" But I didn't do anything, either, and, honestly, this was the first time I actually admitted that to myself. I mean *fully* admitted it. Until that afternoon at Multi, I had somehow managed to use my fragmented half-lives to justify my lack of a whole life. I had told myself for years that I couldn't work as a writer, my trained vocation, because I had children who needed my time. And I couldn't devote all of my time to my children, because, well, I was so smart! I had a degree in journalism! I had a screenplay I was going to start, a children's book I was going to finish. I had convinced myself that I was engaged in this hectic lifestyle, this crazy balancing act of motherhood and career, but I didn't really *do* anything.

Once, when Ruby was in kindergarten, her teacher, Ms. Hill, had grabbed me when I came to pick her up after school.

"Ruby said the cutest thing today," she gushed. "We went around the room and all the kids said what they wanted to be when they grew up, and Ruby said, 'I want to be a nothing, just like Mommy!' "

I managed to smile at Ms. Hill that day and say, "That's

adorable. I work at night . . . when she's asleep. So she'd really have no idea what I do. . . ."

But Ms. Hill had moved on to greet another parent and I remember that I chided myself for caring so much what she thought.

Now, caring very much what the Mommy Gestapo thought, I said, "How do you find the time, Judy?"

"Oh, I do it every year, either officially or unofficially. I know I'm crazy, but I could run the thing with my eyes closed now, so I figure why not do it one more year. Next year will be the first time in nine years that I won't have a child at Multi, so I'm actually kind of feeling a little sad, knowing that this'll be the last time I set up the silent auction, the last time I have to delegate all the little details. . . ."

"I'm furiously taking notes!" said Vicki.

"Vicki and Bunny are going to chair the auction committee next year," explained Judy.

"Great," I said, eyeing my watch. *Where were the kids? Where the fuck were the kids?*

"Anyway, Elaine would be so thrilled to have Joe up there at the podium! I know he was shooting last year, but hopefully this year he'll be able to do it!"

"I'm not sure, but I think he'll be in the middle of shooting this year, too."

"Um, no, they're actually on hiatus the week of the auction," said Bunny.

I was floored. *I* didn't even know when the show's spring hiatus was. "How do you know?" I stammered.

"My sister-in-law has a niece who works as a production assistant on the show, so we got a copy of the show's shooting schedule and set the date of the auction accordingly," Bunny said proudly.

Once, last year, when Ruby was playing in a soccer game, Joe made the mistake of signing an autograph for a mother who was also watching the game. Instantly, a crowd of nannies, parents, and siblings formed around him, and he said, "Sorry, guys, I'm here to watch my daughter's game."

"Okay, just this one," "I'm a huge fan," "Just one for my mom, c'mon," were the replies. Joe signed a few more and then said, "That's it. No more. My daughter's on the field."

I had moved away from Joe when the crowd formed so I could watch Ruby. As the group dispersed, two rejected mothers, obviously unaware of my relationship to Joe, stood beside me, complaining bitterly.

"He's just standing there!" one of them said, and the other replied, "I hate it when people get famous and don't remember to pay their dues to the people who got them there: the fans!"

"I like Tom Hanks. I hear he always signs autographs and poses for fans, and he's much more famous than Joe Ferraro. I didn't even know who he was until you told me."

"It makes them feel more famous if they refuse to sign autographs—as if Joe Ferraro's autograph is worth something." The women ranted on like this until Joe came to stand next to me, draping his arm across my shoulder. The mothers, visibly embarrassed, but giggling, scurried away.

I realized that this was a similar situation. I knew Joe didn't want to be the auctioneer, but since the committee had deliberately scheduled the auction for his free week, in their minds he would just be hanging around doing nothing instead of honorably paying his dues—to his fans and to his dear son's school. I wanted to ask them how they would like it if I found out their husbands' business schedules and arranged some stuff for them to do the next time they had a few days off. Instead, I said, "Great, well, I'll ask him."

Judy's cell phone rang. "Oh, sorry, guys, I have to get this. I think it's the lighting guy for the auction," she said as she stepped away from the group to answer.

"That reminds me, I have to check my voice mail, I'm expecting a call," I said, cursing myself for not coming up with this sooner.

Many times I had stood waiting for Sammy with my phone pressed to my ear, occasionally tapping a button so that the other parents would assume I was checking messages. Of course, I was just using the phone as a prop to keep from having to discuss test scores and ongoing school placements and reading readiness with parents who had allowed their child's life to eclipse their own. Now, as I held the phone tight against my freshly blond hair, it occurred to me that I did have messages to listen to. Joe's messages. I tapped out his number and his code and waited, smiling occasionally at Sammy's classmates' parents as they crossed the street.

"To play your messages, press one."

1.

"Joe, it's Catherine. I've got flight info for you and Julia. Call me."

"Hey, buddy, it's me. There's no basketball on Thursday. Couldn't get court time. We're gonna try for the following Tuesday. I'll let you know."

"Joe, it's Simon. I'm sending that script I was telling you about. It's an offer. It's a great part. I think you should do this one. I know it's going to be tight with your schedule, but I think it's a really great part for you. It's favored nations, so the money's not great, but that's not what it's all about with a project like this. I think it's a once-in-a-lifetime part, man. It's like it was written for you. Call me."

"Hey, Joe. Frank. I saw Leo the other night with that chick and I was thinking about that thing you told me. Fuckin' funny, man. Let's go have a drink sometime. I wanna talk to you about this project I'm thinking of doing."

"Hi, babe. Guess what? I have to work tonight. Damn! I'm sorry, baby. I'll make it up to you, I promise. Call me. I'm really sorry, baby. I love you. Bye."

"Bah." That ridiculous sheep had bleated *bah,* not bye, because of her damned cracker accent. Who? Who was she?

"To delete this message, press seven. To save this message, press nine. To repeat this message, press eleven."

11.

"Hi, babe. Guess what? I have to work tonight . . ."

Bah. I wished I were better at recognizing dialects. The furthest south I had ever lived was Maryland, and we had moved not long after my mom was killed, to Wellfleet on Cape Cod. My dad ran a charter fishing business there until he was forced to retire when he got sick, but I worked for him all through high school and I used to try to guess where people were from based on their accents. I worked on the dock, barefoot, in cut-off shorts and a bikini top all summer long, taking reservations and running credit cards, my skin brown and peeling, or sometimes gleaming with Bain de Soleil, my hair sun-streaked and blond, the front cut into "wings" like Farrah Fawcett-Majors. I remember that people from the South were exceptionally friendly, calling me "sweetie pie" or "angel" while I shyly passed receipts and insurance waivers to them. The boys who worked for my dad would often roll their eyes or make obscene gestures behind the customers' backs, and I would try hard to keep a straight face. I developed crushes on many of these boys, these amiable "wharf rats," as my dad called them, these Tommys, Bobbys, and Steves. If Dad liked a kid but didn't like his name, he'd change it—I fell for a "Skillet" Riley one year and a "Skank" Hanover the next. Sometimes I'd run into these men when I visited the Cape, paunchy family men now, and it was hard to remember them tanned and ripped, flirting with me, kissing me on the beach at night. . . .

I pushed 11 again.

"Hi, babe. Guess what? I have to work . . ."

The kids began scrambling out into the hallway just then, and the parents filed into the school. I shakily swung my phone cover shut, climbed to the top of the steps, and no sooner had I entered the school than Sammy ran into my open arms. I tried to pick him up but he squirmed out of my grip and chased a young friend down the steps and out onto the sidewalk.

Judy was standing beside me, laughing good-naturedly. "Somebody's glad to be going home!"

"Oh," I said, "there you are. I just spoke to Joe. What's the date of the auction again?"

"February eleventh!"

"He'll do it!" I announced, and Judy screamed with delight.

"I can't wait to tell Elaine!" she shrilled.

"Okay, well, just let me know the details when you have them."

"Thank you, Julia! And thank Joe for us!"

"Oh, I will."

Sammy and I walked home in our regular fashion—Sammy racing to the end of the block and then waiting on the corner for me to catch up. "Stay there, Sammy! Wait!" I called to him at the corner.

"I know!" he called back impatiently.

He knew not to cross the street without me, but I still reminded him every time. Boys are so impulsive. So distractible. What if he saw something across the street . . .

"Sammy!" I called, trotting to catch up.

"I know!" he hollered back.

At home, when I slid my key into our lock, the door swung open and Joe was standing there in a pair of sweats and a T-shirt, welcoming us with open arms and a big grin.

"Hi, babe, guess what? I have to work . . ." Was he relieved when he heard her words? He looked so happy to be home.

"Daddy!" cried Sammy, leaping into his arms.

"I thought you had to work late," I said, avoiding his eyes.

"No. We ended up wrapping early."

"What about that difficult stunt?" I asked, but Joe had already turned away from me and was chasing Sammy into the kitchen, with Sammy squealing excitedly and Joe roaring, "I'm gonna get you!"

I'm gonna get you, I thought.

[six]

Rhesus monkeys, *thirsty* rhesus monkeys, would rather watch a videotape of their tribe's dominant monkey than drink their favorite sweetened juice beverage.

Ruby presented me with this interesting kernel of information that night when she wandered into the kitchen and discovered me watching a story about Matt Damon on *Entertainment Tonight.*

It was a distraction.

On weekday evenings, after I put Sammy to bed, it had become my habit to watch TV in the kitchen while Ruby did her homework in her room and Joe studied his next day's lines in ours. When Ruby was little, I never watched TV in the evening because I was trying to write a children's book. *Annie Acorn,* it was called. It was about a little acorn that wanted to be a flower but grew up to be a tree. It rhymed. There were pictures. I never really finished it. Also never finished the screenplay about the three college friends that I started and abandoned a few years back. Or the article about the politics of breast-feeding that Beth had encouraged me to write.

Most recently, I had never finished an application I had requested and received from an adult literacy program. I had decided I would volunteer to teach people to read now that I had such a large part of the day with no kids around. I had started to fill out the application but had gotten hung up in the section that asked how many hours I would be able to dedicate to the program. I had meant to talk to Joe and Catalina about it—how much did they each need me? But I just hadn't had the chance.

Anyway, we had a large flat-screen television for our living room, but I always watched television in our kitchen, where we had a tiny set that sat on the counter under the microwave. "Why don't you watch that on the big TV?" Joe would sometimes ask when he came into the kitchen for a snack, and I'd usually say, "Oh, I'm not really watching it. I just turned it on so that I'd have something in the background while I get some things done in here." Then Joe would look around the kitchen, immaculate from Catalina's after-dinner cleanup, and he'd look at me sitting there with a glass of wine in my hand and he'd say, "Oh." This always prompted me to sputter something like, "I'm just having a quick wine break," and it had become a little bit of a running joke. "Don't bother Mom," Joe would sometimes call to Ruby when she approached the kitchen, "she's working!" and I would leap to my feet and start sorting through drawers and we'd all have a good chuckle. But that night, I'd had no warning and I was caught watching *Entertainment Tonight,* which made me a little ashamed.

"Monkeys watch videos?" I asked Ruby, fumbling with the remote.

"Yep. Given the choice, and two clearly defined levers, the parched monkeys will always choose to watch the activities of their star monkey." Ruby paused behind my chair and watched as the show segued to a piece about Jessica Simpson.

"And the male monkeys, even if they're starving, would rather watch a video of a female monkey's ass than eat food," she said.

"I was only watching because there's supposed to be a segment about Daddy's show," I said, finally finding the power button and switching the TV off. "It looks like they ran out of time. Maybe it'll be on tomorrow."

"On the other hand," said Ruby, who had moved to the fridge to pour herself a glass of iced Kombucha tea, "the monkeys have to be bribed, *with extra juice,* to watch the ordinary monkeys on TV."

I sat for a moment after Ruby left the kitchen and then, feeling a sudden, indignant rage, called after her, "Your father is no ordinary monkey!" to which she replied, "Mom! What are you talking about?" Then she muttered, "Psycho!" and stomped off to her room.

I tried to shrug off Ruby's diagnosis, but the image of those monkeys stayed with me for the rest of the evening. I decided I would do something constructive in the kitchen and began searching the refrigerator for food that had passed its sell-by date, but all the while I thought of the monkeys' hollowed eyes, glazed and vacant from hours of television viewing, their parched, swollen tongues pressing against their yellowing teeth, their fur falling out in clumps as they pulled the lever over and over again. Just to watch that celebrity monkey. And watch him doing what? Preening? Racing about on toes and knuckles? Self-grooming?

And then I wondered about the famous monkey's mate. Did she choose him when he was just an ordinary chimp, before he became famous, when nobody wanted to watch him, much less mate with him? Did she desire him just because she loved his smell or his gait or the way he gazed at her, or did she throw herself at him later, after he was already better than juice—just to bask in his reflected glow?

[seven]

Hi, Julia! It's Alison! I feel like we haven't spoken in ages. Jules, where the hell have you been? Why do I get the feeling you're there and just not picking up? Hmm . . . Okay, well, just wanted to check in and see how you're doing. Not much going on here. Call me when you get this—don't worry about the time difference, I wake up early. Julia? Oh, I thought I heard somebody pick up. Okay. Just checking in. Let's catch up. Call me! Bye!"

Beth had told Alison.

I feel like we haven't spoken in ages. Right. I talk to Alison on the phone every other day. She was feeling left out.

Beth had told, that lying bitch. I knew she was going to tell. I knew it because I probably would have done the same thing—in fact, I have, many times. The friendship that had existed among the three of us since we shared an apartment in college was basically a twisted triangle of deceit. When Beth told me about Walt's gender ID issues, for example, I promised—swore—not to tell Alison. Less than an hour later, I was talking to Alison about something completely unrelated when she said, "Something's wrong with Beth. I sense it."

Blown away by Alison's almost mystical intuitive powers, I allowed as to how Beth might be going through a difficult time.

"Is it Walt?" she pressed.

"I don't think so," I replied.

"Walt's a child," Alison said, and I concurred, and before I knew it, I had spilled the beans about the panties and the shoes and everything. If it had been something else—a health issue or something—I'm sure I could have kept it to myself, but Alison and I always secretly felt that Beth's decision to marry Walt was a serious betrayal. She knew we weren't fond of him—couldn't stand him, honestly—and it seemed selfish of Beth to go ahead and marry him anyway. I knew that Alison and Beth both felt the same way about my marrying Joe, and for that matter, Beth and I had always wondered why Alison had tied herself down with creepy Richard—we didn't care how much he made in his mysterious real-estate ventures. Our standards for one another seemed to be higher than our standards for ourselves, and we each thought that the others had settled for illegitimate, undeserving mates, which is why we felt entitled to speak disparagingly about them with one another.

I had no intention of calling Alison back that morning. I had just sent Ruby and Sammy off to school and Joe was in the shower. I poured myself a cup of coffee and sat at the kitchen table with the telephone. I dialed Joe's phone number, tapped in his code, and waited.

The first two messages were show related: an urgent plea from the wardrobe manager to return a belt and the second AD calling to announce a delayed call time. *Too bad Joe didn't listen to his messages before he took his shower,* I thought smugly.

The next message was from his assistant, Catherine. He had a photo shoot lined up with GQ. A fashion shoot for television's best dressed. And that was it.

"End of messages!" declared the automated recording.

Was it my imagination or was the Nextel voice getting increasingly chirpy? Almost teasingly pert. It was getting on my nerves. I had expected a message from the slutty girlfriend and now I felt let down. Extremely let down. Like some weird lifeline between Joe and me had been severed.

Joe walked into the kitchen, freshly showered and dressed for work, and I closed the phone.

"Coffee?" I asked.

"Yup," he replied, and I got up to pour him a cup. "Thanks, hon," he said, and he gave me a kiss on my forehead. Then he took a sip from his mug, flipped open his phone, and punched in his code. My heart raced. I don't know why I found it so thrilling to know his messages before he did, but I had to steady myself against the counter while he listened. Then he slammed his phone shut. "My call time's not till noon now. I'm going back to bed."

"Oh," I said, but what I thought was, *I know.*

The kids were in school. Catalina was out. Not long ago Joe would have lured me back into bed with him, or I might have beat him back there myself. Because, you know, who doesn't love morning sex? There's something so leisurely and satisfying about that time of day in an empty apartment. The kids off learning. The bed still warm. But now, now that I had to look at all aspects of our marriage with a critical eye, I could see that our sex life had started to deteriorate during the years we tried to have Sammy, and it had never fully recovered. The drudgery of ovulation calendars and fertility drugs and the cruel monthly arrival of my period had slightly soured us to each other. "It'll get better," said my friend Jennifer, who had been through it. "Sign up for IVF and then go back to having normal sex." Jennifer's son, Nathaniel, was conceived in a petri dish. We think Sammy was conceived on a block of ice, in an ice hotel. We're not sure, but that's what we tell people, because it's possible, and it's a good story. In fact, it occurred on a trip that had become part of our family lore. The trip to the Ice Hotel! It was one chapter of an oral anthology that Ruby and Joe and I had compiled over the years, which also contained tales of botched birthday surprises, a kleptomaniac house cleaner, and other amusing anecdotes of our family history that we revisited often, returning like a parched flock to a familiar watering hole.

"Remember the time we drove to Canada, Mom?" Ruby would say suddenly as the four of us sat in traffic on a hot summer day.

"You were visiting me on the set of *Appalachia* in Montreal," Joe would reply. "What was that, 2000?"

"No, it was 2002! It was the winter after 9/11—that's why we drove," I'd reply. That first winter after 9/11, I was still of the mind-set that I'd never fly again, so Ruby and I drove to Montreal during her spring break. We spent a few days hanging around the set, being shuffled behind monitors and standing, breathless, in hushed anticipation of a scene out of context. We watched some of the dailies and met the crew.

"That was the last halfway decent thing Wyman ever made," Joe always said when somebody mentioned the film.

Bill Wyman, the film's director, had his wife and daughter visiting from California, and since Abby was only a year younger than Ruby, they swam in the hotel pool together each morning. The production had a long weekend coming up and Joe and I decided we should take Ruby to visit Quebec City. "Check out the Ice

Hotel," said Kate Wyman when I told her. "It's just outside Quebec. We're thinking of visiting there at some point ourselves."

"The Ice Hotel!" Ruby had declared with delight. "I've always wanted to go to the Ice Hotel!"

Ruby had seen an article about the Ice Hotel in a scholastic magazine the year before and had been fascinated by it ever since. At one point she actually had photos of the Ice Hotel posted on her bulletin board, and it was easy to see why the place was so intriguing to her. The photos revealed what appeared to be a minimalist-inspired hotel interior—except that all the walls, floors, ceilings, and furnishings were made of ice. The beds were blocks of ice with animal pelts for bedding. The artwork was carved into the ice walls, and all of the rooms had an eerily beautiful incandescence that can only be found in a space where light bathes ice everywhere. Everything—the chapel, the lobby, the lounge—was an ethereal blue. It was a pristine winter palace, and in the mind of our daughter, to visit such a place would make us part of its magic. To not visit would be to surrender our lives to an eternity of the carpeted, upholstered, heated damnation that was our only existence.

The hotel was in a park that had other amusements such as skiing, snowmobiling, and dogsledding, and we decided to make a day of it. We would visit the Ice Hotel and also, in honor of Ruby's favorite book, *The Call of the Wild,* we would go dogsledding.

That morning—a bracing, crystal-clear Canadian morning, fourteen degrees Fahrenheit in the middle of March—we drove out to the park. We decided to dogsled first and had been told to arrive at the kennels no later than ten o'clock. Apparently there were some instructions they needed to go over with us.

I was looking forward to the dogsledding. I imagined Joe, Ruby, and me all tucked into a cozy sled together with a Yukon

Cornelius character standing behind us on the sled's runners, mushing the dogs and telling us of his adventures on the old Iditarod Trail. I envisioned noble, courageous sled dogs running us across the frozen landscape, their tongues lolling happily out of their mouths, and of how it would be one of those experiences that Ruby would cherish for the rest of her life.

We arrived to find half a dozen empty dogsleds parked outside a large but dilapidated barn. The sleds were placed in a line, obviously waiting to be hitched up to the dogs, whose shrill voices rose in a cacophonous series of barks, yips, and howls from inside. As we approached the barn door, it suddenly swung open, and the three of us instantly covered our mouths and noses with our hands. The sickening stench of a barnload of dog crap blasted out into the cold morning in an almost visible gust. Then through the door lurched a pair of barking huskies dragging a burly handler along with them. The dogs were strapped into nylon harnesses and their handler was between them, a rough, calloused hand firmly gripping each harness. The dogs were so excited and pulled so hard that their front feet didn't touch the ground, but instead pawed frantically at the air while their hind feet propelled them forward in short hopping steps. The first pair of huskies was followed by a second pair being somewhat restrained by a lanky teenaged boy, and then a third pair and another teenager. All of the dogs grinned maniacally between barks, and their upright two-by-two procession looked like the deployment of a senseless but ferocious army. "Go on inside," said one of the handlers to us. "They're giving the driving instructions." I looked doubtfully toward the massive, listing barn. The cries of the dogs within sounded primitive and foreboding to me, like the lusty song of caged wolves, pent-up, frustrated, boasting of blood and danger. "Go on in," the man said again. Ruby pranced enthusiastically toward the door and we followed her.

Inside the barn, several people stood in a semicircle around an empty dogsled. Next to the sled was a very ruddy French Canadian, who said when we entered, "Ah, here zey are! You made a reservation yesterday. You're with ze child, yes?"

"Yup," said Joe, who then turned to me and rolled his eyes. Later, when he told the story, he would claim that the accent was fake.

"I am Jean-Luc," said our guide. "We will begin our safety demonstration." His demonstration involved much jumping on and off the runners of the sled and stamping on the brake. It wasn't until about halfway through his speech that I came to understand that we were expected to drive our own sleds.

A final pair of dogs dragged their handler past us. The dogs' barks had built into an hysterical crescendo and Jean-Luc smiled as they passed and said, "Zey are excited."

Excited doesn't even begin to describe the emotion I was experiencing. Adrenaline surged through my veins like a flash flood of panic. Even *I* could smell my fear.

"Zee brake under your foot is this metal bar," Jean-Luc was saying. "Ees the only way to slow down the dogs. If the dogs are running, it might mean you must stand on the brake with both feet. With all your weight. *It is important not to lose control of ze dogs.*"

Although the temperature in the barn was about six degrees Fahrenheit, I was beginning to sweat.

Ruby grinned with delight. Joe was clenching his jaw. A bad habit of his. Never a good sign.

"Also, very important," said Jean-Luc, "we will tell you the name of your lead dog. There are eight dogs in a team, but you only need to know the name of ze lead dog. He is the one you talk to. Say the dog's name, then give a command. 'Hup' means forward. Your lead dog will know what you want. *It is very important to keep the dogs moving forward.* If they stop or slow down, they might become entangled in the harnesses. If that happens, *immediately* call for help from one of your guides. When a dog becomes entangled, usually the other dogs will attack it, and there will be a *big dogfight.* So be very careful. Any questions?"

"I can't do this," I whispered to Joe.

"Shhh! Just listen to the guy," Joe said, but I could tell by the way he was clenching his jaw that he was having second thoughts himself.

"Okay, let's go!" said Jean-Luc, and we all followed him out of the barn. The dogs, all hitched to their sleds now, howled and barked and snarled with excitement. Their sleds were anchored to the ground and the dogs lunged against their harnesses, snapping at the air and at one another.

Jean-Luc began assigning sleds to people. When he came to us he said to Joe, "I think I will take your daughter in my sled. Your wife will ride with you. It's easier for you to drive with one person."

I was relieved that Ruby was going to be riding with a professional. At least one of us would survive. And Ruby was clearly thrilled to be riding in the first sled with a real dog musher. Joe and I were directed to the last sled, and when I climbed inside, Jean-Luc threw a filthy blanket over my lap. Then Joe stepped onto the runners behind me and our team of dogs lunged forward so hard that the sled bounced and slid sideways against the strain of the anchor.

"Jesus!" said Joe.

"Whatever you do, don't let go!" I cried. My fear was that if Joe fell off, I would be left alone in a sled with no reins and no way to reach the brakes, behind an out-of-control pack of dogs. I imagined the dogs bolting off so fast that the sled would become airborne with me clinging to it for dear life.

"The lead dog!" I said to Joe. One of the handlers was now unfastening our anchor from the ground. "We never found out the name of the lead dog!"

"Jesus Christ, the lead dog!" Joe screamed. "NOBODY TOLD US THE NAME OF THE LEAD DOG!"

"HELP!" I shrieked.

"It's Lobo," the handler said calmly. He pulled the anchor from where it was lodged in the ground and placed it next to me on the sled and we were off.

The dogs threw their weight into their harnesses, and their frustrated cries turned into playful yips as the sled flew across the snow-covered parking lot. Joe and I screamed in unison at the sled's first surge forward, and I cried, "Whoa, Lobo! Whoa, Lobo!" to the lead dog. But Lobo didn't appear to know his name, which turned out to be okay, because after the first thirty seconds, the dogs ran out of steam. We left the parking lot and headed out over a field, the distance separating us from the three other teams growing larger and larger.

"Hup, Lobo," called Joe. "Hup!"

Lobo had downshifted from a slow lope into a walk. He went to sniff a small fir tree and then stopped to lift his leg on it.

"Hup, hup, hup!" we called out.

Lobo released an agonizingly long stream of urine and then kicked at the earth with his hind legs. He kicked at the ground, and kicked and kicked and kicked and kicked, sending small yellow wads of snow and dirt all over his teammates and me.

"Bad dog, Lobo! Hup!" yelled Joe. Lobo meandered on, but only after pausing long enough for us to understand that he was moving forward only because *he* now chose to. The other dogs in our team stopped and lifted a leg or squatted at the exact same fir tree, each also sending chunks of their marked territory back into my face.

We proceeded across the field at Lobo's lackadaisical pace, the dogs stopping every few yards to have a sniff at the ground, to relieve themselves, or just to have a friendly go at their neighbor's genitals. The first time they came to a complete stop, Joe and I screamed, "Hup, hup, hup!" at the tops of our lungs, but the dogs didn't get tangled in their harnesses or attack one another. They were having a leisurely morning walk and they seemed to be enjoying themselves.

"I feel like one of those dog walkers you see in Central Park," said Joe, and I said, "Is it my imagination or is Lobo one of the most moth-eaten dogs you've ever laid eyes on?" Because once we had started moving, after Lobo stopped lunging and baring his fangs, we were able to get a good look at him, and it was clear he'd seen better days. His coat, where it remained, was graying. It was still thick around his neck and shoulders but started to thin out around the area of his waist, and for some reason, perhaps some kind of canine pattern baldness, parts of his bony hindquarters were completely bare. All four legs were still covered in fur, but the right hind leg was stiff and arthritic and appeared to torque sharply out to the side with each step.

"You know, I'd feel sorry for him if he wasn't such an arrogant son of a bitch," said Joe. "He's not listening to a thing I say."

"I think the handler sized us up and we got the equivalent of the old reliable nag at the dude ranch," I said, and then we both kicked back and enjoyed the ride. The midday sun streamed down on us and I tilted my face up to catch its rays. At the end of the bright windswept field, we turned onto a wide trail that wove its way through a pine grove. The occasional clusters of grass poking up through the melting snow and the promising musky scent of thawing earth made me think of the Easter Sundays of my childhood, of starched flowered dresses and new Mary Janes. Joe squatted down behind me, giving up all pretense of "driving" the dogs, and wrapping his arms around me, he kissed me on my neck. I moved his hand down under the blanket, into the front of my parka and over my breast. The dogs settled into a pace that was just a tad slower than a normal walk and we slid in and out of the dappled sunshine, over a narrow frozen creek, and finally back out into another field that led to the barn. Joe and I untangled ourselves and Ruby turned around in the lead sled to wave excitedly back at us.

"It was like a dream!" she said, after a ten-minute showdown with Joe about why we couldn't buy the lead dog on her team, who was also, curiously enough, called Lobo.

"Let's get to the Ice Hotel before it melts," I said.

The pictures we had seen of the Ice Hotel made the place look like the Winter Palace from *Doctor Zhivago.* The real Ice Hotel was a long, low structure that looked like a gigantic cargo vessel encased in ice. It sat in the middle of a parking lot with Dumpsters and Porta Potties set up outside. By the time we pulled up, there was already a small line of tourists waiting to get in, including the Wymans.

"That's the Ice Hotel?" Ruby asked sadly when we joined them in line and we all wondered how anybody came up with this gimmick in the first place.

But the inside of the hotel actually bore a closer resemblance to the promotional photos we had seen. Something about the way the sun filtered through the thick blocks of ice gave the place a mod, clubby, blue-lit atmosphere. We walked through the ice foyer and the ice chapel and then into the ice lounge, where shots of vodka were being served in ice shot glasses.

"Now you're talking," said Joe, handing shots to Bill and Kate and me. The girls ordered hot cocoa from a waitress. As we tossed back the shots and Joe fetched us each another, I recounted our dog-sledding travails to the Wymans. The first shot had burned going down, but the second was just blissfully warm. Joe grinned at me as I described Lobo, interrupting occasionally with adjectives like *mangy* and *shit-encrusted*. We hadn't really shared an adventure in ages and now we felt reunited by the ordeal. We were actually bent over laughing when we tried to explain just how hard it is to figure out where to look when your dog team has decided to embark on a spontaneous orgy in the middle of a snowy field.

Soon the girls had finished their hot chocolates and set out to explore each and every room in the hotel, and we set out after them. The Wymans followed the girls into one of the guest rooms and Joe and I wandered into another. It was empty except for the ice furniture and the faux fur blankets thrown across the "bed."

"I wonder if people really stay here," I said. "Just looking at that bed hurts my back."

Joe swung the ice door closed and found that it bolted shut.

"Didja ever do it in an ice hotel?" he asked, and I laughed because this was an old running joke between us. Joe and I had discovered, not long after we met, that his sexual experience was a little more . . . limited than mine. Actually, a lot more limited. Joe hadn't had a lot of girlfriends before we met in college—in fact, I've had to take him at his word that he wasn't a virgin before me. I, on the other hand, had had a few boyfriends before we met. I never thought my sexual experiences were that vast until I met Joe and came to realize that maybe I had hung around with a bit of a fast crowd in high school.

"Didja ever do it in a car?" he would ask when we first started seeing each other, and I would say, "Of course, who hasn't?"

"Me," Joe would say. Then: "How about a train," or "a parent's bed, an abandoned building?"

"Yes, yes, yes," I would say and also think to myself, *And a cemetery, a boat, on the beach, in the woods.* Joe would respond to each admission with his "You slut" look and I'd tell him what I'd like to do to *him* in a train, in a parent's bed, and in an abandoned building, and eventually over the years we had made love in all these places and more—private planes, a yacht, a castle, once drunk out of our minds in an Irish peat bog. . . .

Joe checked the bolt on the ice door and then grabbed me by the arm.

"Are you crazy?" I laughed. "All those people out there . . ." But he was already pushing me up against an ice wall.

"C'mon, I'm freezing. Warm me up, baby," he said, and he put his arms around me, sliding his hands into the top of my jeans.

"What about Ruby?" I asked, giggling, and then we were down on that ice-slab bed. When we had finished our hasty, slippery lovemaking, our coats and jeans soaked from the melting bed, it thrilled me to allow Joe to pull me back up onto my feet. For months I had been lying on my back after more purposeful sex, my legs propped up on a pillow, hoping that gravity would help settle the impasse that seemed to have developed between my ovum and Joe's sperm. We had had a quickie in the Ice Hotel—our first in ages—and we had another that night in our real hotel, and another the next morning, and four weeks later I bought a pregnancy test and I peed the line blue. Blue. Finally blue.

[eight]

I met Karen Metzger at Bergdorf's for lunch. Karen and I had been having weekly lunches ever since we met in the late nineties, when Brian directed Joe in *Heartland.* Karen was my only friend who didn't work and had the liberty to dine at places like the Bergdorf Café. Karen always chose the Bergdorf Café. I hate the Bergdorf Café.

"What's to hate?" Karen said this time. "It is what it is. Get the chopped salad."

"I just noticed something," I said. I was whispering now because the tables were so close together.

"Look at them all."

"Who?"

"The ladies who lunch here. The ladies with the fur and hair and nails. They're our age. I've always thought of this café as the roosting place for glamorous grown-ups. Older people. When did I get to be their age?"

Karen looked at me long and hard. "You're too young to be

going through a midlife crisis," she said. "I'm seven years older. Let me have mine first."

"I'm not having a midlife crisis," I said. "I just feel . . . old." For the first time since the first overheard voice mail two days ago, I felt tears gathering.

"Oh, Julia, what is it?" Karen said softly.

I dabbed at my eyes with my napkin. I could feel the lunching ladies on both sides of me making a deliberate effort to not look my way.

"It's nothing. Never mind. Really."

"Is it the kids? Joe?"

I just shook my head.

"Oh my God. Have you been to the doctor? Everybody I know has ovarian cancer all of a sudden. I'm not kidding. Everybody has cancer! Are you all right?"

My emotional lapse was over. I didn't have cancer. Things could be worse.

"I'm fine. I don't have cancer," I said. "Is there mascara all over my face?"

"No. Just a little under your left eye . . . That's it."

"Okay, sorry. I think . . ."

"What is it?"

"I think maybe I *am* having a midlife crisis. That's all."

"Don't be ridiculous."

"I really don't want to go to this party tonight. I feel so . . . hideous."

"Have you been back on the show's Web site again?"

"No," I said, but of course I had. I lurked on message boards on the NBC Web site almost every day. I'd been doing so ever since the show's premiere season. There were constant postings about the show on the site, mostly pertaining to plot twists and speculations about where the season was headed, but there were also comments about the different actors, and Joe had a little harem of regular posters, people who gave themselves screen names like Joesgal and Mitchsbitch (Mitch Hollister was the name of Joe's character on the show).

JF is HOT.

—I'm a huge Joe Ferraro fan. Have been long before series.

—forget it ladies. he's married.

—thought he was divorced

—no, long time married to wife

—I saw a picture of them in a mag. she's not very hot. I was surprised.

—Makes me love him all the more. Didn't leave dumpy wife when he got famous.

—I saw him making out with a blond woman at a bar in midtown a few weeks ago.

—His wife?

—Did she have bad soccermom hair?

—yeah

—wife

—definitely wife

—Awwww, that's sweet.

I hadn't yet started monitoring Joe's voice mail when I read that particular thread, so I assumed, back then, that it was a case of mistaken identity. Joe and I hadn't made out in a bar in Midtown . . . ever.

"You have to go see Dr. Calder," Karen said.

"Who's that, a shrink?"

"No, Julia. Dr. Alexa Calder! The dermatologist. She's famous. She's constantly on talk shows talking about procedures. She's like the first person who did Botox in this country. She does my Botox."

It was only then that I saw that Karen had no lines on her forehead and no crow's-feet.

"Wow," I said, "your skin does look really good. I have to admit I've thought about getting rid of these frown lines on my forehead. . . ."

"I'll give you her number. She can also get rid of those smoker's lines around your lips."

"Smoker's lines? I haven't smoked in years. I don't have smoker's lines."

Karen squinted at my mouth.

"Do I?" I drew my lips together tight.

"That's just what they call them. The little lines above your lip. My friend Helen had them—you know Helen Meyer from DreamWorks? She had Alexa inject a tiny bit of Restylane all around her lip line and now the lines are gone. She looks ten years younger."

Ten years younger. Ten years ago I was one of the youngest mothers in Ruby's class. Now I was one of the oldest in Sammy's. There was certainly something appealing about the idea of having somebody eradicate all the years that had etched themselves onto my face. It occurred to me now that the face I saw each day in the mirror might not look the same to others as it did to me. I saw the Julia Ferraro I once was, with the so-called "great smile" and my father's blue eyes and cheekbones, while everybody else saw the Julia Ferraro who had spent too much time in the sun as a teenager, had smoked too many cigarettes in college, and whose brow had furrowed in constant worry ever since Ruby was born. Julia Ferraro the wife, the soccer mom. The hag.

"Let's order a bottle of wine," Karen said, and although I usually never drink during the day—it makes me too tired—I said, "Yes, let's!"

After lunch I said good-bye to Karen and took the elevator down to the third floor, to the designer formal wear department. The Golden Gobes were only two weeks away and I still hadn't started shopping for a dress. I guess that was because I hadn't quite wrapped my mind around the idea that I would have to *shop* for a dress. I actually thought that as soon as the nominations were announced, there would be a feeding frenzy of top designers vying for my attention, desperate to have the wife of one of the main nominees—Best Actor, TV Drama—wear one of their gowns on the red carpet. I had assumed that everyone was waiting until the holidays were over to call with their offers, but now that the holidays *were* over, I was coming to the dawning realization that Donna and Calvin and Vera and Giorgio were not madly sketching design ideas to propose to me, that in fact as far as they were concerned, I could wear a gunnysack down the red carpet.

It was a weekday afternoon and the third floor was relatively quiet. I wandered into the first of a series of boutiques and I have to admit I was feeling a little rich and splendid. I was all full of chopped salad and wine and chocolate ganache and felt instantly at one with the luxurious finery. The hanging gowns were displayed on racks along the walls. They were carefully spaced several inches apart from one another, bathed in soft halogen light, and I touched them dreamily as I walked past. The salesclerk was a slender, middle-aged man who wore a crisp linen shirt and tailored trousers, and had a shaved head. He was thumbing through a pile of invoices, and when I entered the space, he had nodded to me in greeting. Now that I was touching the garments, he looked up with a slightly bewildered expression and said, "May I help you find something?"

"Yes," I said. I smiled self-consciously, preparing myself for his gushing advances. "I need a dress. For the Golden Globes."

The man nodded. "Mmm-hmm?" he said. Then he glanced back down at the invoices.

"My husband's a nominee."

"Oka-a-ay," the clerk said. He nodded at the dress racks and said, "Let me know if you see something you like," and then returned his full attention to his paperwork.

It wasn't exactly the level of enthusiasm I had anticipated, but I didn't really care, because suddenly I saw something I liked very much. It was a skinny, floor-length black-lace gown by Jean Paul Gaultier, with a clingy silvery-gray lining. It had a rock-glam look, a look that had really worked for me in my youth. The attendant pointed me toward the fitting room, and when I slipped it on, it was as if Gaultier had designed the dress solely with me in mind. The stretchy lining clung to my body in all the right places, and the lacy pattern—delicate roses—seemed to camouflage all the necessary ones. I consulted the sales attendant and he agreed. It was a perfect fit, and as he wrapped it up, and I charged it to my MasterCard, I was very pleased with myself. "It was the first dress I saw," I imagined telling Joan Rivers. "I just wandered into a boutique and bought the first dress I saw."

"It's gonna be hell getting a cab this time of night," Joe said when we left our building that night.

"Joe! A cab? It's three blocks to Susanna's!"

"What're you talking about? It's six blocks, three of them *crosstown* blocks, and it's freezing. . . ."

It's funny, I thought, looking at Joe's clenched jaw and fierce scowl, how a marriage is sometimes like a minefield covered by a beautifully manicured lawn. Or at least ours was. If you saw us leave our building that night, for example, you might think, *There's Joseph Ferraro and his wife. Joe Ferraro from* The Squad! *Look how lovingly his wife gazes at him as he talks to her.* Meanwhile, I was thinking, *Don't get your panties in a bundle, diva-boy,* and he was thinking something along the lines of, *Why can't you, for once, just do things the way I want to do them, you controlling bitch.*

"Let's start walking," I said, and did just that—started walking east on Eighty-fifth Street, which, of course, goes west, so there was no chance of getting a cab headed in the right direction until we reached Amsterdam Avenue. Joe stood for a moment and I could feel his angry glare on my back. I pulled the fur-trimmed collar of my jacket up against my ears and bent my head into the wind. This was an old struggle of ours, the "Let's walk/No let's take a cab" dispute. Joe worked out for two hours every day in a gym, then, for the rest of the day, he went out of his way to exert himself as little as possible. He would take a cab across the street if he could. In my mind, if he could employ somebody to brush his teeth and wipe his ass for him, he would. Joe had befriended (translation: heavily overtipped for a year) a driver from the BLS limousine service, and now Lou exclusively drove Joe. He drove Joe to work and to the gym, and at night he drove us to parties and events (this was his night off). The cost was exorbitant and it was a recurring battle between Joe and me. I wanted to walk to things that were in our neighborhood, the way we used to, and was content taking cabs to other neighborhoods. It bothered me that Lou billed by the hour and spent most of his hours parked outside our building or Joe's gym, where somebody else was paid a huge sum to work out with him. Honestly, the amount of manpower it took to be Joe Ferraro was astonishing. He had started with only an agent, but over the years had acquired assistants, trainers, drivers, more agents, lawyers, a manager, and now he had just added a publicist to the payroll. All on commission or billing by the hour. And it wasn't just the money that bothered me. It was the whole entourage trip that Joe thrived upon. Over time, Joe had come to think of most of these people as his friends, while his former friends fell, one by one, to the wayside. Our old friends, many of them struggling actors, were too "bitter" or "begrudging," according to Joe, while his new "friends" were adoring and worshipful, and over the years, he had begun valuing many of their opinions and ideas over mine. Lately, he would ask me to read a script he was considering for a movie offer, and if I said I thought the script was bad, Joe would say, "Jake loved it." To which I'd respond, "Jake's a personal trainer with a tenth-grade education," and Joe would say, "Who do you think the target audience for this film is?" And then: "Why the fuck do you have to criticize every little thing I do?" *Because you're becoming an idiot,* I'd think, and he'd think, *Bitch!* And together we'd think, *I hate you. What did I ever see in you?*

I heard Joe's angry stride behind me and we walked to the end of the block like that, with Joe hanging back just enough to be separate, and I closed my eyes against the raw east wind. It made my eyes tear, that wind. At the corner, Joe stepped off the curb and stuck his hand out and a cab pulled right up. Joe held open the door while I climbed inside.

When we arrived at Susanna Mercer's apartment building one minute later, the doorman opened the cab door for us. "Good evening," he said when I got out of the cab, but when Joe followed, he said, "Hey! Joe! How's it going, man?"

"Great, great, thanks."

"They're expecting you. Have a nice evening."

"Thanks," said Joe.

"Have you ever been here before?" I asked as we entered the elevator.

"No, why?"

"The doorman seemed to know you."

"I guess he watches the show. Like eighteen million other people," Joe said.

Joe's friendship with Susanna had irritated me on occasion over the past several years, but she was actually the first person I crossed off my mental list of suspects when I heard the initial phone messages. First of all, Susanna is Australian. The accents didn't match. And she only dates billionaires. Plus, I had never heard her swear, and the caller had a younger girl's voice and . . . well, why go on? It wasn't Susanna's voice.

Susanna actually lived in Los Angeles, but as Joe had explained earlier that evening, she was staying in her friend's Central Park West penthouse apartment while she did a few weeks' work on an independent film.

"Whose apartment is it?" I wanted to ask Joe as we rode up silently, but I hated to start with the small talk. It would seem like an apology of sorts. A surrender. Instead, I almost exploded with, "Who the hell are you fucking?" But then the elevator doors opened. They opened right into the penthouse, and there, at the far end of a marble foyer, stood Susanna.

Perhaps she got dressed in a dimly lit room and didn't realize that dress was so see-through, I thought, generously.

Susanna wore a dazzling, and completely sheer, floor-length gown to her birthday party that night. The party that had been repeatedly billed to me, by Joe, as "casual." Her hair was swept up into a complicated, sexy, deliberate mess on top of her head, and on her tanned, perfectly manicured feet she wore a pair of delicate strappy sandals, for which an exquisitely marked snake had obviously been relieved of its skin. Strands of diamonds hung from her wrists. Her eyelashes appeared to have been plucked from the pelt of a lustrous mink, and while her flimsy gown was certainly eye catching, it was also somewhat awkward to look at, because when you did, your eye was naturally drawn to the body underneath it. A body that appeared flawless, and was, except for the small triangle concealed by a pink lacy thong, plainly visible to all.

I was wearing black jeans, clunky boots, and a three-hundred-dollar tank top that some half-wit at Barneys had told me was "elegant and chic."

Susanna greeted her guests in front of a roaring fireplace. The apartment was handsome and stylish, and it occurred to me that although, as far as I knew, Susanna has no permanent place of residence, she possesses such a commanding presence that her surroundings are always, instantly, hers, no matter who the real proprietor is. The yacht she stands on in a *Vanity Fair* photo appears to be her yacht. The beach in the *Vogue* spread, her beach. This gorgeous apartment, with its gleaming mahogany floors and French antiques and illuminated artwork, seemed to have been designed solely with Susanna in mind. In fact, Susanna's whole firelight-enhanced aura evoked a sense of wonder in me. Watching her slender, silky-smooth arms embrace her other guests, I wondered what body-hair-removal process Susanna used, and whether or not it would be appropriate for me to ask her. Her skin was uniformly tanned and I wondered whether she worried about skin cancer. Her breasts managed to stay firmly uplifted without the benefit of a bra, and I wondered how she could imagine that anybody might think they were real. It seemed wrong to stare, so I turned to say something to Joe and I saw that he, too, seemed to be staring at her in a state of wonder.

I know. Meow.

I don't dislike Susanna. In fact, over the years, I've learned a secret about her that the world press, which dogs her every step, has never uncovered. Susanna Mercer is one of the smartest people in Hollywood, and when I say Hollywood, I don't mean the place, I mean the industry. The religion. Of all its members I've known over the years, Susanna probably has the sharpest wit and the most discerning mind. Like many stars, she has her own film production company, but unlike most, she actually runs hers, on the sly, while pretending to be just a simple, sexy, vulnerable Aussie actress.

Susanna has no female friends, unless you count her employees (she does), and instead surrounds herself with platonic male worshippers.

"Hello, Julia. Hello, Joe, darling," Susanna said, kissing each of us on both cheeks. "Joe, I want you to meet Martin. Remember that English producer I was telling you about? Well, it turns out he's just received word that the financing for that project— Oh, Julia, I'm sorry," Susanna said, as if she had suddenly realized that she was rudely speaking a foreign language in front of me. She stood on the tips of her toes, managing to obscure Joe's face from me with her bosom. "Nikki! There she is! Nikki, will you come and take Julia over to the bar and help her get a drink, darling?"

Nikki, Susanna's longtime personal assistant/makeup artist, approached with a giddy, ambling stride and greeted us with enthusiastic kisses to each cheek. Nikki was a short, blond, voluptuously plump British girl who had worked for Susanna for years. She was holding a near-empty martini glass that had sloshed its remains onto her short black dress with each springy step.

"Nikki . . ." Susanna said quietly, eyeing the glass.

"Not to worry," chirped Nikki. "I'm pacing myself. Hello, Julia! You look thirsty, can I get you a drink?"

"Why don't you show me where the bar is?" I said, desperate to be away from Joe. Nikki grabbed my hand, and I followed her through the crowded room, and as I did, I looked around to see what the other women were wearing. That's when I came to discover that, other than Nikki, Susanna, and me, there were no other women at this party, only men. Gay, straight, short, tall, some famous, some not, some gorgeous and some not—Susanna's apartment was packed full of men, but even in their company I felt like a clod. I had left home half an hour ago feeling casual and hip and cool, and now, compared to Susanna and Nikki—in fact, compared to half the men at the party—I felt plain and manly and dull.

"I wish I'd worn something a little more . . . festive," I told Nikki. "Joe told me that this was going to be a casual thing."

"Don't give it a thought, Julia," Nikki said. "Susanna forgets that casual here means jeans, while casual in London, where we've been the past year, means 'Leave your dinner jackets at home.' " She squeezed my hand. "So, what'll you have to drink?"

"What are you drinking? A martini?"

"Yes, but there was something wrong with it. I really didn't care for it at all." She placed the empty glass decidedly on the bar. "I'm switching to a Cosmopolitan. Umm, so sorry, bartender, I've forgotten your name again."

"John," replied the bartender, smiling vacantly. He was gazing across the room at Susanna.

"Right. Johnnie. Do you want one, Julia?" Nikki asked me.

"Yes," I said. "Why not? Thanks."

"Two Cosmopolitans please, Johnnie. Wait. Better make it just one for my friend Julia here. I have to watch what I drink tonight." Nikki turned to me and whispered, giggling, "I got absolutely shit-faced the other night, and this morning Susanna gave me a little lecture. About my drinking."

"Oops," I said.

"Oh, fuck it. This is a party. Give me just one more. But make it weak please, John."

"Hmm," said John. He looked at the bottles before him and pondered the challenge of making a cocktail, whose ingredients are almost all alcohol, weak. Then he poured vodka, triple sec, and a splash of cranberry juice into an ice-filled shaker, shook it, and poured the contents into two glasses. He left a little room at the top of Nikki's glass, topped it off with cranberry juice, then handed us the glasses.

"Cheers, John!" said Nikki. "Cheers, Julia!"

The vodka was smooth and the tiny slivers of ice that had made it through the cocktail shaker's strainer sat on my tongue for a moment before they melted. I'm a wine drinker, but now I wondered why I rarely had cocktails when I went out. The effect of the crisp, citrusy drink on my raw, angry nerves was immediate. I took another sip.

Nikki led me off to a corner of the room where there were two chairs and a table, and we sat down. A tray of hors d'oeuvres had been placed on the table and Nikki's eyes lit up when she saw them.

"Ooooh, shrimp tempura! And what's this other little item here, all wrapped in pastry dough?" She plopped one into her mouth.

"It's heavenly, Julia, have one!" she said, passing the tray to me. We gobbled the shrimp, and the pastry thing, dripping sauce all over the table. I was pleased to see that Nikki, despite spending nearly every waking moment in Susanna's presence, had managed to escape her boss's devout abstemious influence. Unfortunately for me, Joe hadn't been so lucky.

Joe first met Susanna on location in Mexico in the winter of 1998. They were shooting *Mercy Killings* (you probably haven't seen it—it went straight to video), and Joe told me over the phone that the famous beauty was very generously sharing her personal trainer and dietitian/chef with him. The full effect of Susanna's generosity, however, wasn't apparent to me until the end of that shoot when Ruby and I met Joe for a week in Puerto Vallarta. When we settled in at the resort and Joe stripped down to his swim trunks, I was astonished to discover that a large percentage of my husband was missing. All the soft, fleshy stuff around his middle and the beefiness around his shoulders and upper arms—all of it was gone. Joe was now as wiry and lean as a whippet, and I couldn't help but stare.

"I know," said Joe, proudly giving his taut midsection a slap. "I've been working out a little." Then he sauntered out to the beach.

Every day that week, around noon, Joe would say, "Hungry?" and although I was usually starving, had been since about half an hour after my morning pancakes (he had a piece of fruit for breakfast), I would casually reply, "Oh, I don't know . . . maybe a little."

Then he would say, "Let's eat now so my food has time to digest before my workout," and we would wander over to the restaurant to order our lunch.

At lunch, the waiter would try to give me Joe's order and Joe would say, quite sanctimoniously, "No, the mixed baby greens salad with the dressing on the side is for me," and the waiter would place before me the cheeseburger with fries that I had ordered. The first day, I actually offered Joe some of my french fries, to which he shook his head in disgust and said, "I don't think I could even eat one of those anymore. Once you start cutting out the grease and the salt and the fat, you actually lose your appetite for that kind of junk."

"Really?" I said. I was sucking a fry. I had started sucking them to make them last longer, to savor the grease and the salt and the fat.

"Your body's like a machine. Like the engine of a car. Eating too much fat is like putting sludge in your engine. . . ."

"Right, right," I said, nodding seriously. I was trying to look like I was taking it all in, but what I was thinking was, *Give it a rest, Gandhi.*

I thought that Joe's new fitness mania was a fad, and that once we returned to New York, his zeal for health would, like his boyish crush on Susanna, fade away. But I was wrong. Joe had changed. Gone was the man who ate, with gusto, whatever I put on the table. In his place was a salad-obsessed exercise nut, and although Joe no longer ate carbs, he loved to talk about them. Preaching about the benefits of a low-carbohydrate diet actually sent him into a sort of ecstatic reverie, and it was difficult to get him off the subject once he was on it. My friend Lindsey came to visit us at the beach one weekend around that time, and soon after she arrived she asked Joe if he had lost some weight. I frantically tried to signal to her the danger of that line of questioning, but I was too late and soon she was treated to a lecture on the uselessness of carbs, the benefits of protein, and the joy of a daily two-hour workout. Throughout the speech, I sat on the kitchen counter eating handfuls of carbs and staring dully into space. Finally, much later, eyes glazed and stomach rumbling, Lindsey was able to escape to her room, where she spent the better part of the weekend.

Here's the thing: Before Joe got fit, I was fit. Not because I worked out or counted calories. I just didn't eat too much. Food had never been an issue for me. Once Joe started making food seem shameful and naughty, however, I couldn't get enough of it, and for the first time in my life I started to put on a little weight. My ass started to get a little fat, and while I knew that it was still not technically a fat ass by most people's standards, it was getting to be a fat ass by New York standards, and I put the blame squarely on the sculpted shoulders of Susanna Mercer.

Take that, Susanna, I thought as I popped the last fried shrimp into my mouth. *And that!* I thought, washing it down with a gulp of my Cosmo.

Nikki was gleefully telling me about how a certain famous musician and his wife had given up bathing with soap (too many chemicals) just around the time they'd taken up tantric yoga, and how they were now quite infamous among their friends for their horrific combined reek.

"Susanna won't have them in the house," laughed Nikki. "The last time the odor lingered for days!"

There's nothing better than a tipsy personal assistant, really. With very little encouragement I was able to get her talking about Cate Blanchett, another friend of Susanna's. I nodded and smiled at Nikki as she described Cate's eating habits, but my eye was on Joe now. He was across the room, on a long chocolate-brown suede sofa, sitting next to Susanna and surrounded by many of her other guests. Susanna was lolling back on the oversized throw pillows, smoking a cigarette and laughing languorously at something Joe was saying. He began making broad, flapping movements with his arms, and I knew that he was telling his story about the day, last summer in Amagansett, when he hit a wild turkey with his car.

"There I am, going sixty miles an hour," he was saying, "and suddenly my windshield is covered with turkey!" I couldn't hear his exact words from where Nikki and I sat, but I had heard the story a few times before, and it was both frightening and funny the way he told it—the awkward flapping of the giant bird, its panicked expression the moment before it collided with the windshield, the way its wingspan completely obscured Joe's view, causing him to spin off onto the side of the road. I saw Susanna and the others watching him and laughing, and then I saw Joe as they must have seen him: handsome and funny and raffishly charming. Joseph Ferraro standing on a sandy roadside, his Porsche covered in feathers and entrails, signing an autograph for the state trooper who had stopped to help. Not the awkward, shy, borderline dork I had met in college—the one I had taught to drive a stick shift and to shoot pool and, really, how to dress. The Joe Ferraro I first met in 1986 wore Levi's corduroys and oxford shirts and Adidas. After a couple weeks with me, Alison, and Beth, I'm not kidding, he looked like one of the Ramones, only handsome. Now the warm, blinking glow of the fireplace altered his profile slightly, highlighting his cheekbones and pale blue eyes and the whiteness of his smile, and I saw, in that moment, the Joseph Ferraro you've seen in magazines and on the side of buses and on billboards. On *Letterman* and *Leno,* with Barbara Walters and Katie Couric, and maybe just walking down the street with his gaze fixed just past you, but his slight smile revealing that he knows *you know* who he is. Joe Ferraro, the star.

"Julia," Nikki said, "finish up that drink. Mine's completely gone and you're making me feel like an alcoholic!"

I gulped the rest of my drink, and since Nikki was on a gossip jag, I asked, "What was that story I recently read about Susanna? I think it was on 'Page Six.' . . . Something about her saving a choking man?"

Nikki hooted with laughter. "Oh, Julia, I have to tell Susanna you said that! Did you really read that? Was it 'Page Six'? Susanna and I made it up for a laugh!"

"C'mon!" I said. "How?"

"Well, Susanna loves to Google herself, and sometimes we go on Gawker.com just to see what people have said about her."

"Seriously?"

"Yeah, Gawker or Perez Hilton. Oh, you know, those sites where people post celebrity sightings in Manhattan, like, 'I saw Kevin Bacon standing on the corner of Fifty-ninth and Fifth.' Or 'I saw Julianne Moore adjusting her knickers,' that kind of thing. Anyway, Susanna and I remembered when *Mission: Impossible* was coming out, the press was full of stories about Tom Cruise saving people in real life. He rescued some drowning French people, he saved someone who was hit by a car. . . . There was something else, too. I forget. So we started wondering how his press agents or the Scientologists managed all that—Susanna was convinced the items were made up—so we decided to put up an entry about her saving a choking person on Gawker.com, just to see what would happen. And sure enough, it got posted and picked up by the tabloids. Her publicist's phone was ringing off the hook the next day, and she told every reporter that Susanna denied helping any choking person, but lots of papers ran the story, anyway! Just goes to show you," said Nikki. "Well, I'm ready for another drink. I think I'll have a real one this time—the last one was mostly cranberry juice. Ready, Jules?"

"Sure," I said, rising unsteadily. "I'll get them!"

Just then Joe stepped up, balancing three pink drinks in his hands, a cigarette dangling from his lips.

"Here. I told the bartender to make up some more of whatever you girls are drinking, but this time I told him to use normal glasses."

"Jesus Christ, Joe," I said, laughing helplessly. He had Cosmo highballs in his hands.

"Have you got a fag, Joe?" Nikki asked.

"Nah, just the wife here," Joe said, nodding at me, and then he laughed jovially at his own little joke. He pulled a pack of cigarettes out of his pocket and handed one to her.

"I'll have one, too," I said, and Joe held one out for me. I reached into his jacket pocket for his lighter.

"Do you smoke, Julia?" Nikki asked.

"No!" I replied, lighting up.

"Never?" asked Nikki as I lit hers.

"Really never." I inhaled deeply. "Only, you know, occasionally when I drink."

Joe was watching my every move. He loves it when I smoke. I looked at him and blew smoke out of the corner of my mouth. He gave me a slow, simmering smile, and I couldn't help it, I had to smile back. I smiled and looked away.

"C'mere," he said.

[nine]

Mommy?"

My eyes slammed open. Sammy's face was so close that our noses were almost touching.

"Hi, sweetness," I whispered. Then I lowered my eyelids. Darkness.

"Mommy?"

"Mmm-hmm?"

"What smells?" he asked.

I opened my eyes again. Sammy had clamped his nose between his thumb and forefinger.

"I don't know," I said.

"Oh," Sammy said. Then he said, "Maybe it's you."

I blinked at him.

I blinked and then I tried to sit up. Something in my frontal lobe—and I could somehow distinguish between my throbbing cerebral lobes—was killing me. My skull seemed to have shrunk overnight and the resulting pressure on my brain made me whimper.

"Can I have breakfast now?" asked Sammy. He rolled off the bed and trotted toward the bedroom door.

"Okay. Yeah. I'm coming," I said, and the lungful of air accompanying those words settled around me like a noxious shroud. I had the breath of a two-day-old corpse. It actually hurt to inhale. I saw that I was naked and, glancing over at Joe, I saw that he was, too, and then it all came back to me.

Lighting cigarettes. Many, many cigarettes. Lighting cigarettes off cigarettes. Stopping off at the Dublin House for a drink with Nikki and a drunken young actor she had hit it off with at the party. Joe amiably signing autographs for a group of college kids. More smoking. Drinking beer. I remember we switched to beer so we wouldn't get too drunk! Laughing at Nikki and her new friend making out at the bar.

Did I drag Nikki into the ladies' room to try to talk some sense into her about hooking up with that guy? I did. I remembered now that Joe told me to. Nikki had slipped going into the bathroom and I had tried to force her to drink water and we had almost fallen over with laughter. Later, Joe and I, our arms around each other, walked the few blocks home, laughing and whistling and trying to remember the theme songs to old television shows. Somberly greeting the night doorman, and then, the minute the elevator doors closed behind us, the way I pushed Joe back against the wall and began kissing him on his lips, his throat, his chest, Joe pulling my lowering head close with one hand and attempting to cover the security camera above him with the other. The rest of it rushed back then, like smash cuts in a bad movie.

I stood.

I pulled on a robe, shuffled into the bathroom, and brushed the night's accumulation of Cosmos and cigarettes off my teeth, all the while trying to find some way to blame Joe for what I considered to be an outright violation the night before. I had vowed to myself after the first overheard phone message from Miss Hornyasamother-fucker that any future sex with Joe was out of the question. Those days were over. The shop was closed. I had held out for two days (held out! as if anyone was asking) and then last night I had blown it. Literally. And no matter how I tried to turn it around in my mind now, I knew that I had been the culprit. The aggressor. Each drink had diluted my resolve. During dinner I glanced over, and when I caught Joe's eye I thought, *When did his hair get so long? I love him with floppy hair.* Later, when I saw Susanna delicately pick up a piece of cake with her fingertips and then place it in Joe's mouth, I thought, *Nah, she doesn't have a Southern accent. And who could blame her for flirting? Look at him!*

"Mommy!" Sammy called from the kitchen.

"Yeah, okay. Here I come."

On the floor of the kitchen lay Joe's coat, and a few feet away, completing this shameful tableau, my new Marc Jacobs jacket lay in a heap, all limp and used looking, the fur collar as lifeless and vulgar as roadkill. The kitchen table had been pushed away from its usual place against the wall. A bowl of fruit had been knocked onto the floor.

Had we . . .

Yes, I remembered. Indeed we had. We had said good night to Catalina, locked the door behind her, and . . .

"Can I have pancakes?" asked Sammy.

"Sure, honey," I said, thinking, *Thank God Ruby slept at Emma's last night.* "I'll make you some pancakes and then let's go out—to the park. Look how the sun is shining! And it's Saturday!"

An hour later, somewhat fortified with coffee, pancakes, peanut butter, and Advil, I followed Sammy out of our building. We left the stale, heated lobby, stepped out onto West Eighty-fifth Street, and the late-morning air felt clement and pure and forgiving. It was early January, but the slicing wind that had whipped down the avenues on recent mornings had blown off the island of Manhattan and a mild breeze had taken its place. Sammy ran ahead to the Korean deli on the corner, where the owner's wife was placing large buckets of flowers out on the sidewalk beneath a long, low pyramid of fruits and vegetables. I caught up with him, and as we waited for the light to change, we watched the woman, whose name we didn't know but whose face we saw many times each day, carrying two buckets at a time from the inside of the store to the sidewalk. She seemed to just place the buckets haphazardly in a row, but there before us was a multitiered exhibition of color and texture and fragrance so vivid and promising against its dirty graffitied backdrop that most mornings even Sammy was compelled to stop for a moment to take it all in. It was like a seam had ripped in the corner of our building's aged facade and this ripe, multicolored brilliance had burst out. There were tall buckets of irises with their impossibly blue spearheads pointing out in all directions, soft clouds of white hydrangea, interlocking tiered stems of fragrant blue-green eucalyptus, and scarlet-veined Easter lily buds, swollen and ready to bloom. We stood on the corner waiting for the light to change and we watched a frail, elderly couple filling a bag with apricots. The man's hands shook and his body swayed slightly as he held the bag open for his wife. *Maybe Parkinson's,* I thought, my hand touching Sammy's shoulder. The old man seemed to be clutching the bag for all he was worth. He patiently held the open, shaking bag while the woman examined each apricot with bony fingers, rejecting three for every one she placed in the bag. The man just stood there with head bowed, clutching that bag as if his life depended on it, and his wife scrutinized the fruit as if they had all the time in the world.

"Walk!" said Sammy when the light changed, startling me a little. He reached up for my hand, which was the rule, and we started across Broadway.

"Hippo or dinosaur?" I asked Sammy.

"Hippo!" Sammy hollered. When we reached the far corner, Sammy dropped my hand and began his sprint up the block.

"Wait for me at the corner, Sammy! Don't cross!"

"I know!" he called back.

"Wait!"

The Hippo Park is nestled beneath the shade of centuries-old trees at the foot of a steep hill in Riverside Park. Like the Dinosaur Park six blocks north, the Hippo Park's proximity to the Hudson River always makes it feel about ten degrees cooler than everywhere else in the city, which is a good thing in the summer. In the winter it's usually a windswept no-man's-land. When we first moved to the neighborhood, during Ruby's preschool days, the playground was being renovated. First the old-fashioned metal swings and rickety jungle gyms were removed and replaced by newer, safer models that were installed above rubber mats. And then came the hippos—hollow concrete sculptures that children scramble onto and jump off of, or straddle like a horse. In the summer, water squirts from the gaping hippo mouths and children dart in and out of the spray in sopping underwear or bathing suits. The hippos were meant to have children climb inside and stick their heads out through the massive benign jaws, and at first the kids loved to do just that until one morning when a little boy climbed in to discover that a presumably homeless person had decided the inside of the hippo was the perfect place to move his or her bowels. Not long after that, thanks to some frenzied calls from the more vocal members of the playground committee, the parks department filled the hippos with cement.

When Ruby was little, I was on the playground committee. We were playground regulars. Weather permitting, we could be found at the Hippo Park every day. Sometimes twice a day. I had friends I would meet up with in the park—other stay-at-home moms—and we would talk about the news, our husbands, and our kids, about sex and books and our favorite television shows and our annoying mothers and our reproductive cycles while our kids stomped around the fenced-in playground, imagining they were princesses and warriors and ninjas and fairies.

After Sammy was born, though, we could afford to have Catalina work for us full time, and she was usually the one who took Sammy to the park. The two of them developed their own network of friends, so now, on the rare occasions when I took Sammy to the playground, I felt like a bit of an outsider.

"¡Hola, Samicito!" a woman called out as soon as we walked through the gates, and Sammy called back, *"¡Hola, Señora Berta!"* and ran into the woman's arms for a hug. *"¿Dónde está Tía Catalina?"* the woman said, and to my astonishment, Sammy replied, *"En su casa. No trabaja hoy."* This was a kid who had been recently labeled "possibly speech-delayed" by his preschool teacher, Lauren, during our parent/teacher conference in October.

"Really?" I had said. It was true that Sammy usually chose to speak in monosyllables, but I knew grown men—my brother, Neil, for example—who used words almost as sparingly. "Joe's mother told me that Joe didn't speak a word until he was two and a half," I told Lauren. "Sammy's sister and her friends do everything he wants, so all he has to do is grunt and point. I think he just hasn't seen any reason to talk in complex sentences yet."

But Lauren urged me to have him tested and the results shed a different light on Sammy than the soft, easy one through which we had always viewed him. Sammy had "issues," according to his tester. He was "immature." Informed of this diagnosis in a follow-up meeting, Joe had concurred. Sammy was indeed immature. He was four years old.

"We mean he's immature compared to children his age," said Lauren. She stared impassively at Joe, and I could see that she was determined to convey an "I'm unimpressed by celebrity and for that matter anyone with a penis" attitude. When asked for an example of his immature behavior, Lauren said, "He still thinks potty humor is funny."

"That's because potty humor *is* funny," said Joe.

Lauren smiled tolerantly.

I said, "I think what Joe is trying to say is that we've probably encouraged him at home by laughing at silly potty jokes. He has an older sister—"

"No, what I'm saying is that potty humor is usually pretty funny." I could see that Joe was clenching his jaw. Really a bad sign.

"And what's this business here about sequencing problems—" I tried to continue, but was interrupted by Joe: "Seriously. I defy you to tell me something about . . . poop that won't make me laugh."

"Okay," said Lauren, smiling condescendingly. "*Poop* is a natural function that helps our bodies eliminate waste."

"HAHAHAHAHAHA," Joe laughed maniacally. Lauren gazed at him with a look of controlled anger that I had seen her give Sammy when he got a little wound up. The tester, a meek girl named Paige, began explaining to me about "normal" sequencing and "delayed" sequencing, and it all got jumbled together in an incomprehensible, unsequenced mess in my mind, and all the while Joe shook his head and chuckled to himself. But despite Joe's objections (he's just a little kid), I had scheduled Sam for speech therapy and occupational therapy. Now I wondered if his speech therapist knew that he was bilingual.

"Hi," I said to Berta as Sammy chased a little boy over to the climbing apparatus. "I'm Julia. I'm Sammy's mom."

"Hi. I know. I'm Berta, Catalina's friend. I babysit with Alex."

"Oh, of course . . ." I said, and then I tried to recall which little boy was Alex and I had no idea. I used to know all the kids in the playground. When Ruby was little.

The playground was rather busy on this bright morning, but as I gazed around I saw nobody I knew except Adam Heller, who was seated on one of the benches reading the *Times.* His daughter Katie was playing with another little girl on the climbing apparatus. The girls hung on to the lower bars and swung their feet back and forth, singing and laughing. Adam glanced up at them occasionally but seemed otherwise engrossed in his newspaper.

Adam Heller was a stay-at-home dad whose wife supported them with her income from a big law firm. He had been a source of fascination for me ever since his wife, Elizabeth, told me about how Katie had come to be potty-trained. We were in the park one Saturday, when Sammy and Katie were not even two, and while I was changing Sammy at one point, Elizabeth said, "Glad those days are over."

"Really? You're all finished with potty training?"

"Finished?" she said. "I never even started. I was on a business trip one weekend and when I returned, I noticed we were out of Pampers. I told Adam I was going to run out and get some and he said, 'We don't use those anymore.' Honestly, the first thing that came to my mind was that Katie had had some kind of horrible accident or . . . operation while I was away. Then Adam told me that when he realized we were out of diapers, he figured she was probably old enough to start using the toilet, so he told her that from now on, she should just *go in the toilet.* He doesn't read any books about raising children, so he just thought that's all there was to it. And in Katie's case that was all there was to it."

I loved this story and recounted it to all my friends, who also got a kick out of it (eventually, the story became an urban legend—I once heard somebody at a cocktail party tell the story and they had never met Adam or Elizabeth). Adam Heller had disproved a silent understanding we mothers shared: that our children, left in the hands of their ill-equipped fathers for more than a few hours, would quickly regress to the point of becoming feral, unspeaking, self-wetting animals. The Adam Heller story forced us to consider the possibility that perhaps we mothers sometimes get in our own, and our children's, way with all our fretting and researching and managing, and that maybe we should just trust our partner's instincts a little more.

I wandered a little closer to the climbing equipment and saw that the little girl playing with Katie belonged to Nancy Grickis, another Multi mom, who was, herself, trying to read a section of the *Times* but had positioned herself almost underneath the apparatus.

"Hi, Julia!" Nancy said. "Annie, that's high enough." The girls had started to climb up the jungle gym. Each wanted to be higher than the other. Nancy's daughter Annie stopped climbing but Katie continued her determined ascent.

"What's Katie's dad's name again?" whispered Nancy.

"Adam. Adam Heller."

"Right. I only really know the wife," Nancy mumbled. Then she called out, "Adam?"

Adam looked up from his paper.

"Look where Katie is!" Nancy was forcing a smile.

Adam looked up from his paper at Katie, who was now almost at the summit. He nodded and smiled. "She's a good little climber all right," he said, and then returned to his paper.

"Oh my God," Nancy angrily mouthed to me. Then she whispered, "Elizabeth would be pissed, and I would be, too, if I was working my butt off at a big law firm and my stay-at-home husband couldn't be bothered to watch out for his own daughter."

"I don't know," I said. "She actually is a good little climber. It's supposed to give them confidence to let them try things like climbing up high."

"It also gives them spinal cord injuries if they fall," Nancy snapped. She stared at Adam, then she shook her head in disgust.

"Mommy, Katie's at the top. Why can't I go up?" Annie whined.

"Because Mommy wants you to be safe!" Another angry look at Adam.

Annie moved herself up a rung.

"That's it! No higher!"

"But Katie gets to go higher!" Annie's whine had turned into a shrill, fake cry.

"I'm not responsible for Katie. I'm responsible for you. And I want you to be safe!" Nancy fully glared at Adam. He read on, oblivious.

Annie moved herself up another rung.

"Okay, Annie. That's it. You're not listening to what I say, so I want you to come down. Now."

I knew where this was going, so I turned around to look for

Sammy. He was playing king of the hill on the slide with a group of little boys. Sammy was climbing back up the slide like a monkey. Another little boy followed him.

"One!" Nancy called out sternly. I looked back at the jungle gym. Annie clung to her perch defiantly.

"Two!"

Annie moved one hand up to the next rung.

"Three! Okay, that's it. Time-out! A three-minute time-out, Annie. Do you want to make it six minutes?"

I'm certainly no expert, but I had learned through bitter experience with Ruby and Sammy that one must never start counting if one can't snatch up the child immediately upon the arrival at three to drag his or her screaming little body away. Nancy couldn't reach Annie. Annie knew this. Nancy could count all day, but she and Annie both knew she was screwed.

I glanced at Adam to see if he was purposely trying to antagonize Nancy with his indifference, but it was clear that he had no idea she was furious at him. He was placidly reading the newspaper, his daughter was playing with a little girl, and two women whom he vaguely knew were watching their children. This was the extent of his awareness, and I have to admit I was a little envious of his casual oblivion. I had witnessed it on other occasions as well. Adam would drop Katie off at birthday parties that were clearly meant to be attended by children *and* their parents, and then he would be late picking her up. He threw a birthday party for Katie last year, invited only half the girls in the class, and held the party right after school! The mothers of the girls who weren't invited harped about this for months. And, according to Liz Kelleher, whose daughter was invited, he gave out fistfuls of gum and candy instead of the usual beautifully prepared party bags. *Why couldn't I be more like Adam Heller?* I wondered. *Why did I have to succumb to the unspoken tyranny of the playground Nazis and Montessori Mumsies?* I was constantly apologizing for Sammy, forcing him to share when he didn't want to, smiling over a glass of wine at a group of dull parents at a spoiled child's birthday party. Why didn't I just act like Adam Heller? Like it was all beyond my own comprehension?

"One more time, Annie! I'm going to give you one more chance!" Nancy keened. Just then Adam glanced up from his paper. He grinned naughtily at me, rolled his eyes at Nancy, and then he said, "Hey, Katie, let's go."

Okay, so he was doing it for his own amusement in this instance. I still wanted to be like him.

Katie climbed down two rungs to where Annie perched and then she launched herself into the air, landing slightly wobbly on her feet just a few feet away from Nancy.

"Taa-daa!" Katie declared.

"Annie . . . don't you dare . . ."

Of course, Annie jumped, too, but she was obviously less experienced and rolled forward onto her knees upon landing, scuffing them sharply on the hard rubberized mat. There was a pause. Then a shriek.

Every mother in close proximity offered wipes and tissues and Band-Aids. Somebody ran over to the soda vendor for ice. Adam simply tucked his papers under his arm and headed home, his daughter happily skipping by his side.

The afternoon was so mild that Sammy and I stayed in the playground until the sun had begun to settle across the river, and then we began the long trek back to Broadway and Eighty-fifth Street. Waiting for the light on West End Avenue, I wished, once again, that we lived closer to a park.

Joe and I had actually started looking at apartments the previous fall. We were looking primarily on Central Park West and across the park on the East Side. The apartment we currently lived in was large enough, but the location wasn't great. Too far from Ruby's school and Sammy's playgrounds, and it was on Broadway, which was noisy and crowded. We had bought the apartment six years earlier, using the income from Joe's first two movies as a down payment. It was a co-op and our "financials" were a disaster, according to our real-estate broker. We had no credit history, except for some long-overdue student loans that had been hastily paid off just months before, and when we met with the co-op board, the president had voiced his concerns.

"What if you can't keep up with your maintenance payments? What if you don't get any work next year and you have to foreclose?" But Joe had charmed him. He showed him a recent article in *Variety* that listed Joe Ferraro as one of Hollywood's hottest up-and-comers, and the contract that he had just signed for the Ralph Fiennes movie. Then he gave all the board members tickets to an off-Broadway show he was going to be starring in the following month, and the board was enchanted. "This kid's gonna be a star," the president told our broker when he called to announce the board's approval. "I can feel it!"

The evening after we closed on the apartment, Ruby, Joe, and I took the subway uptown from the East Village, where we had been living, and we had a picnic on the broom-clean floor of our new home. Now that the former owner's furnishings had been removed, the space seemed grand and cavernous, and when we entered the foyer, our footsteps and voices echoed off the high plaster ceilings and walls. "It sounds like school in here," Ruby had said.

It was a classic prewar apartment, a bigger one than we had

thought we could afford. We had gotten a deal on the place because the kitchen and bathrooms sorely needed updating. There was a formal entryway, with a door leading to an old kitchen with matching Kenmore appliances in avocado green, circa 1975, then a central hall with a living room on one side and a formal dining room on the other, and at the end, a master bedroom on the left and two other bedrooms on the right. The hardwood floors were dull and scratched and the original wooden trim around the doors and windows had years ago lost their edge, swathed as they were in decades' worth of hasty paint jobs. The place needed work—even the broker had conceded that it was a little "shabby"—but after years of loft living, there was something enduring and solid about the thick walls and the carefully considered floor plan of apartment 6B, an old-world warmth and vitality that had been lacking in the modern high-rise apartments that we had been seeing.

We ate takeout on the floor of our new dining room that first night, and through the windows we could see the rosy twilit sky above the neighboring buildings, the western light so foreign and strange to us. Ruby ran in and out of the rooms singing a song about whales, and from somewhere in the building came the do-re-mi-fa-so-la-ti-do of a child's piano scales, careful and precise. I wondered how many first meals new tenants had enjoyed in that very room. How many Thanksgiving dinners, seders, Christmas breakfasts, New Year's brunches? Joe had run down to the corner for a bottle of champagne, and we toasted our new lives in the pale light of that late-June evening, just me and Ruby and Joe, and it seemed then that the kindly ghosts of the former families of apartment 6B toasted our cozy future along with us.

"There's a thing about you two on Gawker today," Ruby said that night over dinner. We were having take-out Chinese, as we did most Saturdays when Catalina took the night off.

"On what?" asked Joe.

"On Gawker dot-com."

"That's funny," I said. "Somebody was just telling me something about that Web site last night."

"Well, according to Gawker, it's surprising you remember. It sounds like you two had yourselves quite the time at . . . where was it? The Dublin House?"

"Wait, you read Gawker? I thought you hated everything to do with celebrity and show business," said Joe. Then he said, "I don't want you reading that crap."

"Is the Dublin House that place on Seventy-second Street?" Ruby continued. "That place looks like a dump. Why were you there?"

"Why aren't we monitoring where she goes on the Web?" Joe said to me. "I thought you were doing that."

"Monitoring?" I said. "You know I don't know anything about computers. I trust Ruby not to go places she shouldn't. . . ."

"Don't you read the fucking papers?!" Joe shouted at me. A piece of moo shoo pork was stuck to his lower lip. "There are *predators* on it looking for kids to—"

"Jesus Christ, Joe!" I exclaimed. Then, carefully lowering my voice, I said, "You don't have to shout."

"Yeah, don't you read fucking papers?!" shouted Sammy, sending Ruby into fits of giggles.

"Don't laugh at him, Ruby!" I yelled. Then I took a breath. "Sammy, that's a grown-up word," I said.

"I'm not the one who said it," said Ruby.

"Fuck!" said Sammy. Then he looked devilishly at Ruby.

"Great," I said to Joe. "Just great."

"Sammy. Quit it now," said Joe. His face and neck were red, and I could see by the bulging vein in his forehead that he was furious but was trying to remain calm. He turned to Ruby. "I thought you were on some kind of a kids' limited-access Internet plan. How could you get onto Gawker?"

"Dad, I was on that kiddie plan when I was like six. You can't use the computer for research when you have those blocks."

"So you can go anywhere you damn well please on the Internet. That's nice," said Joe, looking accusingly at me "I mean, what kind of research are you doing on a sleazy site like Gawker, Ruby?"

Ruby visibly bristled at the sound of the word *sleazy* in the same sentence as her name.

"I Googled you! I wanted to read about you! And I'm just reading about people on the sleazy Web site. I'm not one of the sleazy people in it," she said quietly. Then she jumped up and ran to her room.

"Oh, Jesus Christ," said Joe. He slammed his fork down on the table and stood up. "I just want to know where she goes on the Internet," he said to me. "That's all!" Then he walked to the back of the apartment and could be heard knocking on Ruby's door. "Ruby?" he said quietly. "Ruby, kitten, open the door."

"All done," said Sammy, climbing out of his seat.

"Okay," I said. "Fifteen minutes of Nickelodeon and then bath time."

Sammy trotted happily into the living room and I started to clear our plates. I finished off the wine in my glass, the blessed, merciful hair of the dog that had buoyed me through dinner. I was tired when dinner had arrived, but now I was waking up a little bit. Joe's tirade had provoked me, to say the least. I had been lulled that day into a hangover-induced state of forgiveness and compassion. I honestly hadn't checked Joe's voice mail once. The unbidden flashbacks to last night's intimate romp had softened me a little and made me wonder if all my doubts were unfounded. "I love you, baby," he had whispered into my ear last night. Walking back from the playground, I thought about that and about how all the messages could easily have been from some chummy wardrobe girl who liked to joke around with Joe. I had almost decided that I would take Beth's suggestion and at least ask Joe about the messages, even though doing so would bring an end to my access to them. It is wrong to spy on another person, I had thought, chasing Sammy down our block that afternoon. It's just wrong. Now, dumping out a half-eaten plate of broccoli with garlic sauce, I thought, *It's also wrong to cheat on your wife.*

That night I stayed up late, eating ice cream and watching a movie after Joe and the kids had gone to bed. It was the film version of *The Crucible,* and I was quite taken aback by Joan Allen's heroic speech to her husband at the end. "It needs a cold wife to prompt lechery," she had said to Daniel Day-Lewis during their moment of reckoning before his execution. "It were a cold house I kept."

Was our house—our marriage—cold? Had I caused Joe to stray? There was certainly no disputing that our sex life wasn't what it had been before we had kids. Whose was? Babies change you. Before I was pregnant with Ruby, I used to watch mothers tend lovingly to screaming babies and toddlers, and I worried that I might never be able to summon up the appropriate maternal instincts toward any future offspring of my own. In my mind I was witnessing an extremely annoying little person and an adult with an almost Christ-like capacity for love, tenderness, and forgiveness. I didn't understand their history the way I do now. The history of the mother and child's love for each other, which, for me, began almost immediately after Ruby was conceived. Nine months before Joe ever saw or touched Ruby, I was awash with her, my every waking moment consumed by thoughts of her. Then, in those first days and nights of her life when she needed to suckle almost hourly, everything beyond her spiky pink hair (really, it was pink), those dimpled knees and elbows, those gorgeous lips . . . everything beyond Ruby disappeared into a sort of soft-focus backdrop. We spent endless hours gazing into each other's eyes. Nobody had told me about the urge to gaze, about the instinct that compelled Ruby and me to peer at each other, over and over again between feedings, passing the gaze back and forth. All night and all day, milk, breaths, gazes, and sighs were passed back and forth between us like life-giving transfusions until both of us were just pumped full of love for each other. And every now and then, from somewhere far off in the murky distance, I'd hear Joe's voice saying, "I got a callback for that Barry Levinson film. It's not a big part, but it could be good because . . . ," and when he was finished with whatever nonsense he was droning on about, I'd say something like, "The skin on her cheek is so soft, it's like kissing air. Kiss her. It's like kissing nothing. I can't stop kissing her."

When I read *The Crucible* in high school, and later when I saw the play, I had imagined that "Goodwife" Proctor was probably not such a great wife at all, and I always felt that her personal revelation at the end was simply too little, too late. She was obviously not giving her husband enough sex, so he *had* to go elsewhere. Now I didn't feel so generous. Why couldn't men see that the children grow, they leave the bed? Then, eventually, they leave the home. Someday there'll be just the two of them again, the husband and wife. I saw now that the whole mess—the witch hunt, the trial, and the executions—all of it was John Proctor's fault. He had seduced an unstable girl, then he had cast her aside. The girl was enacting her revenge and his wife and kids were the victims.

A parable of the McCarthy trials, my ass.

My big, fat, whopping ass.

When I went into the bedroom, I saw that Joe had fallen asleep with his laptop open on the bed next to him. I went to move it and wondered if he had been looking at the Gawker site. I crawled into bed next to him and placed the laptop across my thighs. I went to Gawker.com and typed Joe's name into the search box at the top of the page. A series of dates appeared on the screen. It hadn't occurred to me that there would be an archive of previous Joe Ferraro sightings, but indeed there was. I clicked on January 6, which was the night before.

> Spotted Joe Ferraro and two women walking into the Dublin House on the Upper West Side. Appeared to be wife and younger woman. Threesome drank at bar for almost an hour. Wife and younger woman disappeared into restroom together for about ten minutes, then returned to the bar looking disheveled. The Ferraros left around 1:00, Joe helping giggly wife who appeared to have had one too many.

Ruby had read this. My sweet Ruby had read about her drunken mother. I read and reread the line about Nikki and I going to the ladies' room together and I wondered what Ruby had made of that.

"Joe?" I said. I said it before I had a chance to think. I just said it because I felt so alone.

"Hmm?"

"I'm scared," I said. It felt like I might start crying, so I focused on my breathing.

"What?" Joe mumbled.

I closed the laptop and I placed it on the floor next to the bed. Then I shut off the light. Breathing in and out.

"Honey?" Joe mumbled.

"Yeah."

Joe rolled over toward me and I turned away. He put his arms around my middle and pulled me in to him, pulled my shoulders back up against his chest and cradled my breast in his palm. Joe has always found great comfort cupping something while he rests, his balls or one of my breasts, either will do. He held my breast in his palm and he dozed back off. I could feel his sleep in the heaviness of his limbs on me and in the steadiness of his breath, and the disgust I had felt toward him was slowly displaced by the familiar warmth of his skin against mine, his chest pressed into the curve of my back, our bodies intertwined as they had been thousands of nights before.

[—]

"So?" Beth had said after he left that first morning. That blistering hot July morning in 1986. She was trying not to laugh, I could tell.

"What?"

"Just a little surprised to see the Spaniel here this morning, that's all."

We called Joe "the Spaniel" back then.

"Okay, well, don't tell Alison." Alison was our other roommate.

"Soooo . . ." Beth grinned, kicking a chair out for me to sit on and handing me her pack of Marlboro Lights. "What happened?"

"I took him to see that band."

"Uh-huh."

"Uh-huh, because you wouldn't come!"

"Oh, so this is my fault. I see." She grinned again.

"He called last night to see what we were up to and I asked him to go to CBGB's. Because nobody else would come . . ."

"Because we knew it was going to be a hundred fucking degrees in that place . . ."

"Well, I still wanted to go."

"Because you thought the Weasel was going to be there!"

We called this guy Eddie "the Weasel."

"Did you make coffee?" I asked Beth, trying to change the subject.

"Yeah. I had to use toilet paper for a coffee filter again. It's your turn to go to the store."

"I know."

"So let me get this straight. You took Joe . . . stalking with you? That's an interesting idea for a first date."

"Scalding coffee," I said, pouring myself a cup, "about to be dumped on your head." I was giggling now, because I was deliriously tired and a little hung over. It was still early morning and I was already drenched in sweat. "It wasn't a first date! I've known Joe for months."

"Well? Was Weasel there?"

"Yeah, he showed up toward the end of the set. He was with that freaky redhead who always wears the boots."

"You mean . . . his girlfriend?"

I shuffled over to the refrigerator and removed a carton of milk. I smelled it and then poured some of it into my coffee.

"You know, I think you're right. I think they *are* going out," I said.

"Julia, they've been sleeping together for months—he told you that! Why do you deny this obvious fact?"

"I don't deny it," I said, "and I don't really give a shit anymore."

"Wow! You and Joe must have had some big night." Beth laughed.

This was when we were living in the loft on Avenue B, Beth and Alison and I. Alison and I were both at NYU—Alison was a drama major, I was supposed to be a journalism major, and I have no idea what Beth was supposed to be studying at the time. She was at Parsons—drawing or illustrating or something. Anyway, we lived in a huge unfinished loft that had once been occupied by Alison's brother. He had moved to Amsterdam with his boyfriend but he still held the rent-controlled lease, and he sublet the place to us for something crazy like three hundred dollars a month. Almost the entire sixth floor of an old warehouse building, it had two long walls of floor-to-ceiling arched windows and was only approachable by stairs that were littered with beer bottles and cigarette butts. Beth had a very useful boyfriend when we first moved in—a sculptor named Chris who was handy with tools and drywall and paint—and he lived with us for a while and built a few bedrooms in exchange for rent. The only toilet was in an old-fashioned water closet down the hall, and we shared it with a frail but kindly former junkie who lived on the floor below us. We lounged on colorful thrift-shop furniture and bathed in our industrial-sized kitchen sink, which sounds ridiculous now, but this was the eighties. The city was filthy and crime ridden. We threw great parties and were comped at all the best clubs and once had a short feature written about us in *New York* magazine. Sam Shepard showed up at one of our parties. Somebody whom Alison and Beth swear was Joe Strummer appeared briefly at another (he was gone by the time I got home from work that night). The graffiti artist Zephyr tagged one of our walls one night in big, loopy orange and gray letters.

We had a gigantic old black Garland stove, but none of us cooked, and on occasion, when Alison came home a little tipsy, she would decide to have a nice hot soak in the sink next to it, and if Beth and I brought friends home later, we would have to explain why there was a naked model sleeping in a sink full of dirty dishes next to our front door.

Joe has said during interviews that I was a model when we met, but I never really modeled. I did a fashion show once for this Israeli designer we hung out with, stomping down the runway in a clear cellophane blouse, leather pants, and heavy combat boots, and I was on the cover of a Chemo Haze album (they had a hit song in the early eighties—you'd know it if you heard it) because Alison was seeing their bass player at the time, but I wasn't a real model. Alison was a real model. She had been signed by Eileen Ford the first week she arrived in Manhattan and she did a lot of runway stuff and features in *Elle* and *Harper's Bazaar.* She also auditioned for films and television shows and NYU productions, and that's how we met Joe. He was in a play with Alison. It was Bertolt Brecht's *Baal* and he played the wino. Alison was in love with the guy who played Baal. She'd had a one-night stand with him and now she wanted Beth and me to come to opening night and to the after-party so we could tell her if we thought he was straight.

"You slept with him but you want *us* to tell you if he's straight?" Beth had asked.

"Well, I think he might be kind of bi."

"Based on what?" I had asked.

"Just a feeling. I dunno."

"Did he have . . . problems in bed? The night you guys were together?" asked Beth.

"Yeah, a little."

"But you said you were both drunk. That's probably why," Beth replied. "You're just being neurotic."

"No, it wasn't just that. He told me he's been with a guy."

"What?!" I said.

"Alison!" Beth cried out.

"It was just once," Alison said. "He was just experimenting! Jesus, you guys have such a naive view of sexuality. Lots of people try homosexual sex when they're young."

"Yeah, I know," Beth said. "And those people are called homosexuals."

"Wait until you meet him," said Alison. "He's gorgeous. I mean, I'm sure everybody comes onto him all the time, male and female, and he just . . . well, just come. You won't think he's gay when you meet him."

So we went to the play, and at the party afterward, I met Joe. I had hated the play and didn't really notice him onstage. Joe wasn't as noticeable then, especially near Ben Grier, the lead who—Alison was right—didn't seem gay. Or maybe it was too difficult for women to imagine that he was gay because he was so gorgeous. Tall, lean, yet muscled. Tousled sandy-blond hair. He's on *All My Children* now, but at the time we all thought he was going to be the next Marlon Brando.

Joe was more heavily muscled—even a little chubby—back then. "That was baby fat," I would later tell Ruby when she laughed at early pictures of Joe and me. "You still have baby fat in your twenties?" she asked, and I said, "You do if your diet consists entirely of waffles, macaroni and cheese, and beer."

Joe wore unflattering glasses, and his dark hair was short, but still somehow always messy, and he usually had rough stubble on his cheeks and chin. He always had those great eyes, of course—

"seaglass blue" was how a critic would describe them years later—with those thick brown lashes, and his lips that turned up at the corners like a kitten's. He had a shy way of tilting his head down a little when he was talking to me, then glancing up quickly and looking straight into my eyes and then looking away.

I had a thing for a guitar player at the time, a tall, skinny Irish kid named Eddie O'Malley (the Weasel) whose band opened for Aimee Mann one night at the Bottom Line and now there was a record label interested. Or so he said.

I was crazy about Eddie O'Malley but, unfortunately, he just wasn't that into me. He *was* into the press ID I had forged that got us backstage at all the shows. I was doing an internship at the *Village Voice* then and had altered my intern identification into an ID that said:

JULIA MANNING
MUSIC CRITIC
VILLAGE VOICE

But Joe—Joe was into me. He asked Alison about me all the time, and when the play was over, we would invite him to our parties and he would talk to me with his head tilted down a little, glancing up now and then to shoot me a look, and then away. Those puppy-dog eyes! That's why we called him the Spaniel. His eyes and his loyal, tagalong determination to be with me even though I didn't really encourage him. Finally one night, during that long July heat wave, I couldn't get anyone to go out to a club where I thought I might run into Eddie, so I asked Joe. We had a few laughs and a few drinks at the club and then, just when we were heading out the door, Eddie arrived with the redhead. They said hello and walked into the club, and I was about to suggest to Joe that we go back inside when he put his arms around me and kissed me. He backed me up against the building, right there on the corner of Bowery and Fourth Street, right in the middle of that killer heat wave, and he kissed me like he would die if we stopped, and all those obsessive thoughts about Eddie sort of melted away.

We walked back to my place and I remember that the streets were soaked from the spray of unplugged fire extinguishers. A regatta of chicken bones, beer bottles, cigarette butts, and the occasional condom was floating along the gutter, causing us to leap on and off of the curbs. God, the city was filthy back then. It was late—probably around three in the morning—and the sidewalks were crowded with partially clad drunks and preppy college students and noisy transvestites and whores and addicts and teenaged clubgoers. Because the frontier had already been crossed, because we had already kissed and pawed each other for a good fifteen minutes outside the club, Joe kept pulling playfully on my jeans pockets and sliding his hot hands under my T-shirt and across my belly and up over my breasts and we tripped over each other as we made our way east. When we got back to the loft, we forgot all about the heat and didn't worry about the broken fan in my room, we just threw the dirty clothes off my unmade bed and dove right in.

It was Joe's urgency that got me. He couldn't get his clothes off fast enough. At one point his jeans got stuck around one of his ankles and he staggered, groaning and cursing, until he had kicked off one bunched-up denim leg, and then the other. I pulled my T-shirt off over my head, but I left my bra and jeans on, and Joe looked at me for a second and then the bra and jeans were being pulled off. Although the sex didn't last all that long, the next morning with Beth, and later at my internship, every time I thought of that night, of those brief, steamy moments, my heart literally ached for him. I replayed all of it in my mind, over and over again. Especially when we were ready to sleep, the way he put his arms around me and pulled me in to him, pulled me right up against his warm chest and tucked my hips into his, cradling my breast in his palm.

[—]

[ten]

I sat at the kitchen table with my laptop in front of me. I was multitasking—Googling Joe while listening to his phone messages—my fingers poised above the keyboard, the handset of the cordless pressed to my ear.

"To play your messages, press one."

1.

"Hi, Joe! Laney here. Barbara Walters is interviewing some nominees the Saturday before the awards. She's having Spacey and Kiefer on and she wants to interview you, too. Call me either way."

Laney Atwood was Joe's new publicist. I hadn't met her yet, and while it was clear from her New York accent that she wasn't Joe's girlfriend, it occurred to me that she could have a foulmouthed young assistant who might have crossed paths with Joe somewhere along the way. I typed "Laney Atwood" into the Google search bar and clicked on "Images."

Just then, Ruby walked into the kitchen and I fumbled with the phone, battering the "off" button with my thumb, and clicked the cover of my laptop closed.

"I think it's unnatural. I think it's sick. It's diseased," Ruby said, pouring herself a cup of organic coffee.

"What?" I asked. I held the phone below the table, on my lap. "What's unnatural?"

"Mom!" Ruby spun around so that she was facing me, and I could see that she was holding her cell phone to her ear.

"Oh, nothing," she said, turning back away from me. "It's just my mom. She's trying to be a part of my life by talking to me about my *private* phone conversations."

Ruby grabbed a carton of soy milk from the fridge and carried it out of the room with her coffee, saying into the phone, "That's a cult, not a religion. It's like Kabbalah . . . with Jesus. I told him that."

I sat for a moment. Joe had taken Sammy to his gym. There was a young trainer there who watched Sammy while Joe worked out, and it had become a Sunday-morning tradition that Sammy loved. They went to the gym, and then out to breakfast at a diner in Hell's Kitchen where Joe had been eating Sunday breakfast for years. I listened now to make sure that they weren't back early, and I listened for Ruby, but all I could hear was the faint sound of yoga music coming from her room.

I silently tapped out Joe's number on the phone, my heart pounding.

I hit the number 1 and had to listen to Laney's message again.

I saved the message and waited for the next.

Joe. Jake. Tomorrow? Eight o'clock workout? Gimme a beep.

The next message was hers.

Hi, baby. Callin' you back. Bye.

I played it again. Then again. I listened for subtleties in her voice, for subtexts. Clues.

Hi, baby. Callin' you back. Bye.

Who?

I opened the computer and found that the screen was covered with tiny jpegs of Laney Atwood. I clicked on the first one and waited for the enlarged photograph to appear. And there it was. A middle-aged woman dressed in black, standing, wineglass in hand, next to Julia Roberts. The caption read, "PR agent Laney Atwood, from the Atwood/Neilson Agency, and Julia Roberts, *Leominster Square* premiere." I clicked on the other images and saw Laney posing with Ben Affleck and Sarah Jessica Parker and Cuba Gooding Jr. Then I clicked on a photo with the caption "Laney Atwood, Lizbeth Neilson, partners in the Atwood/Neilson Agency, at the Tribeca Film Festival."

Lizbeth Neilson? She was younger than Laney, and younger than me. But still, not quite right for the part. Too urban looking. There was no way the woman in this photo had a Southern accent. I realized that I had attached a soft-focus image to the voice in my head. A beautiful girl/woman who wore yellow printed minidresses and pigtails. It was Elly May Clampett, or Jessica Simpson, fresh and sweet and naive (despite the potty mouth). I could see Lizbeth's dour cynicism even in the still on-screen image. Why go *out* for dour cynicism when you can have it at home?

I typed "Joe Ferraro" into the Google search bar, and I spent the better part of the next hour reading about Joe, revisiting all his film roles, scrutinizing photos of him—sometimes with me, sometimes without—taken over the past ten years. There we were at the premiere of *Gangs of New York,* at a *Star Wars* screening with little Ruby, and at various awards dinners. There was Joe's weird haircut that he had gotten for his part in *Rum Runners,* and there I was in my favorite Donna Karan dress—the one that covered my post-pregnancy fat after Sammy. Joe with Hillary Clinton at a benefit. Joe jogging on a beach in Nevis. Joe and me backstage at the U2 concert last summer . . .

I started Googling scenarios like "Joe Ferraro mysterious woman" and "Joe Ferraro hotel," but these searches got me nowhere, so I just scrolled through the pages with Joe Ferraro in boldface type.

It occurred to me that I was stalking my own husband.

I listened for any sounds coming from the rest of the apartment, then I dialed Joe's number again.

I am out of my friggin' mind, I thought. That's what my dad would have said. Out. Of. Your. Friggin'. Mind.

I hung up. On impulse, I dialed Dr. James. Dr. Benjamin James. I had never called him Benjamin, or Ben. Always Dr. James. Beth and Alison called him Dr. Boyfriend. To me it was only funny once, but they kept calling him that, even after I had stopped seeing him.

I expected Dr. James's voice mail to answer, especially with this being a Sunday morning, so when I heard his actual voice instead, I wasn't sure what to say.

"Hello?" he said again.

"Dr. James? It's Julia Ferraro."

"Well! Hello!" he said. He sounded surprised, but in a good way.

"What are you doing in the office on Sunday?" I stammered.

"Taking care of some paperwork. Why are you calling me on a Sunday?" he asked.

"I'm having a kind of . . . situation. With Joe. Could I possibly come in to see you?"

"Uh . . . well. Let me see," he said.

I was dying. I really wouldn't have blamed him if he had said no.

"I have a cancellation Friday. Ten o'clock?"

"Okay," I said. *Okay.*

My gynecologist was the one who first sent me to see Dr. James. This was when Sammy was about eighteen months old. I had been having crushing anxiety and consecutive nights of insomnia ever since I weaned the baby, and when I called my doctor for a Valium refill, she referred me instead to Dr. Benjamin James. His office was on the ground floor of a gray prewar apartment building on Eighty-sixth Street, just off Central Park West. On that first Tuesday, when I told the doorman who I was there to see, he nodded politely and pointed down the hall to his left. I recall now that I sort of mumbled my thanks and then scuttled off with a strained smile, my head tilted up as if I was studying the ceiling tiles. I sensed that the doorman sized up all of Dr. James's visitors to see which were more visibly unbalanced, and this idea, for some reason, made me move down the hall like a crazy woman trying to appear sane. I had never been to a shrink before. I was incredibly nervous and was really only going in the hopes that the doctor would prescribe me something so that I could sleep. I got to the end of the hall, found Dr. James's door, and gave the buzzer next to it a hesitant tap. After a short pause, I was buzzed into a waiting area that held six empty chairs and two flat baskets filled with magazines.

The kids and I were at a stage, at that point, that required us to roost, frequently, in one waiting room or another. Ruby had broken her wrist playing soccer that past fall and Sammy had recurrent ear infections. Ruby's mild asthma was not yet under control and she had just had braces put on her teeth. Even Joe's old cat, Clover, was sick. She had cancer. The orthodontist, allergist, pediatrician, orthopedist, physical therapist, dentist, and veterinarian were all haphazardly recurring destinations scribbled in my daily planner, and I spent many long hours corralled in their holding areas, looking at my watch, tending to my children, and leafing through magazines.

The magazines in Dr. James's office were superior to those found in most of the other reception rooms. I noticed this at once. Unlike the glossy parenting magazines that issued shaming edicts (*End Homework Hassles! Lose That Tummy NOW! No More Clutter!*) from the paste-colored laminate tabletops of the other waiting areas, Dr. James's magazines had articles about Islam and Darfur and God and Tony Blair. There was nothing else in the small windowless waiting room, just the good magazines and hard chairs. Not a clock, nor a table. Just the chairs, set facing one another. Two groups of three. At precisely twelve o'clock on that first day, and on many, many Tuesdays afterward, Dr. James opened his door and invited me into his office.

Like I said, I had never been in therapy before, and in the beginning it was hard to figure out what to talk about. But as the weeks went by, I was comforted by Dr. James's kind, intelligent manner and his keen, alert attention to every word that came out of my mouth, his eyes staying on my eyes when I gazed off and then remaining on them when I looked back at him. I told him about my mother's death and my father's nightly drinking and the times that Neil and I awoke in an empty house and my fear of bridges and my first kiss and first fuck and my lonely semester abroad. I told him about how I learned, through my aunt, that Mom had been with a Navy buddy of Dad's that night she died. They were killed in a car crash—both drunk—and nobody knew why they were together in her old VW. We talked about how Dad and I lost Neil to Christ, after he quit alcohol and drugs and married an Evangelical Wisconsinite who disapproved of us both, and how I missed having a mother more than ever once I had my own children. We reviewed my stint as the breadwinning girlfriend/wife of a nonworking actor and the hesitation and misgivings I initially had about marrying Joe. Eventually, the well began to run dry and there wasn't much left to discuss—my depression had more or less cleared, but still I didn't want to terminate my sessions with Dr. James. I was in love with him.

I didn't exactly "fall" in love with him the way I had fallen in love with Joe. Instead, my feelings for Dr. James came to me in tiny allotments. Tiny measured doses. An encouraging word here, an understanding look there, each flitting connection touching me like a drop of precipitation so small that I hardly took any notice until one day I found myself drenched in a sort of relentless fascination—a heavy, almost mournful longing for the man who sat opposite me every Tuesday for precisely fifty minutes. Dr. James would ask me about my week: Was I writing? Was I communicating with Joe better? And I would give him a general summary of my days and nights, but all the while I was imagining Dr. James and me rapturously intertwined on the couch . . . on the floor . . . sprawled across his desk, the files of his other patients knocked hastily aside. What was it that I found so alluring about Dr. James? Had I seen him walking down the street, a complete stranger, I wouldn't have taken a second glance. Somehow, something happened in the "analytic space" that transformed Dr. James from an average-looking, nice middle-aged doctor into a demigod of unfathomable sexual potential. One day, in the middle of one of these sessions, in a fit of desire so intense that I thought a steamy aura of sexual heat might be visible in the air surrounding me, I had finally blurted out, "I . . . I . . . think I have a . . . crush on you."

Dr. James smiled casually and responded, "Oh, well, thanks."

I sat dumbfounded for several minutes and then said, "That's all?" To which he replied, "Well, it's very common to develop these feelings for a therapist. It's a normal part of the psychotherapeutic process."

I stammered, "Do you mean to tell me that you've had other patients who have told you . . . that they're in love with you?"

"Yes. Of course," he responded, matter-of-factly, as if I had asked him if he was in the habit of brushing his teeth each morning, or breathing air.

Ever since that session, I started to have a good, hard look at the patients who left Dr. James's office before me, and who waited for him when I left. The majority of his patients were women. Most were older than me, but one very attractive blond couldn't possibly have been twenty. I wondered if each of these patients blew into his office the way I did, tempestuous and unstrung with longing, and I imagined Dr. James holding fast in his large leather chair like a ship's captain who has lashed himself to the mast in a raging storm.

Transference is what they call it. It's supposed to be normal. It's not the therapist you desire, it's one of your parents. All I can say in my defense is that I was under a lot of stress at the time. The crying spells and insomnia and anxiety. Plus, Joe was never around. He was in L.A. doing that mob film. Then he was in Toronto doing something else. . . .

I sent Dr. James a present once. I rushed to Bergdorf's one cold December night when Joe unexpectedly arrived home early from the holiday party for the cast and crew. I told him that I wanted to do some last-minute Christmas shopping now that he was home to watch the kids, and when he said, "Yeah? And just who might you be shopping for?" in a half-drunk, flirty voice, I responded, "Oh, somebody," with a suggestive smile, and he had accompanied me to the door with explicit details about a certain tennis racket that was being held for him at a pro shop in Midtown. I didn't go to the pro shop, but instead spent the following two hours agonizing over what to purchase for Dr. James. A patient, dignified older salesclerk walked me around suggesting ties, scarves, and cuff links for the "colleague" I told him I was shopping for, and finally he opened a long, thin sterling box and tilted it up so that I could behold the enclosed "writing instrument" that he said had been masterfully designed in Switzerland. It was a sleek, streamlined, black pen with subtle platinum details, but it wasn't until the clerk actually removed it and pressed it to a piece of ivory stationery that I was swayed. The tip floated across the page in the salesman's delicate cursive, leaving a trail of shiny resin that looked as opulent and rich as oil. He carefully wrapped the box in gold tissue under my watchful eye, and the next day I sent it anonymously from a mailbox near Sammy's speech therapy class, so that it wouldn't bear the postal code of my neighborhood. The following Tuesday, Dr. James held the pen in his hand during my session, and I pretended not to notice it. At one point he pressed the bottom of it to his lower lip in a show of thought, just for a fleeting moment, just touched it there, making a tiny impression in that soft area at the center of his lower lip, and then he moved it back to rest upon my file on his lap. I wondered if Dr. James was gauging all his patients' reactions to the pen, and I allowed myself to gaze at it impassively while he jotted notes in my file about a lonely Christmas memory from my childhood. "Lovely," I imagined him writing, "her eyes, her lips, the way she crosses and uncrosses her legs . . ."

"Stuck," is probably what he really wrote, the letters scratched hastily onto the page in a doctor's illegible scrawl, his mind on lunch. "Stuck in transference."

"He's a paid boyfriend. You're still hot, you can get a real boyfriend for free," Beth used to scoff. She calls her shrink Carol. She and Alison have always laughed at me for calling mine Dr. James. It's just that my dad has ruined most first names for me. I didn't even want to know if Dr. James was a Ben or a Benjamin because the first conjured one kind of man and the second, another, both equally unappealing. And I needed to use the title Dr. as a constant reminder of the clinical reality of our relationship, a reminder of the "boundaries" of the clinical setting, the ethical boundaries that Dr. James was always harping about.

Ethical boundaries. At one time, I viewed Dr. James as quite noble for respecting them; now I wondered if it was just a polite way of rejecting me. He was probably violating boundaries left and right with that blond chick who had the eleven o'clock slot.

I Googled *Joe Ferraro* one more time.

That night, I modeled my Golden Globe dress for Ruby. She had been begging me to show it to her ever since I brought it home, but I hadn't exactly been in the mood. Now I decided that modeling my new gown was just the thing to snap me out of my brooding angst-cycle. "Don't come in yet," I called to her when I heard her fidgeting at the doorknob. I wanted her to see it looking perfect, but now the lining was all bunched up around my thighs. "Hold on," I said, and then when I had it all sorted out, I said, exuberantly, "Okay, Ruby. C'mon in!"

Ruby threw the door open with an expectant smile. She stood there for a moment and the smile slowly disappeared.

"Well?"

"Mom," she began, "no offense, but . . ."

"What?"

"It's seriously goth. You look like . . . like you're going to Ozzy Osbourne's funeral or something."

"I think it's cool," I said.

"It's covered with spiderwebs, Mom. It looks like a Halloween costume. And the bottom is all frayed. It's not even finished."

"Those are flowers, not spiderwebs," I said, but when I looked down at them now, I wasn't so sure. "It's supposed to look frayed and unfinished. That's the look."

"You're—*we're*—just at an age where we have to think carefully about what we're wearing," Beth said later that night, after I'd convinced her to come over for a second opinion. "That dress would look great on Mary-Kate Olsen. It would have looked great on you when you were nineteen, too. Now, though, it looks a little . . . spinsterish."

"I'm going to pretend you didn't utter that word," I said, and as I pulled the dress over my head, Beth said, "You'll find a great dress. You deserve a perfect dress. There's still time."

I called Jonathan at the salon first thing Tuesday morning and he took matters into his own hands. He called me back ten minutes later and said, "Monica at Vera Wang will meet you in the showroom this afternoon at two."

"Great," I said. "It's on Madison in the eighties, right?"

"No, dear, that's the shop," Jonathan said. "The showroom is in the thirties, in the design district."

At two o'clock I met a pretty young woman named Monica at the showroom. She was about twenty-three, and her dark brown eyes were lined with charcoal liner, her smiling lips were glistening and red. She wore a pencil skirt with a crisp white blouse neatly tucked into it, and a pair of ballet flats. I followed her into a large dressing room where she had hung about a dozen gowns.

"Jonathan told me you're probably about a six," she said, but she was looking at my midsection doubtfully.

"A six . . . or an eight," I said.

"Okay, well, why don't you just slip something on and we'll get started?" she said, gesturing toward the hanging gowns.

"Great," I said, and waited a moment before I realized that Monica wasn't going to leave the dressing room. Back in college, Alison and her model friends used to talk about how they spent most of their time in designer showrooms in the nude. Still, I was overcome with shyness about removing my clothes. First of all, I was wearing an unflattering pair of white cotton underpants and a heavily padded bra. I just hadn't expected anyone to see them. Also, it occurred to me that it was entirely possible that petite Monica had never seen a normal middle-aged body up close before, and that the shock might be too much for her. Should I explain about the little pouch of skin that hangs over caesarean scars? Would she faint dead away when she saw that without the bra, my bosom consisted of two tired, deflated sacs? As Monica stood there, smiling patiently, I adopted the psychological split that is used by people with multiple personality disorders, and all women at the gynecologist's office, and I disrobed.

The first dress resolved the size issue for us. I was an eight, not a six, and Monica cheerfully darted out of the room and returned with a pile of size eights. What can I say? Vera Wang gowns are beautiful and flattering, and we quickly settled on a simple gown, elegant and blue. Monica immediately brought in a seamstress to start the alterations.

"This is the first fitting, but I think we'll need two, especially since you need to sew inserts into the front panel," Monica said. "We're short on time, so I think you should have your second fitting in Los Angeles."

I stood in front of the three-way mirror, and while the seamstress pinned up my hem, I dialed Joe's number.

[eleven]

Dr. Alexa Calder's office was on the ground floor of a Park Avenue apartment building. I had expected to find a waiting room filled with taut, pinched socialites that Wednesday morning, ten days before the Golden Globes. Instead, there was a middle-aged businesswoman typing madly into her BlackBerry and a harried-looking mother with a teenaged son who, with his cheeks an angry road map of acne, was clearly the patient. The receptionist asked me to fill out a form that she handed to me on a clipboard. I chose a seat across from Acne Boy and his mom and began to answer questions about my skin.

As questionnaires go, this one was pretty dull. *Do you use sunscreen? Does your skin react to products with fragrance? Have you noticed any moles that are new or seem to be changing in size or appearance?* I normally enjoy medical questionnaires for the most part. I mean, how often do you get to describe your organs to somebody who is actually interested in the fact that your uterus is tipped or that your breasts are fibrous? Not often enough, in my opinion. Skin, though, skin is boring, and in my case, a source of tremendous guilt. Of all my organs, my skin has been the most abused. I spent my youth self-basting in Bain de Soleil while working on boats and docks and napping on beaches. My nose and shoulders peeled all of their seven layers of skin each summer. Now I had fine lines on my face and not-so-fine lines on my chest. I had inherited a scowl from my father and a nicotine addiction from my mother, and though I had quit smoking before Ruby was even conceived, I was starting to get little vertical lines above my lip. A long horizontal mirror was mounted on the waiting room wall opposite me and I scowled into it for a moment, seeing the familiar deep groove in my forehead, right between my eyebrows. *Maybe I should leave,* I thought. *I'm not in the mood for a lecture on how poorly I've treated my skin. Maybe I should just go.* But I didn't leave. I filled out the rest of the questionnaire and returned it to the receptionist.

When I sat back down, I grabbed a brochure from the holder on display in the center of the magazine table. The boy with the acne was called inside and so I picked up one of the brochures. "Now you can look as vibrant as you feel!" said the headline. There was a gorgeous woman with flawless skin and sun-streaked hair standing on a mountain, gazing serenely off into the distance. The brochure outlined the range of "injectable fillers" available to the clients of [here, somebody had stamped Dr. Alexa Calder's name and address]. There was Restylane and Dermagen, CosmoDerm and bovine collagen and even human collagen. Human collagen, I learned as I flipped through the brochure, is harvested from the discarded foreskins of babies.

Women are paying doctors to inject babies' foreskins into their lips. Why had I never read or heard anything about that? I thought of all the women I had seen shopping in Bergdorf's and Barneys, with lips as protuberant as duck's bills. What would an alien culture make of a world where the mothers at the upper stratum of society ritually inject discarded tissue from mutilated baby penises into their lips? I wish I could say that I rose from my chair in indignation and strode from the office, slamming the door behind me. But I didn't. I made a mental note to ask the doctor if she had any plans to inject human tissue into my face, and if the answer was yes, to ask her if the tissue had been tested for HIV. Beauty had suddenly become an "every man for himself" proposition for me, and I couldn't afford to worry about whose flesh was going where.

Ten minutes later, I was seated in an examination room into which Dr. Calder stepped calmly, all smiles and glowing, uncreased skin. She introduced herself and asked me what I'd like to have done. She spoke in a professional, soothing tone and she smiled as she spoke, but all the while her eyes moved hungrily around my face.

"I'm going to the Golden Globes and I want to get rid of this frown line," I said, pointing to my forehead. Dr. Calder glanced up at it and nodded. Then her gaze wandered to the other parts of my face.

"Here's what I'd like to do . . ." she began.

When I left Dr. Calder's office, two hours and twenty-eight hundred dollars later, I stopped to look at myself in the same waiting-room mirror. My skin was a little red, but except for some minor swelling around my upper lip and some tiny injection marks above my eyebrows, I looked pretty much the same as when I first came in, which was surprising, considering what I had been through.

"Microdermabrasion. That's a given," Dr. Calder had said after a few minutes of pinching and pulling at my face. "And when's the last time you had a glycolic peel?"

"Well, I've never had one."

"Never? Okay, I certainly recommend that you have regular

facials and include a glycolic peel. It'll help get rid of a lot of this dead skin—this crepey-looking skin around your forehead and chin. I have glycolic facials all the time and my skin always looks amazing afterward. Today we'll just do the microdermabrasion since you have an event in, what, almost two weeks?"

"Yes," I said.

"I know because I have three other clients going. Two are nominees. Now, what about these smile lines?"

"I know. The crow's-feet. I just don't think they're that noticeable."

"They're actually smile lines. They're just not noticeable to you because you don't smile in the mirror the way you smile at other people. You have smile lines that run halfway down your cheeks. It's actually the first thing I noticed about you when I walked in here."

"Really? They're that bad?"

"They're not bad, they're not good. They just say, 'I'm not thirty-five anymore.' Without those lines you'd look younger."

And so it went. I was talked into microdermabrasion, as well as Botox in my forehead, in my smile lines, and in my chin, where Dr. Calder said I was starting to get some "dimpling." "You want to start immobilizing these muscles now," she said, and I wondered how the immobilization of muscles squared itself with the Hippocratic oath. Restylane, a synthetic filler—"Nobody's foreskin," Dr. Calder had laughed when I asked her—was to be used on the little vertical lines above my lip. "Chances are you would have gotten them even if you'd never smoked. They're from puckering your lips. We all do it all the time," she assured me, and then she said, "I'd like to put just a little bit in your lips. Just a little around the edge of the lip. Just to plump them up a little." She assured me that nobody would notice that I'd had anything done. "You'll just look, generally, younger."

How do you say no to looking generally younger?

"It'll feel like the exfoliating part of a facial. It doesn't really hurt," Dr. Calder said as she began the microdermabrasion.

"I don't care if it hurts," I replied, because it seemed like it should hurt, this stripping of years. Like all female transformations—onset of menses, sexual maturity, childbirth—all these female milestones were marked with blood and pain, so why shouldn't this one?

"Now the Botox. Just a little prick," Dr. Calder said. She began poking my forehead with the tiny needle, and it really wasn't that bad when she was working on my forehead. She moved on to the area around one of my eyes.

That hurt.

Then she stopped, busying herself at the counter where a nurse had laid out an arsenal of syringes.

"All done?" I asked.

"No, my needle was just getting dull, so I had to change it. Here we go." Then she attacked my needle-dulling hide with a fresh needle. She poked here and there, over and over, and each time, just as I became used to the cold pain of the stainless-steel needle in my raw skin, she withdrew it and inserted it someplace else.

"Now for your lips," she said, and she whipped out the bigger needle. She pumped Restylane into my lips, a process that was slow and excruciatingly painful. Tears streamed from my eyes. My fingers seized the examining table and I tried to remember all those childbirth breathing techniques.

Breathing. I knew that breathing was key.

"Just a little more." "Hold on." "Just a little more over here," said Dr. Calder, the experienced coach. Then, finally, she was done.

"There'll be a little swelling for the next couple of days, but it'll go down, so don't be alarmed."

I had said it already, but I said it again: "I don't want to be one of those fish-lip ladies."

"Oh no, no, no," said Dr. Calder. "Trust me. You're gonna love it. In a few days."

Ruby had a basketball game that afternoon at Trinity School and I arrived in the gymnasium a few minutes before the game was scheduled to begin. I followed several other parents up into the bleachers, and when I looked down, Ruby was standing with her teammates in a circle around her coach. She had her arm draped casually over the shoulder of one of her teammates and she was nodding at something the coach was saying to her. Then the girls fanned out across the floor for their pregame drills. I watched Ruby lope across the court, her strawberry-blond ponytail bouncing playfully over the word *Ferraro,* which was emblazoned on the back of her jersey.

I always love to watch Ruby play, especially during warm-ups when everything is a little more casual and relaxed. I followed her long, muscular legs up and down the court and admired her athletic ease and the cool camaraderie she shared with her teammates. Somebody passed her the ball and she jogged down the court, dribbling it once, then twice just in front of her; once, then twice off to the side; and then, just before turning back to the drill line, she placed one hand beneath the ball, one hand behind it, and sent it arcing up and into the basket with a clever little flick of her wrists.

"Go, Ruby!" I wanted to call out. But I didn't say anything, I just smiled and clenched my fist. It's uncool to call out to your kid during warm-up. Ruby had taught me that. Other important game-watching "don'ts" I had learned from experience included: bounding across the court when your child is hit in the nose; calling the referee a jackass; shouting "Yes!" when a girl from the opposing team makes a blunder; shouting "Go, Rube!" or "Nice shot, Rube!" or anything with the word *Rube* attached.

"People probably think you're calling me names!" Ruby had sulked after a game, before I had kicked the Rube habit. "I'm not a Rube!"

"Why did you have to name me Ruby?" she used to ask us regularly. Ruby hated her name. "It's so ugly!" "It's a fat person's name." "It's what you call a Labrador."

Joe once made the mistake of telling her the partial truth, which was that we loved the name because it was in so many great songs. The rest of the truth, which we kept to ourselves, was that my dad didn't know any Rubys. He had no opinion of them—we had checked.

"Songs?" Ruby cried when we told her. "Normal people are named after saints. I'm named after . . . songs?"

"We were young when we had you," was all I really had to offer.

The game was about to begin. I saw Ruby glance up into the bleachers a few times. Finally she saw me and gave me a dismissive nod, then it was her turn to shoot. She dribbled the ball around to the side of the net and popped it in again.

Yeah, Rubes! I thought, but I didn't say anything. My lips were sealed. Throbbing, but sealed.

When the game began, and moderate cheering was allowed, I called out to Ruby and her friends—"Go, Catherine!" "Nice shot, Lily"—but then I had to stop moving my lips. The lip pain had been mild when I left Dr. Calder's office, but it had slowly built up into a searing, pounding crescendo of white-hot agony before the first quarter of the game was over. When I ran my tongue over my lips they felt huge, but I pacified myself with the thought that a canker sore often feels massive to the tongue when it's barely discernible to the eye.

By the end of the second quarter, my eyes were watering and I was fantasizing about my lips being packed in ice. *Ice, just a big bucket of ice,* I thought, *and I'll never ask for anything else in my life. Heat and pain. Hot. Pain.* These were my only thoughts until the halftime bell rang. From clear across the gymnasium I saw Ruby glance at me as she joined her teammates on the bench, and then I saw her do a double take. Her eyes fixed in panic upon my face, making her leap up from her seat and run across the court to where I sat near the top of the bleachers.

"Oh my God, Mom! What happened to you?"

"What?" I said. I tried to position the flotation devices that I used to call lips into a smile.

"Your lips! They're all bruised and swollen!"

Now the parents sitting around me all craned their heads around to have a look.

"Oh God," said the man in front of me. He winced and looked away.

"Oh," said his wife, looking a little bit longer. Then she turned and whispered something to the husband, who turned back for another look. My hand flew to my lip.

"The door," I mumbled. "I slammed my mouth against . . . the door."

"What door?" asked Ruby.

"The door to a taxi. It's fine, really, Ruby. Great playing out there . . ."

"Mom! Don't you think you should go to the emergency room or something?"

I could see the shoulders on the woman in front of me shake with mirth.

"No! I'm fine!"

"Jeesh!" said Ruby. "Okay."

Somehow I made it through the rest of the game. I called Dr. Calder's office the minute I got home. "My lips are killing me. And they're bruised and swollen as hell!" I cried.

"They really shouldn't be that painful, but bruising and swelling is normal," she told me. "The swelling should go down in a few days, and the bruising should be gone by the end of the week."

"I wish you'd told me all this before I went to my daughter's basketball game!"

"You went to a basketball game? Oh my God, I'm so sorry, Julia. I just assumed you knew. It's all spelled out in those release forms you signed."

"Who reads release forms?"

"I always do. Look, tell people it's from the microdermabrasion. Some people do get all swollen from that. And call me if the pain continues. It sounds like you might be having a reaction to the Restylane. Even if you are, the pain should subside in the next day or two."

"Oh Christ!" I said.

"You're gonna love it in a few days. Trust me."

I hung up the phone and I dialed Joe's number. Dialing it had become almost a reflex during the past few days. I did it pretty much any time I was near a phone. Of course, sometimes Joe would answer and then we'd chat about the kids or our plans for dinner, but often enough, I'd get his voice mail.

On the day of the lips I had a little breakthrough.

"Hi, baby. It's me. Jenna. I was thinking of stopping by the set today. I

had visions of strolling into the makeup trailer and rubbing my hot little body up against yours when nobody's looking. How'd you like that, baby? I'm getting all horny just thinking about it. Call me!"

Jenna or Gina? I played it back five times before I knew for sure. Jenna. The only Jennas I had ever known were still in preschool. I'd never met an adult Jenna, had never heard my dad describe one. *Young* was the only thing I could associate with her name. She was young, that was for sure, with a name like Jenna.

"How'd you like that, baby? I'm getting all horny just thinking about it. Call me!"

Horny this, horny that . . . *This slut needs a new line,* I thought. Would she never shut up about her alleged horniness? And the thing that killed me was that the word actually sounded cute and sexy when she said it. Something about her little accent and the breathiness of her youthful voice. I knew that if I ever called Joe, or anyone else for that matter, and nattered on about being horny, it would come across as nagging and whiny, or even worse, offensive and threatening—not sweet and beguiling like Jenna.

The fact that Jenna felt as if she could just pop into the makeup trailer made me wonder if she worked on the show. I knew a woman named Andrea who was the head of makeup and always gave Ruby makeup lessons and false eyelashes whenever she visited the set, but she was an incorrigible gossip and Joe would never allow his secret girlfriend to visit him there.

I knew all the women who had regular parts on *The Squad.* There was Tanya Irwin, Hope Ball, Ilana Wakefield, and Jane Wendell. None of these women were from the South. But there were also the smaller recurring roles to consider, and I found the boxed DVD set from last season and scanned the list of credits. I found no Jenna, but then again, they only listed regular cast members. I logged onto the show's Web site and did a search for the name *Jenna* but came up with nothing. But while I was there, I decided to peek at the message boards.

—How friggin' hot was Joe during last week's episode? the scene where he was kissing that callgirl?

—HOT

—I don't like the whole callgirl story line. I don't believe a guy like Mitch Hollister would actually fall in love with a ho

—she's supposed to be like a Heidi Fleiss girl. A notch above ho.

—lol. Not too ho. Just the right amount of ho. I don't care about the girl. I heart JF.

I had always lurked the boards in the past, but, of course, had never posted anything. Suddenly my fingers flew to the keyboard and typed in the "Post Message" box:

He's gay in real life.

I didn't send it right away. I sat there for a moment, reading the sentence over and over, relishing the sense of power, the utter wickedness of it. Honestly, if her name hadn't been Jenna, I never would have done it. I can see that now. If it was a name that was at least close to my age—something like Jennifer or Susan or even Brooke—I might have had a clearer head, but the sheer profanity of the name Jenna, the almost criminal youthfulness of it, was like a slap in the face. And my face hurt so much already from trying—trying so hard . . .

I clicked "Send" and then quickly closed the cover of my laptop. It was time to make dinner and help Sammy get ready for his bath.

Later, after the kids had gone to bed and before Joe came home, I logged back on and scrolled down to the thread about Joe. To my great surprise, right beneath my line about Joe being gay, somebody had posted:

—I know. I've heard that too.

—What? Gay? Really?

—Not true. He's married. With kids.

—That doesn't mean anything.

Good point, I thought. Then I typed:

—I know him and his "wife" in real life. He's definitely gay.

I logged off *The Squad*'s message board and logged on to Gawker.com. I typed Joe's name into the search box and began to read all the sightings of him. There were quite a few, averaging one or two a week just over the last year alone. Gawker is New York–based, so the New York celebrities—Kevin Bacon, Kyra, Ethan Hawke, Sarah Jessica Parker—are all site regulars, with occasional appearances by more exotic personages like Madonna and Amy Winehouse. The Joe sightings were, for the most part, pretty innocuous:

> Saw Joe Ferraro with teenaged daughter walking into Virgin Records. Followed them inside. Daughter was shopping for something in the Soundtrack section. Joe followed her around talking on his cell phone. I saw a teenager approach him for an autograph and he shook his head, still talking on the phone.

Or this:

> Joe Ferraro standing in line at the Angelika Theater with wife. It was a dark, cloudy day but Joe still wore his sunglasses inside theater lobby. I guess he was afraid nobody would realize he's a celebrity if he took them off.

I could have submitted that entry myself. It never ceased to embarrass me the way Joe wore his sunglasses indoors. "You're actually calling attention to yourself," I always said. "I didn't even realize I still had them on," was usually his response.

The Gawker posts were all listed in reverse chronological order, the most recent sightings first. There was even a "Gawker Stalker Map," which actually highlighted, on a map of New York City, where each celebrity was sighted. Most of the sightings of Joe occurred in our neighborhood, but a handful were in the West Village.

> Saw Joe Ferraro leave a black Escalade in front of a brownstone on West 11th Street. He was impatiently pushing a buzzer to get in the building and finally was buzzed inside.

The date of that sighting was last October. October 27th. I got out my calendar and looked up the date. It had been a Thursday. There was nothing listed in my date book, which meant that I had been home that night. If Joe wasn't home, he was usually working or playing basketball. Instead, on this night, he was visiting somebody in a brownstone downtown. It couldn't be a coincidence that last fall was when I started obsessing about Dr. James. Joe was running off to his girlfriend's house and I was lusting after my poor shrink.

I clicked on the "Tips" box on the sightings page and typed:

> Saw Joe Ferraro leaving Bungalow 8 with a young male, very early this morning.

Then I paused. My lips throbbed. I entertained various scenarios in my mind and then typed:

> Ferraro's chauffeur-driven Escalade was parked outside and he seemed to be trying to persuade the young man to get in the car with him. After a few minutes of discussion, the man got in the car with Joe and they drove off.

I had forgotton how much I liked to write. *I'm good,* I thought. Why had I been studying journalism in college when clearly I was meant to write fiction? I closed the laptop. I knew my behavior was nuts. I thought about Dr. Boyfriend.

My last session before Dr. James's summer break, I had arrived at his office slightly unraveled. His impending vacation loomed. Joe was shooting every night (he said) and I was having trouble sleeping again. At the beginning of the session, I had tried to talk about issues regarding my children and my marriage, but before the hour was half over, I started talking about my feelings for Dr. James. Again.

"You know, I think about you all the time," I said.

"All the time?" he asked, frowning and cocking his head to the side. There it was, the frown, the head cock. Nothing was new. His actions and reactions were hopelessly predictable, but rather than being bored by their sameness, I was always entranced by their comforting reliability. *There,* I thought when he nodded encouragement at me. *There,* when he furrowed his brow with concern. *There,* when he cast me a sidelong look of doubt in those moments when he felt I was selling myself short . . . *There, there, there again.*

"I just feel so hopeless about this process. I don't think it's normal to become so . . . infatuated with your shrink."

"Well, I think what you're going through *is* normal. It's not really me you're attracted to. You know this. We've discussed this."

"Yeah," I said.

"Your attraction to me is really a longing for connection. Probably to your father. It's really quite common."

"I guess . . ." I said, unconvinced.

"You don't even know me," he said. He had said it before.

"I think you're wrong about that. I think I know a lot about you."

There it was—the sidelong look of doubt.

"I know that you're honest," I began. He *was* honest. There had been times when I had asked him very pointed questions—questions about himself—and he always answered carefully and honestly.

"You're reliable," I said. He never canceled appointments, and his appointments began and ended on time. Always. Okay, so now I can see that this isn't much to set store by. Really, though, when I was going through this, it was enough. I felt I knew everything about Dr. James that I needed to know. He was perfect.

I had been staring at the floor, but now I looked up and saw that he was studying me. He looked into my eyes and I looked back, blinking, into his. We had been locked in looks like this before, but no matter how I tried to delude myself, I knew he wasn't trying to engage me in some kind of hypnotic stare of seduction. He was studying me with a clinician's eye and it was always me who looked away first.

"What's going on with Ruby? You were saying that you were having trouble setting limits with her?" he asked finally.

"Ruby?"

"Yes. You felt that she sometimes bullies you. . . ."

"What would you do if . . . one of your patients . . . unbuttoned her blouse? If she showed you her breasts?" I glanced at him quickly, then stared, blushing wildly, at a point on the ceiling.

There was a very long pause, then: "What would I do?"

I glanced back at Dr. James. He was looking at me very carefully now. He didn't look happy.

"Julia?"

Outside, a car alarm started, and after three or four identical rising screeches was shut off. I remember those moments in that room now as if they had just happened, it's so clear in my mind. A small child could be heard laughing and chattering right under the window, and the solid, heaving bass notes of a reggae tune pulsed from an approaching car. *It's already August,* I thought. I would need to make appointments for the kids' school physicals. I would need to register them for fall sports camps. Where had the summer gone? The music got closer and louder, throbbing for several minutes right outside the window, and then it faded off up the avenue.

"I don't know why I just said that," I said. "I would never do anything like that, you know."

"I know."

"I'm just curious about all the crazies you must get in here," I said. "The situation with Ruby is better. We had a talk. I think a lot of it is hormonal. . . ."

And I talked to Dr. James for the rest of my fifty minutes. I recalled a dream about a house that was actually a ship, and as I recounted it, he took notes. I described my efforts to communicate better with Joe and my difficulties setting limits with Ruby, and when my time was up, Dr. James told me so by glancing at his watch. Then he followed me to the door, and this time he paused for a moment before his customary handshake. *Who could blame him,* I thought, but when I went to sidle past him, he reached out and clasped my hand in his. I had a fleeting sense of pulling up on him for balance—a feeling that his solid presence made it possible for me to stand. The day, the daughter, the August afternoon—he was handing me off to my life, cutting himself free with his brief, workmanlike grip that said, *Keep trying, you're fine.* Then it was over. Then I was on my way. We had left it that I would call him when Joe and the kids and I returned from Amagansett in early September. But I never called.

[twelve]

How can you not have Vicodin?" Alison asked.

I was right: Beth had told Alison. Beth had told Alison and now I was glad, because Beth had a job and wasn't available to talk to me endlessly about the Joe situation. Alison was. I called her with an update every time there was a new message and we mulled over any possible "clues," but today I hadn't called just to talk about Jenna or Joe. Right after I dropped Sammy off at school, I called because Alison lived in Los Angeles, had a very wealthy husband, and had started messing with her lips and her crow's-feet when she was in her thirties.

"My lips always kill for at least three days after I get them done," Alison said. "I don't like Calder's work. She does my friend Sasha . . . you know, Sasha Millicovic?"

"Mmm-hmm." It was always a little annoying when Alison did this—dropped a name like Sasha's just so everybody would know that while she might not have been on the A-list herself, many of her close friends were.

"Well, anyway, my doctor would have given me something for the pain, and I always keep plenty of Vicodin and OxyContin around. I can't believe you don't even have a single Percocet lying around! Have you and Joe become Christian Scientists?"

"No, Alison! Nobody I know takes that stuff. Unless they've had surgery or something."

"Wow," said Alison. "The Upper West Side sounds so different from the New York we lived in. Whenever you talk about your life up there, it all sounds so . . . wholesome."

"It's not!"

"Honestly, I picture all you moms walking around in Amish clothing with giant aprons. . . ."

"Right," I said. "Well, I'm not looking very Amish with these lips."

"Are they still swollen?"

"Not so bad. They look a lot better today. Just a little bruising on one side. It's pretty easy to cover with makeup. So that's why I'm calling. I think I can actually go out in public today, and I have some time before I get my extensions this afternoon, so I want to pop in unexpectedly at the set. To see if Jenna's there."

"Excellent," said Allison.

Alisons are "game," my father said. He always loved Alison.

"How will I know where they're shooting?" I asked. "They shoot in different locations each day."

"Look at his call sheet," Alison replied. "Doesn't he come home with one each night, telling him which scenes they're shooting the next day?"

"Oh yeah," I said. "I think so."

I recalled once opening Joe's gym bag—the male equivalent of a purse—and finding it full of loose change and protein bars and many crinkled-up call sheets. Here I'd been listening in on his private phone messages but hadn't had the wherewithal to open his gym bag!

"He keeps them with him, though," I said. "And I want to go today."

"Just call somebody at the production office. They'll know," Alison replied.

"I wish I knew if Horny Jenna was planning to stop by for a body-rubbing session."

"Even if she doesn't, there's a lot you can learn on the set. People gossip, they're resentful, they let things slip. If you can find some time alone with somebody on the crew, you'll be amazed at what you'll discover."

"Right. Of course," I said. Alison's half-baked career in television and films was now paying off for me. She had worked on scores of sets.

"And remember, the makeup girl's going to be your biggest resource! They never shut up, any of them. Also, the prop truck is a good place to get information. Okay, I have to go now. Pilates."

The Squad was shooting in Harlem that morning. Off 125th Street, next to the West Side Highway. "Right behind Fairway," a member of the production staff had told me on the phone. Back when I did all our grocery shopping, Fairway was my favorite store because, in addition to having arguably the city's best selection of meat, produce, cheese, and breads, it has free parking right across the street alongside the Hudson River Parkway. Where else in New York can you drive your car to the grocery store and load it up, just like a regular American mom? When Ruby was little we used to go to Fairway and buy chocolate-chip cookies that we would eat sitting on the tailgate of our old beat-up Subaru while we watched barges being pushed up and down the Hudson by tugboats that Ruby would give names—like Josabelle. Josabelle the tugboat! That was going to be the name of another children's book I was going to write. *When I have the time,* I told myself then, when I was really quite busy being Ruby's mom, keeping our apartment clean, and encouraging Joe while his career lagged. Now I recalled that there was a certain comfort in not having the time to do the things I wasn't sure I could really do. I had the time now. I had all day, each day, that I could be working on projects. Somehow, instead of writing a book, or even an essay, I was being a nothing. A husband-stalking nothing. *When I've sorted all this out,* I told myself now, *when I've sorted it all out with Joe, then I'll write the book about Josabelle, and the one about Annie Acorn. And the screenplay. And the article about breast-feeding.*

I arrived at the set just before ten, hoping that I would get there around the time the crew would break for coffee. (Everything on a television and movie set is more or less dictated by union standards, including the timing and duration of coffee breaks and meals.) I wanted to be there when everybody was acting all chummy and perhaps rubbing up against each other.

There was very little traffic as I drove up Broadway, and as soon as I turned left on 125th Street, I could see the caravan of long white trucks, vans, and trailers that always strike fear and loathing into the hearts of New York City residents. Their presence indicates that a movie or television show is using that spot as a location and that the people who normally inhabit the area will be treated like annoying but easily removable pests. The roped-off sidewalks were busy with electricians unloading lighting equipment and dollies loaded with heavy pieces of scenery. There were plenty of empty parking spaces on the street around the trucks because *The Squad* had commandeered all the spaces. Those cars whose unlucky owners hadn't taken heed of the numerous orange flyers forbidding parking by anyone not associated with the production were being towed.

When Beth, Alison, and I lived on Avenue B, film productions frequently used our block when they needed a "ghetto" location, and we were always outraged by the sense of entitlement these movie people felt when they came barging into our neighborhood. One morning I was late for work, as usual, and when I went to run across the street in front of our building, I was stopped by an enthusiastic young towhead wearing a black parka and holding an oversized walkie-talkie.

"Excuse me. You can't cross here. We're shooting a scene," he whispered.

I looked across the street where there was a large crowd of people standing around a cluster of video monitors. A few feet down the sidewalk, lights shone on two male actors, or perhaps stuntmen, simulating a fight. The rest of the street was lined with those dreaded white trucks, vans, and RVs.

"But I have to cross here. I have to get a bus."

"Shhh!" he whispered. "We're rolling." He gave me an "Isn't this exciting!" look and I said, "I don't give a fuck!" I couldn't believe this little creep.

"Look, we're *shooting a feature film.* That's Wesley Snipes over there," he said, quite superior and condescending. "I can't let you cross here. You can cross on the next block."

"What makes you think your job—or Wesley Snipes's job—is more important than mine, huh?" I asked, furious, and louder than necessary. "I'm late. This is *my* street. Why should *I* have to change *my* life so that Wesley Snipes can make millions of dollars shooting a film in *my*—"

"Cut!" came the command, garbled and static, over the production assistant's walkie-talkie. A police officer, whom I had thought was an actor, walked over to where we stood.

"What's the problem here?" he asked.

"I don't see why my life has to be . . . altered, just so these people can make their stupid little movie."

"Oh. Okay, then, I'll explain why your life has to be *altered,*" said the officer. A large African-American man with a round belly, he used the slow, patient, authoritarian voice that I had heard my father and other former military men use my whole life. "This production has purchased a permit from the city of New York that enables them to shoot here and also to direct pedestrian traffic in the immediate area."

God, I thought I was cool back then. I think I gave some kind of haughty, wise-assed reply and then flipped the PA the bird over my shoulder as I stomped off down the block. Now driving along, feeling slightly old and conspicuous in our shiny black BMW, I thought of Ruby's youthful outrage at similar ridiculous situations and I had to smile.

I pulled in behind a large RV parked a few empty spaces in front of a smaller RV. Joe had top billing on the show, which I knew guaranteed him the largest trailer. This was perfect. I pulled in behind the vehicle and then sat waiting to see if anyone was going to try to chase me out of the spot, at which point I planned to icily tell them that I was Joe Ferraro's wife. Members of the production crew walked hastily back and forth on the sidewalk, but nobody seemed to notice or care that I was there. I removed a piece of lined paper from one of Ruby's notebooks in the back and with a broken crayon that I dislodged from Sammy's car seat, I wrote, "JOE FERRARO'S CAR." I placed the paper in the windshield. Then I removed the paper and squeezed in the word WIFE'S so that it read,

"JOE FERRARO'S WIFE'S CAR." Then I removed the paper, crumpled it up, and threw it on the floor.

I opened my purse and removed a lipstick that I had borrowed from Ruby recently. Pink Expectations, it was called. I liked it because it was a darker pink than I usually wore and it covered the bruising that still lingered on the left-hand corner of my lip. Otherwise, I thought as I studied myself in the rearview, not too bad. Although Dr. Calder had told me that the full effects of the Botox could take a week or two, I could already see a slight difference in my face. That worried, angry look seemed to be gone, or was it my imagination? The furrow between my brows seemed less severe. And my lips, except for the little bit of bruising, looked more voluminous than they ever had, even in my youth.

Suddenly there was a rapid knocking on my window. I screamed and Ruby's lipstick flew out of my hand. I looked up to see Catherine, Joe's assistant, waving excitedly to me from outside the car.

I composed myself and jumped out of the car. Catherine gave me a big hug.

"Joe didn't tell me you were coming!" she exclaimed.

"I know, I wasn't planning to, I just happened to be in the neighborhood. I was on my way to Fairway and when I saw the trucks I wondered if it was you guys."

"Cool!"

"Is my car okay here?"

"Yeah, I'll have one of the PAs keep an eye on it."

"Where's Joe?" I was trying to be casual and breezy.

"Oh, you just missed him. He was in his trailer all morning because they had some problems setting up his shot, but now he's on the set. It's down at the end of the block. I'll take you there."

As Catherine and I walked down, I marveled, as I always did, at the number of people it took just to shoot one small, uncomplicated scene. Production assistants, assistant directors, personal assistants, electricians, sound technicians, script supervisors, child wranglers, and caterers were either racing around doing their jobs or standing around waiting for somebody else to do their job, sometimes for hours on end. The first time I ever visited a movie set I expected to find something out of Truffaut's *Day for Night.* I thought that the crew would be made up of glamorous and sexy young men and women who, when they weren't flipping through pages on their clipboards and chasing down wayward actresses, would be sipping espresso, discussing Bergman and Fellini, and seducing one another in the wardrobe truck. Instead, what I found was a typical workplace full of ordinary-looking people who, like workers anywhere, were doing their time in a job where they often felt bored, resentful, and unfulfilled.

"I just have to stop in Joe's trailer for a minute," Catherine said, and I followed her inside with some enthusiasm. Since Joe wasn't there, I could snoop to my heart's delight.

The TV had been left on, tuned to ESPN. An overflowing ashtray and several empty cans of Diet Pepsi sat on the table. Newspapers were strewn everywhere. A half-eaten plate of fruit salad was sitting in the sink, surrounded by dirty drinking glasses. I wandered casually to the back of the trailer and glanced into the small bedroom. Joe's gym bag and coat were thrown onto the bed, which was completely made up in a tacky, seventies-inspired psychedelic bedspread. I realized that Joe would never bring his girlfriend here for sex. For one thing, people like Catherine were always wandering in and out.

And also, Joe's trailer stunk.

Catherine seemed to notice this as well. She sniffed the air a few times and then threw open the door to the tiny bathroom.

"Shit!" she said.

"What's wrong?"

"Somebody took a shit in Joe's toilet again! Goddammit! Joe is gonna freak!"

"He is?"

I could hear Catherine pushing the flush button over and over again.

"Yes!" she said. "He is."

"Umm . . . How do you know it wasn't Joe?"

"It wasn't Joe!" Catherine said. She emerged from the bathroom and began looking wildly around, apparently for clues. "Joe already went this morning!"

Wow, I thought, *no wonder Joe felt that I didn't pay enough attention to him at home.*

"Somebody keeps sneaking into Joe's trailer and shitting in his toilet, and then just leaving it there. And Joe is freaking out!"

People aren't kidding when they say there's really nothing glamorous about show business. My heart swelled with pity for Catherine, who, having worked for Joe for almost a year, was his longest-employed assistant yet. The last one had lasted four months.

"Joe just left his trailer about ten minutes ago, so maybe somebody saw somebody go in," said Catherine as she sprang for the door.

Outside, we encountered a young production assistant stomping his feet and warming his hands around a cup of coffee. Catherine marched up to him.

"Hey!" Catherine said. She looked him over carefully.

"Hey," the PA responded tentatively.

"Were you just in Joe's trailer?" Catherine demanded.

"Me? No!"

"How long have you been standing here?"

"I dunno. Five, ten minutes?"

"Did you see anyone besides Joe go into his trailer?"

"I saw . . . her." The PA nodded at me.

"Yeah, well, that's Joe's wife. She's allowed to go in his trailer!"

"Hi," I said, smiling awkwardly. I struggled with whether or not I should reach out to shake the man's hand, but he was being interrogated about a freshly committed bowel movement and I just couldn't.

"And you didn't run into Joe's trailer to use the bathroom?"

"No!"

"Because I know it would be convenient, especially if you had to take a big . . . you know what. It would be an awful lot more convenient just to go in the trailer than to go all the way over to that disgusting bathroom in the church that they're using."

"Look," said the kid, his face reddening, "I just told you I didn't go in there."

I half expected Catherine to grab the guy by the shirt collar, drag him into Joe's bathroom, and spank him with a rolled-up newspaper. "No!" I could hear her scolding him. "Bad!" But she just glared at him and then stomped off, with me at her heels.

"They're shooting in an old church. It's a pedophile episode," Catherine explained, oddly calm again, as we began walking over there.

"Didn't they already do an episode about a child molester this season?" I asked.

"I think that was a nanny. This one's about a priest."

"Oh."

"It's going to air during sweeps week!"

That explained it. Nothing like a pedophile priest to guarantee viewers during sweeps week!

A small crowd had gathered outside the entrance to a charming but run-down old Baptist church that I had never noticed on this block. A police officer was standing in front of a street barricade where sidewalk spectators stood around with their cell phones poised to take pictures of whoever might come walking out of the church.

"Who the fuck do these people think they are, telling me I can't walk down my own street? Man, this is fucked up," a guy in dreadlocks was ranting. The cop nodded at Catherine as she walked around the barricade and I followed her into the church.

In the entryway, a production assistant stood guard in front of a closed door. "They're rolling," he said to us quietly, and Catherine and I stood waiting. After a moment, a voice came over the PA's walkie-talkie, saying, "Cut!" and the PA opened the door for us.

The inside of the church was dark and warm and it smelled like lemon oil and wood and musty leather. I imagined that when it wasn't chock-full of people and equipment, it must be quite a peaceful sanctuary. The thick stone slab walls blocked off the noise of the city and the nearby highway. I pictured the pews lined with Sunday worshippers wearing hats and white gloves, singing hymns, joining their hands together in prayer. Today the pews were fillled with technicians and teamsters, and the floors were littered with Dunkin' Donuts cups and napkins. At the front of the church near the altar, several large lights shone on an old man and a younger man about Joe's age and height, with Joe's exact haircut—Joe's double.

"Julia!" somebody called, and I turned to see Andrea, the makeup girl, waving to me from a nearby pew. Just the woman I wanted to see.

"Hi, Andrea," I said, and she motioned for me to come over.

She cleared away a large tote filled with makeup and I sat down beside her.

"They're just setting up this shot. I think Joe and Frank are in the back running through their lines. He'll be out in a minute."

"Great," I said. "So how're you doing?"

"Good! Good."

We both looked toward the front of the church.

"Have you met Doug yet?" she asked me as I tried to think of what to say next.

"Doug who?"

"Doug McCarthy? He's a new director. He did episodes three and four this season."

"No, I haven't met him, but I know Joe really likes him."

"Oh yeah, he's great. Everybody likes him. I'm sure Joe told you about Brant getting fired."

"Uh, no . . . I'm not really sure who Brant is."

"Oh, I know you've met him. He was the head of wardrobe," Andrea said, and she started in on a long and generally uninteresting diatribe about Brant's unfortunate history on this production. While she talked I thought, *Alison was right. Makeup girls love to chat.*

". . . Joe couldn't stand him. We have a new guy now, Al, and he and Joe get along great. He's funny. Everybody's been teasing Joe about that thing in the *Post* this morning, so Al put a 'Gay Pride' T-shirt in Joe's trailer with the rest of his wardrobe and—"

"What thing in the *Post*?"

"Joe didn't tell you?"

"No, I haven't spoken to him today."

"Oh, well, it's one of those blind items, where they don't say who it is they're talking about, but it sounds like they're talking about Joe, you know. There must be a *Post* around here someplace. Let me see if I can find one. . . ."

Andrea stood and wandered down the rows, looking for a paper, and I started to get a sinking feeling. She returned to our pew, riffling through the pages of a beat-up newspaper.

"Here it is," she said, handing the paper to me.

There at the bottom of "Page Six" was:

> *What married male star of a hit cop show was seen picking up an attractive young man at a popular New York club recently, adding fuel to the, um, flaming online rumors that his marriage might be a sham?*

I read it over several times. Then I said, trying to conceal the panic in my voice, "And people think this is supposed to be Joe?"

"Yeah, well, not really, but everybody's been giving him a hard time about it. You know, married star of a cop show . . ."

"Oh yeah, I see. . . ."

"I mean, they could mean Richard Davis from that show *Rookie,* but that shoots in L.A. and this happened in New York. . . ."

"There are tons of cop shows," I said. "Doesn't Kiefer Sutherland play a cop on that show *24*?"

Andrea's eyes lit up. "Kiefer Sutherland is gay? How do you know? Are you and Joe friends with him?"

"No, I wasn't saying he's gay, I was just saying that there are a lot of cop characters on TV."

"I don't think he plays a cop on *24.* Wait a minute, here comes somebody who'll know. . . ."

I followed Andrea's gaze to see a very beautiful young woman approaching us. She was cheerful-looking and petite and she wore the type of clothing that looks lovely on the cheerful petite but clownish on the rest of us. She had a little red wool ski cap that perched at a jaunty angle on her head. Long, silky auburn hair flowed from beneath the cap and over her shoulders. What had looked like a hand-knit sweater from a distance turned out to be a multicolored poncho. She wore very tight jeans that accentuated her slender hips and slim thighs, and on her feet were a pair of lime green moccasins. I tried to imagine the same getup on my five-foot-eight frame, with my abundant (although somewhat less noticeable these days, due to stress) butt. I would have looked like a big pear-shaped oaf in those jeans, with that crazy short poncho. She looked like a young Audrey Hepburn. I knew it was Jenna.

"Hey, what a great surprise!" said Joe's voice behind me. I turned to see him entering my pew from the opposite side.

"Hi, honey," I said. Joe gave me a kiss and I whipped my head around to see what Jenna's reaction would be. She remained calm and composed.

Andrea called out to her, "Katie, do you watch *24*?"

"I've seen it. It's not, like, a regular show of mine. But I've seen it."

Not Jenna. This girl Katie had a thick Long Island accent. She wasn't Jenna.

"I didn't know you were coming," said Joe. Behind him, a pair of teamsters was trying to make their way toward the altar with a life-size bronze-painted Jesus on a crucifix. "Coming through!" one of them called out, and Joe moved forward into the pew, allowing Jesus to be schlepped down the aisle behind him. He was obviously constructed out of Styrofoam, because the two men held Him high above their heads, each effortlessly bearing the cross with one hand.

"Is Kiefer Sutherland supposed to be a cop on his show?" Andrea asked Joe.

"I think he's a spy or something," said Joe. "Why?"

"Julia and I were trying to figure out who that blind item was about."

"Oh, it was definitely meant to be me. My publicist just found out that there's all this stuff about me being gay on Gawker. They have dates when I was apparently out with some guy, but she's going to go back over my schedule and figure out what I was doing each night to prove that that site is full of lies. I'm thinking of suing."

"Is there any way for them to figure out who posted those tips?" I asked calmly. *Breathe,* I told myself. *Breathe.*

"Of course they can. Everyone who posts on the site has to register. They'll have to track the people who wrote those lies, and maybe I can sue them, too."

A group of boys in choir gowns were now being led down the aisle behind Joe, his cue to get ready for his next scene.

"You should stay and watch these kids sing, honey," Joe said to me, kissing me good-bye. "They're real members of the Harlem Boys Choir."

"Yeah, they sing like angels," said Andrea, then when Joe walked away she said to me, "Have you read this week's script?"

"No, I never read the scripts anymore," I said. "I used to. . . ."

"It's great. The priest has been abusing one of the boys in the choir. The boy's going to be doing the solo—they're supposed to be rehearsing—and while the boy sings 'Ave Maria,' there are tears streaming down his face. . . . That reminds me, I better make sure I have the eye drops." Andrea started rummaging through her makeup bag. "Here we go. . . ."

"So what happens?" I asked.

"Oh, so the boy is singing and crying, and the priest is all evil looking and laughing at the boy, and then Joe comes storming in and they get into a skirmish and Joe goes to shoot the priest and accidentally shoots the boy! It's a 'To Be Continued' episode."

Oh Jesus, I thought, looking apologetically up at the Styrofoam

Savior hanging above the altar. Even He looked embarrassed. No wonder I stopped reading the scripts! I looked at my watch and realized that I was due in Jonathan's salon for my hair extensions in less than an hour and still needed to drop our car off at the garage.

"I gotta go," I said to Andrea. "Will you please tell Joe and Catherine that I said good-bye?"

"Sure, sweetie," said Andrea.

I ended up being early for my appointment with Jonathan, so I sat in the waiting area and flipped through a gossip magazine that somebody had left on the seat beside me. It was the one with a regular column called "Stars—They're Just Like Us!"—a two-page spread of candid photos showing celebrities doing things that are supposed to be surprisingly normal.

"They eat with their hands!" said a caption under a photo of Will Smith popping a morsel into his mouth at a sidewalk café.

"They forget their umbrellas!" said another, showing a drenched Zooey Deschanel trudging through a Manhattan downpour.

I thought about the contributions I could provide with my own exclusive access to one particular luminary. "They floss on the bed while watching TV!" "They leave milk out on the counter until it spoils!" "They cheat at Scrabble!" I came up with a variety of annoying things Joe did, little domestic crimes, but I knew that none of them, perhaps not even his adulterous affair, equaled the hateful slander that I had posted on Gawker. Why had I done it? Ever since I left the set, my mind kept wandering back to the poisonous posts and the various "what ifs." What if, at this very minute, Joe's lawyers were serving Gawker with a summons or a warrant or whatever else would enable them to gain access to a list of the site's registered users? I imagined the slow, disbelieving smiles appearing on their faces as they learned that the poster was actually his wife. I thought about the way that they would pass on the shocking information to Joe. "We've got some . . . bad news," they would say. "You'd better sit down."

I was still playing out this revelation of my betrayal when Jonathan came to collect me for my extensions. He sensed my somber mood and didn't talk much throughout the process, which was much more complicated than I had anticipated. Jonathan took long, thin strands of human hair in various shades of blond and fastened them to my own hair with some sort of glue-gun/flat-iron contraption. He began at noon. By three o'clock, when I was well into imagining my lost custody battle, Jonathan finished with the gluing, and my hair, once barely past my chin, now hung halfway down my back. My scalp was tender and sore from the pulling, and my hair looked eerily similar to my Barbie doll's the time I decided to give her a haircut when I was a little girl. It didn't taper at the bottom but instead ended in long, chunky, uneven sections. Not a great look. Jonathan sent me off to be shampooed and I winced in pain as the shampoo girl scrubbed the tightly glued sections that lay in hard knots all around the top of my scalp. Back at the chair, Jonathan started to trim the bottom of my hair. "Not too much," I said, not only because the extensions were expensive and it felt wasteful to cut them, but also because I started to realize I looked younger with long hair. I momentarily stopped fretting and admired the way my hair swung around my shoulders in long, silky, sandy-blond waves. My hair had never looked this good.

I left the salon and hadn't walked two blocks before I encountered—get this—two firemen, walking toward me all geared up.

One was talking on his phone, but the other looked me up and down and then said, "Hey!" with a big smile. Before I had a chance to think about it, I said, "Hey!" with a big smile right back. Not "Fuck off" like I would have said fifteen years ago, but "Hey!" with the big smile.

I walked home wondering why, in my youth, I used to get so terribly annoyed by the catcalls from workers on construction sites or from gangs of teenagers lurking on corners. I had no idea then that one day I would no longer be noticed by men at all. I would become, as far as most men were concerned, invisible.

But this didn't happen, as one might suspect, when I became pregnant with Ruby. Actually, I discovered that there is a huge segment of the male population that finds pregnant women quite sexy. *"¡Hola! ¡Mamacita!"* these men would call out to me with accompanying kissing noises as I waddled across the street. Joe and I were still living downtown then (Alison had moved to L.A. and Beth had gotten married and moved uptown). They flirted with me in local bodegas and eyeballed me on subways and sang to me when I walked past their stoops.

And then, when Ruby was born and all my forays into the outside world included her, it was as if I suddenly possessed a hideous physical deformity. Men didn't look at me—if anything, they averted their gaze as I struggled down the steps of my building or onto a bus with her stroller. Catching my eye would instill an obligation to assist, and most men in my neighborhood had their own women and kids they weren't helping out. After Ruby was born, I only received attention from old women who descended on the stroller like pigeons, cooing lovingly at Ruby and scolding me in Russian or Spanish for not having her head covered or having enough layers on her.

Now, though, walking through an early-evening snow flurry with my fresh long locks cascading around my flushed cheeks, I felt beautiful, mysterious, blond, and young . . . looking. Nobody would ever find out who sent in those posts, I decided. Joe would never bring legal proceedings against Gawker—it would just draw more attention to the gay charges. At the corner, while waiting for the light, I noticed that the driver of a delivery truck was staring at me, and when the light changed he gave me a little honk and a big smile. I gave him a big smile right back.

In our lobby, I was greeted with startled exuberance by our doorman, Luis, and when I opened the door to our apartment, Sammy ran into my arms, as he always did. He galloped right into my open arms, and when I lifted him joyfully up onto my hip, he pulled back his little hand and slapped me across the face as hard as he could.

"You're not my mommy!" he cried.

It was a reflex. His hand had connected with a part of my lip that was still agonizingly sore from the injections, and my own hand shot forward, landing flat on his little cheek with a crisp slap. He blinked, startled for a moment. And then he screamed.

Ruby stood, wide-eyed and motionless, at the end of the foyer.

"It's okay!" I mumbled as Sammy thrashed hysterically in my arms. "It's okay!"

Then I burst into tears.

[thirteen]

Just let it all out," said Dr. James. He was holding fast in his large leather chair while I sat, hunched over, snotting and sobbing in mine.

I was in control when I nodded hello to the building's doorman and felt a mild, almost pleasant sense of nostalgia when I saw the good magazines and hard chairs, but when I saw Dr. James, I lost it.

"He's fucking somebody from his show," I whimpered. "I hit my baby," I cried. "I'm out of my mind!" I practically screamed, in summation. (And I wondered why Dr. James wasn't attracted to me.)

"What do you mean, 'out of your mind'?" Dr. James interrupted.

"You know what I mean. I'm crazy!" I was in snot city. I ripped tissues from the box on the table next to me, and a sizable discard pile of them had already formed on my lap.

"No, you're not crazy," said Dr. James.

"Please," I said. "Look at me."

"I am."

"Tell me that you don't think a lunatic who throws herself at her shrink, who sends him a stupid pen for Christmas, who cyberstalks and spreads rumors about her husband and abuses her children—tell me that that woman isn't completely insane."

"You sent the pen?"

"Yes!"

"Hmm," he said. He looked down for a moment. "Did you also send the basket of cured meats?"

"What? No!"

"Oh."

"Cured meats? What kind of nut would send you cured meats?" I asked. Then I couldn't help it. I started to laugh a little. Dr. James was also smiling, despite himself.

"What else have people sent you?"

Dr. James shrugged the way he always did when I tried to ask him anything personal about himself. Questions such as "How old are your children?" "Are you happy in your marriage?" "Do you find me attractive?" "Do you think about me when I'm not here?" were always met with a little shrug and countered with a question about me. *Here it comes,* I thought, sniffling, and he said, "What do you fear most right now, in this situation with Joe?"

I had to think about that for a moment. Finally I said, "I guess I'm afraid of growing old by myself."

"Why would you grow old by yourself?"

"I mean, if Joe left me for this chick Jenna, I'd be by myself."

"More than you are now?"

"I'm not by myself now."

"Exactly."

What a field day my dad would have had with Benjamin James—a man with two first names.

"I really hate my husband," I said. Sobbing again. "I hate his guts."

"It's okay to cry," said Dr. James.

"You have to stop crying," said Beth an hour later and you know, in my experience, friends always offer better advice than shrinks. Beth was right. I really had to stop. We were at Starbucks, seated at our usual spot in front of the window, but that afternoon, even though it was dark and shitting frozen rain outside, I wore sunglasses and wept.

Except for a few short intermissions at Dr. James's office, I had been crying nonstop ever since I slapped my poor son the night before.

"What is it, PMS?" Joe had asked when he came home and found me weeping in bed.

"Yes, you son of a bitch," I had sobbed.

Now Beth said gently, "Try to stop."

My skin, which had been sensitive ever since the microdermabrasion, was raw from the salt in my tears, and my hand shook as I raised my coffee cup to my lips. The hardened glue that was attached to almost every strand of hair on my head cut into my scalp like a crown of thorns.

"Joe . . . could . . . take . . . the kids!" I whimpered.

"What?" Beth said. "Just for a little slap? Come on! My mother slapped us all the time. She still got custody when my parents split up—not that you and Joe are going to."

"Things are different now. You should have seen the way Ruby was looking at me."

"She was just upset. Didn't you tell me that she calmed down once Sammy stopped crying?"

"Yeah."

"And that Sammy kissed you and said he loved you when you put him to bed?"

Now my tears turned into sobs again.

"You need to talk to somebody," Beth said.

"I just came from Dr. James's office," I said.

"No, I mean a lawyer," Beth said. "Call Ivan Samsonoff. He's the best."

"But getting a lawyer seems so final. I mean, Joe doesn't even know I know what's going on."

"Nor should he, until you get some good legal advice. It kills me that you're sitting here feeling like the villain when you're the victim! Joe obviously has no regard for your marriage, and as far as I'm concerned, that translates into having no regard for his children. But like you said, he could use something like the little incident last night to his advantage. You just need to protect yourself."

Through the smeary glass windowpane I saw a Starbucks employee trying to shovel a path through the slush on the sidewalk, but it was too wet. It was like trying to shovel beach sand once the tide had risen.

"Let's go," I said, and when we arose Beth said, "Have you lost weight?"

"Yeah, I think so. I can't eat. It's the one good thing that's come out of this. I'm thinner."

We walked outside and then Beth grabbed my arm. "Look, I know it must be hard feeling like you have to compete with whoever this Jenna person is. But . . . I'm saying this as your friend. This cosmetic-treatment stuff is a bottomless pit. I see it all the time. The more stuff you do, the more you feel like you have to do."

"What're you talking about?" I said.

"I'm talking about you, Julia! When I first knew you, you didn't even wear makeup, but you were always the one everybody noticed, wherever we went."

"No I wasn't. Alison was."

"No, *you* were. Because you had so much to say, so many funny stories . . ."

"Well, I was eighteen. Of course I didn't need makeup. And everybody has funny stories when they're eighteen."

"I'm just saying, maybe you need to start thinking about what you're going to do with your life . . . no matter what happens with Joe. In the meantime, I'll e-mail you Ivan's number. Call him today."

Beth grabbed a cab heading downtown, and as I stood on the corner of Broadway and Eighty-fourth Street waiting for the walk signal, I saw them. I saw them, but it was too late to do anything about it. It was Judy and Vicki, the Multi-Culti auction organizers, and they were waving gaily at me from the other corner. Once they're waving gaily, it's too late to duck into the CVS. The light changed and I swear they skipped across that intersection, they were so excited to see me. So, I stood there with my swollen, tear-stained face. I stood there, smiling broadly, and thought, *Fuck.*

"Finally!" said Vicki. "We've been calling and calling. Did you get our messages?"

"Look at your hair! It's so long!" said Judy. "How did it get so . . . long?"

The truth was that I actually hadn't listened to my own voice mail in days—I only listened to Joe's messages now. But of course I didn't say this. Instead, I said, "My phone was stolen."

I said it like that, without giving it a thought. Joe's lying skills were starting to rub off on me.

"Oh my God!" said Judy. "Right out of your purse?"

"Yup!"

"But can't you check your messages, anyway?" asked Vicki.

"No," said Judy, "she had to stop the phone service!"

I hadn't thought of that, but it was good, so I said, "Yeah, and I haven't gotten around to getting a new phone and phone number and everything."

"What a pain," said Vicki.

"Wait," said Judy. "I just called you this morning. Who's your service provider? You must have the same shitty service that I do. I don't think they shut off your service yet, because I just called you this morning and heard your voice mail. Whoever stole your phone is probably racking up thousands of dollars in overseas calls. . . ."

Judy opened a pocket on the side of her Chloé bag and removed her cell phone. "Here," she said. She held the phone at arm's length and squinted at the front of it. She pushed a few numbers and then said, "Here, let's call you now. Maybe the guy who stole it will answer it." Judy handed me the phone and I could hear the ringing coming from the earpiece before I got it anywhere near my head. A millisecond later, my phone could be heard loudly ringing from somewhere in the dark fathoms of my oversized bag. It didn't actually ring; it played a ring *tone* that Ruby had decided to surprise me with several months before. It was the song that broadcast: *I like big butts and I cannot lie* . . . Ruby had downloaded it onto my phone as a joke after I complained about my weight one too many times. I pretended I didn't hear the song in my purse and Judy and Vicki pretended with me. When I heard my recorded voice through the earpiece and my bag stopped playing, I slapped the phone shut and said, "You're right. It's still on."

"Right," said Vicki. "Okay."

"I'll have to get that taken care of."

"Well, in the meantime, we were calling about the auction," Judy said. "We want to put a notice in next week's Multi newsletter about Joe doing the auction, and we were wondering if we could get a head shot or something."

I hadn't asked Joe about the auction yet, but I knew what his answer would be. What had seemed to be a wonderfully vindictive move at the time—committing him to the auction—would have no effect on him at all, I realized now. Once I told him about it, he would just refuse and he would never have to see these women. But I would.

"Joe can't do it. I'm really sorry. I just found out this morning. He's . . . working."

"What?" cried Judy.

"Oh, no," said Vicki. "Eileen is going to have a nervous breakdown. The auction's only five weeks away!"

"I'm really sorry," I said. "I have to go." And I started across the street just as a delivery truck was pulling away from the curb. The driver leaned on his horn and stayed on it, even after I stopped dead in my tracks and glared at him.

"Get the fuck out of the road!" he called to me.

"I've got the fucking light, you asshole!" I shrieked.

The driver motioned angrily at the pedestrian light, which steadily illuminated the DON'T WALK command.

"Fuck you!" I yelled, and I continued across, almost getting sideswiped by a Vespa in the process. I didn't look back at Vicki and Judy, I just walked on across the street, trying not to think about the playdate lists from which Sammy's name would soon be crossed off. Vicki and Judy were talkers, and I could just hear their reports about how "unbalanced" I seemed. How "unstable." I had heard these words used to describe other mothers, and I have to admit I avoided playdates with their kids. Who wouldn't?

When I got home, the apartment was empty. Catalina must have gone out to the grocery store, I thought, and then I started to tear the place apart. I was like an addict looking for a fix. I pulled out all of Joe's clothes drawers, looked in his pockets and in his gym bags and in his medicine cabinet. I searched under his side of the mattress and on top of our tallest armoire. I had no idea what I was hoping to find, but I was feeling the adrenaline rush of the hunt and flew through the house like a madwoman. I dumped out the drawers of Joe's desk and riffled through his receipts, looking for evidence of presents or hotel rooms—and I found dozens of receipts for presents and hotel rooms. Actors are always buying presents and they're always staying in hotels. The receipts really told me nothing, but I was getting a second wind. His computer! I grabbed his laptop and was just about to open it when I heard the front door open.

"Hello?" sang Catalina from the front hall. I heard her set down a grocery bag on the hall table before wandering into the living room. I was seated at Joe's desk with papers strewn all around me.

"Hi, Catalina," I said. "I'm just looking for something." I pretended I had an itch in my eye. I didn't want her to see that I had been crying.

"I'll help you," Catalina said with a sympathetic smile.

"No, it's not here," I said. "It's okay."

"Are you okay, Julia?" Catalina asked.

"No," I said. "I really don't feel very well."

"Is because you no eat!" Catalina said. "I bought the favorite chicken soup. From the Jewish store. I make you lunch."

"No, thanks, Catalina, you go ahead. I'm not hungry."

"No, come eat. You feel better after! *¡Barriga llena, corazón contento!*" Catalina had said this many times to the kids.

Full tummy, happy heart. A peasant's credo.

"Okay, let me put this stuff away first."

I stuffed the papers back into the drawers. I pushed the file cabinet back under the desk and fixed a pile of books I had knocked over. Catalina had discovered this amazing chicken soup at a nearby kosher deli, and she and the kids and I ate it at least once a week. Sometimes with noodles. Sometimes without. Now the smell of the soup being reheated on the stove made me a little hungry and I walked into the kitchen, where Catalina was setting up a place at the table.

"Sit," she said, smiling warmly, and I sat. Catalina had sliced a baguette, still warm from the French bakery, and placed it on a plate with some butter. I watched her ladle the soup into a bowl and I thought about her own children, as I often did when Catalina was taking care of me, as she was now, and as she had done right after Sammy was born. Her kids were grown now—her son managed a Days Inn in New Jersey and her daughter was getting her master's in education from Hunter College—but I thought about them waiting when they were children, waiting just like me, for their meal, for their mother's warm touch.

[—]

"Do either of you have parents who live close by?" the attending nurse had asked me between contractions the night I had Ruby. It was small talk, meant to distract me, I knew. She had already asked me, in her crisp, lyrical Irish accent, if we knew the sex of the baby and whether we understood that our sleeping days were over. Now she wanted to know if any grandparents would be visiting soon.

"My parents are down in Florida," Joe had answered. I had given him the job of chat deflector. After being in labor for several hours, the chatter of the various attendants was starting to get to me.

"What about you, Julia?" the nurse had asked. I was bracing myself for the next contraction.

"Where's the anesthesiologist?" I whispered.

"He'll be along soon. He's coming."

"That's what you said an hour ago," I said, and then, as I moaned through my pain, I heard her say, "I know it seems like hours, sweetheart, but it's only been twenty minutes since you asked."

"What if I die?"

"Honey!" said Joe.

"The doctor's coming. So are your folks looking forward to being grandparents, then?"

"No," I groaned, after a few seconds, when I could. "My dad's not too well."

"Oh, I'm sorry," the nurse said.

Not as sorry as you're about to be, I thought, and I said, "My mom's dead. She died when I was eight."

"Oh," the nurse said. "I am sorry, sweetheart. I lost my own mum, too . . . and this is the time I missed her most. When I had my first baby. After I brought him home. That's when you want yer mum, sweetheart, I know. But you'll do a grand job of it. . . ."

I looked at the nurse then—I mean, really looked at her for the first time since she had come into the room. She was tall and slightly heavyset, with pale, blotchy skin and age spots on her hands, but when she said the word *mum,* I could see her as a little girl in some green place, some idyllic lace-windowed home, listening to the clicking noise her mother's sandals made when they met her heels.

"You'll be fine," the nurse said. She patted my hand and then she left the room, and as I gazed longingly after her, Joe said, "How about a little TV? I know I saw a remote control around here someplace."

The only birth I had ever witnessed prior to Ruby's was the litter our cat Sable had when I was about five years old. My mother awoke Neil and me before dawn that morning to watch the birth, in the hopes that we'd learn something about the facts of life, and all those years later, as the anesthesiologist finally arrived and shot numbing agents into my back, I recalled the strange, metallic scent of blood in my parents' closet—Sable's chosen birthing space—and the furious purring of Sable as she licked the slimy, writhing kittens clean. When the doctor left and Joe and I waited for the epidural to kick in, I told Joe about watching the cat's birth with a combination of wonder and disgust, and about the dried blood and umbilicus stuck to the shirt my father furiously held up in front of my mother later that morning. "You watched her have her kittens all over my best shirt?" Daddy had raged.

"I couldn't move her," my mother replied indignantly. "She had chosen that spot as her nesting place! That's sacred!"

"Was he drunk?" Joe asked.

"No, of course not," I answered angrily. "He never drank during the day then. I've told you that."

"You're having a contraction," Joe had said.

"Get out," I said, laughing with relief.

I hadn't felt a thing.

[—]

[fourteen]

The last place I wanted to go that afternoon was the Multicultural Montessori School. I was sure that Judy and Vicki had already reported to Eileen that Joe had backed out of the auction and I feared an angry confrontation, but I wanted to pick up Sammy myself after what had happened the night before. When I arrived at the school, Judy and Vicki were nowhere in sight, much to my relief. I waited a few doors down from the school, not right in front, and I was just pulling my cell phone out of my bag when I heard a man say, "How'd your hair grow so fast?"

I turned toward the voice. It was Adam Heller. He was staring at my hair.

"Is it a wig?" he asked.

"Are you serious?"

"Yeah."

"You're asking me if I'm wearing a wig?"

"Yeah."

"Okay. You don't think that's rude?"

"Why?"

"Because . . . Well, what if I was wearing a wig because all my hair had fallen out from chemotherapy treatments? Wouldn't it be rude then?"

"I dunno. Did your hair fall out because of chemotherapy treatments?"

"Jesus Christ! They're hair extensions, okay?"

"Oh."

"I got them because I'm going to this . . . event." Over the past twenty-four hours, I had made this coy reference to an "event" in response to comments about my hair, and everybody had followed with the question "What event?" to which I casually replied, "The Golden Globes. Joe was nominated and I got these extensions to wear that night. Just for fun." It made me appear slightly less superficial, I thought.

Adam didn't rise to the bait, so I said, "It's a big, stupid Hollywood thing."

"What is?"

"The event."

"Oh."

"It's the Golden Globes. Joe was nominated."

"Joe who?"

I looked at Adam then to see if he was joking. He wasn't. It was clear he had no idea what I was talking about. I knew that Elizabeth, his wife, knew I was married to Joe. Apparently she hadn't shared this with Adam. *Apparently,* I chided myself, *people have more interesting things to talk about.*

"My husband. He's Joe Ferraro."

"Oh, yeah?"

"Yeah."

"What's he, an actor?"

I laughed indignantly. "Yeah. He's an actor."

"Oh."

Parents were starting to leave the school with their kids, so Adam and I walked toward the building.

"I'm taking Katie over to the diner for a hot chocolate. Do you want to come with Sammy?"

I normally would have said no, but I knew that Sammy would consider it a treat. Also, I was intrigued by Adam, to say the least. He was either very dull and stupid or very quirky and intelligent, and I wanted to find out which, so I said, "Okay."

To my great relief, Sammy ran into my arms when I arrived at his classroom. I kissed him tenderly on his cheek, which didn't reveal a red outline of my hand, as I had feared. He was fine.

"I'm a little worried about Sammy," his teacher, Lauren, said to me quietly while Sammy removed his belongings from his cubby.

"Why? What happened?" I asked. *He was fine!*

"We're worried about his behavior. He's very distractible and it has us concerned."

"When you say 'us,' you mean . . ."

"I mean me, my assistant teacher, Dina, and Joanna, the school psychologist."

"This school has a psychologist? The oldest kids in the school are what, five?"

Lauren smiled at me patiently. "He has a hard time sitting quietly in group. At this age, children are constantly experimenting with the ways that they move their bodies through the space around them, but they should also be able to control their bodies for short periods of time and focus on external information so that they can process it appropriately."

"He's bored," I said. "Group is boring the way you run it. I watched you on Parents' Day, and *I* had a hard time sitting still." I said it impulsively, the words moving through space like Sammy's active limbs, wild and uninhibited.

Lauren opened her mouth to speak but was having a hard time forming the right words. It occurred to me that she was having a hard time "processing" what I was saying to her, so I decided to put it in other words. "He's a boy. He has a lot of physical energy that he isn't able to exert in your crowded classroom. He's bored and frustrated, and that's why he has a hard time sitting still."

It took a moment but Lauren managed to recover her impassive, indulgently condescending expression and said, "I'm hearing that you have issues with my teaching methods. It would be more appropriate to discuss this in a meeting. Next Friday, if that's okay."

"Next Friday I'm going to Los Angeles."

"Oh. Well, this is pretty important. We're only trying to do what's best for Sammy, and Joanna is only here on Fridays."

"I'm Sammy's mother. I know what's best for him. I'll meet with you when I get back from L.A. In the meantime, I'm going to have Catalina pick him up every morning before group next week. There's no reason he should have to bear another week of it if he's as restless as you're describing."

"Fine," said Lauren, blinking furiously.

When Sammy and I exited the building, we found Katie and Adam waiting for us. Katie and Sammy ran ahead to the corner while Adam and I walked along behind them. My heart was pounding and I was aware that the adrenaline that was pumping through my veins, causing me to clench and unclench my fists, wasn't anger or rage but rather a sense of victory and triumph. I realized, suddenly, that I had always regretted giving in so readily to the suggestions about having Sammy see a speech therapist. I knew him better than anyone. I was his mother. What a sense of power I suddenly felt, knowing this.

"Wait, Sammy!" I called.

"I know!" Sammy called back.

At the diner, Adam and I drank coffee and the kids drank hot chocolates. Sammy wanted to drink his cocoa with a spoon, and after arguing this with him for a few minutes, his voice growing increasingly whiney and loud, I gave in and let him—something I never would have done with Ruby. "Never negotiate with terrorists," was my mantra then, knowing that if I gave in once, I'd pay the price later. Now I was too tired and I still had lingering guilt from the slap. I had slapped my small child in the face. "Go ahead," I said to Sammy, and when he smiled up at me, I had to blink back tears.

"So when is this big event of yours?" Adam asked, stirring his coffee.

"It's a week from Sunday. We leave next Friday for L.A."

"Oh, so the Golden Globes are in L.A.?"

"I can't tell if you're making fun of me, or if you really don't know anything about the entertainment business."

"Why should I know anything about the entertainment business? I'm a writer. What do you know about the publishing business?"

"Well, a little, actually. I was a journalism major at NYU and I worked at the *Village Voice,* then I worked at the *Daily News* for a while before I had Ruby."

"Oh, yeah? As a writer? Editor?"

"I had two pieces published in the *Voice* . . . well, *pieces* might be too grand a term—they were small, paragraph-long reviews of bands. And I was basically a gofer at the *Daily News.* I did some research work for Jimmy Breslin."

"Wow. Cool," said Adam. He actually seemed semi-impressed. "What kind of writing do you do?"

"Essays—science writing mostly. I'm working on a book about

climate change and how it affects various animal species. Otherwise I write for magazines. Probably the only thing you would have ever seen is a thing I wrote for *New York* magazine about the city's rat population last year. It got a lot of attention."

"Oh my God. Yes, I remember that. The part about the mother finding the rat licking the baby's bottle in the gazillion-dollar penthouse—that really got me."

"Yeah, I know. Disgusting."

"And the thing about rats squeezing their way into the plumbing fixtures . . . getting into people's tubs. You know, we lived in this really neglected building in the East Village for years and we never had a rat in the apartment. We used to see them on the streets all the time, but I never saw one inside."

"They were in the building for sure," replied Adam, "but there was so much garbage on the streets in those days, they didn't have to find their way into people's kitchens the way they do now. Plus, there probably wasn't a lot of construction going on when you lived down there."

"No, that was all starting up when we moved."

"Well, that's what stirs up the rats. When everybody starts trying to make everything look better."

I nodded, twisting a strand of fake hair around my finger. "I suppose you sort of got used to them, when you went in the sewers with those sanitation guys."

"Not really. One ran across my foot down there and I screamed like a schoolgirl."

I laughed, shivering.

"Do you still write?" Adam asked.

"No. I was working on a children's book, but I let that drop. I just never got around to finishing it."

"Why not?"

"Oh, I don't know. I guess it seemed really lame after Madonna and Fergie and everybody started writing children's books."

"It's not lame. And I think you'd have a good chance of getting it published, having a famous husband and everything."

"That's what made it seem lame." I was eager to change the subject, so I asked Sammy how he liked his hot chocolate and he gave me two thumbs-up. Katie copied him and they both jammed their thumbs in the air, laughing fitfully, then Sammy went back to drinking his cocoa from a spoon.

"Your hair . . . it looks so real," Adam said.

I smiled and then started laughing. "Wow, that's just not a compliment I ever thought I'd hear."

Katie had decided to imitate Sammy some more, and started using the spoon to drink her cocoa. That only worked for a few moments, both of them giggling and slurping their drinks, until Katie managed to knock her cup over with her spoon. Adam lifted Katie from her side of the booth just before the drink cascaded onto her lap, and I grabbed a pile of napkins from the dispenser on the table and started mopping up the mess.

Katie looked at the spoon in her hand and started to cry. Adam held her on his lap and kissed her brusquely, then told her to stop crying, and she did. I wondered then what it would be like to be married to Adam. This is how I had begun to assess men after I had children, even Dr. James (no doubt a perfect father). Before I had children, whenever I met interesting guys, usually through work or sometimes just in the neighborhood, I would wonder what they were like in bed. Now I wondered what they were like in a car when the wife was driving. Or what they were like at three in the morning when a baby was sick. Was Adam a man who hollered when he was angry at his wife, punching walls and slamming doors, or did he silently stew? Did he leave globs of spat-out toothpaste in the sink without a thought about who would have to chisel them off later? Did he hog the remote? These were the real issues. I knew that now.

I had a boyfriend in high school who once told me that I was an ideal girlfriend because I was practically a guy when it came to just hanging around. I told this to Joe early on in our relationship, and he concurred. He thinks it's because I was raised in a house with just a father and a brother, after my mom died. Basically, I follow sports and I'm not prone to excessive chatter. I've told Beth and other single friends that just working these two little traits into one's personality can make such a difference when dating a guy. Now I supposed my stock as a relationship guru had fallen. Apparently having a wife who watches ESPN loses its appeal after a while.

On the way home I thought about what it would be like to be single now. I had thought about this quite a bit over the past several days, actually imagining various dramatic scenarios surrounding my divorce from Joe. First there would be the confrontation with Jenna. Even though Joe was too obtuse to realize this, I knew she was only after his money and status. She wanted to be a celebrity wife. She was working her little ass off for a role that was basically just handed to me. I wasn't looking to marry a celebrity when I met Joe, and his chances of making it in show business back then were as good as anyone else's—not very good. No, I married him for a nobler reason, I told myself—for love. But now I was a little riled. If I was going to leave the marriage, it was going to be with the money and status that Horny Jenna so greedily desired. I imagined Aaron Spelling-esque confrontations with Jenna. Perhaps we would meet at a party. Somebody would introduce us and I would say, "I know who you are. I know *exactly* who you are." She would feign ignorance and I would sidle up to her and whisper into her ear, "He's still my husband. Keep your filthy paws off him." Then I'd say, "You can have what's left of him . . . after the divorce."

But that was about as far as I could get with the divorce fantasies, because once I got beyond handing Jenna the comeuppance she so richly deserved, there wasn't much else to look forward to, and there was a lot to dread. Of course, all our friends would side with Joe. He was the one who could get anybody house seats to anything. Who could, if you were with him, get you whisked past security lines in airports and invited aboard yachts and onto private jets. I'd have to date and eventually reveal my body to another man. The breasts that had shrunken after nursing Joe's babies, the loose skin on the belly that had expanded to accommodate Joe's offspring—what kind of offerings were these to a man who had no claim on the children who marked me, forever, as the former estate of another?

When Sammy and I arrived home, Ruby and Catalina were sitting together on the living-room couch watching MTV. Over the years, Ruby had gotten Catalina hooked on all her shows and favorite bands, and Catalina, as a result, was the hippest sixty-year-old on the Upper West Side. She watched *TRL* and *The Real World*. She hated Eminem, but loved Shakira, of course, and also Muse, Kanye West, and the Arctic Monkeys, and would drop anything if a Gorillaz video came on TV. Now they were watching *Cribs* and knitting. Catalina had taught Ruby to knit when she was quite young, so Ruby knit compulsively, whenever she watched TV.

"Hi, guys!" I said. Sammy ran across the room and leaped onto Ruby's lap.

"Sammy, watch it!" said Ruby.

"Hi, Julia!" said Catalina. I smiled but Ruby looked straight ahead at the TV, her knitting needles clacking angrily against each other.

"How was school, Ruby?" I asked.

Silence.

"Ruby?" said Catalina.

"Ella abusa niños," Ruby said to Catalina.

"Ella no abusa niños," Catalina scolded. *"Hablas con su madre."*

Because my spoken Spanish is so bad, Ruby and Catalina think I can't understand what they're saying. I understand enough.

"¡Abusa niños!" Catalina said again, rising now and laughing. "Americans! In my country, if a child hit his mother and she no hit him back . . . *that* is child abuse! Because he might grow up and think nobody ever care enough about me to teach me anything about what is right and wrong."

Then she said, "I'll finish the dinner," and she kissed Ruby on the top of her head.

"Thanks, Catalina," I said, and she looked like she was going to give me a little hug, but I must have given her some kind of nonverbal indication that her touching me would cause me to dissolve into a sodden pile of tears, because she just touched my arm and went into the kitchen.

"I guess she knows where her bread is buttered," Ruby muttered.

"RUBY!" I shouted. "THAT'S ENOUGH!"

The decibel of my shouting caught Ruby and me both by surprise and Ruby looked at me, startled. Then she started to cry. I wanted to keep shouting. I wanted to tell her to give me a fucking break. That I was obviously in over my head when it came to parenting. That what little I knew about being a mother I had learned from Catalina—a woman who went to Mass every morning and mysteriously crossed herself whenever she heard a siren. That Ruby's whole life, the best I could do was act as if I knew what I was doing. But I didn't keep shouting. Instead, I sat next to Ruby and put my arms around her, and she didn't pull away. She hugged me back and sobbed. Sammy patted her and said, "No crying, Ruby! No crying!"

"Everybody at school is asking me if Daddy's gay!" Ruby sobbed.

"What?"

"It's what all the kids at my school are talking about. Daddy picks up guys at nightclubs and is secretly gay."

"Ruby, you know that's not true," I said.

"How am I supposed to know it's not true?"

"You'd know if your father was gay!"

"There are gay men whose *wives* don't even know they're gay."

"Okay, I've told Catalina again and again, I don't like you kids watching *Oprah.*"

"Why all the gay rumors, then, if Daddy's not gay?" Ruby sniffed.

"People are sometimes jealous and resentful of celebrities and they make up things out of spite. A miserable, miserable, pathetic person made up those stories about Daddy. Everybody'll forget them soon, don't worry."

"Also . . . I want a chin implant. I know that's adding to my insecurity about Daddy. . . ."

Ruby was playing on my sympathy here. She is a beautiful girl, but she had decided almost a year earlier that she had a weak chin. "I have *no* chin," is what she said, and she'd been angling for a chin implant ever since.

"How does a thirteen-year-old even know about chin implants?" Joe had asked after she first broached the subject. I guess Joe doesn't get to see a lot of daytime television in that trailer of his. I had told Ruby again and again that she was too young for cosmetic surgery, but now I felt my resolve weakening. I felt like one of the world's worst mothers. It would be so easy to ingratiate myself with Ruby again by giving in on this issue. I couldn't take back the ridiculous rumors I'd started about Joe, or the fact that I had slapped Sammy, but I *could* make her an appointment with a surgeon and buy her a new chin!

Then I came to my senses.

"No," I said.

"Why not?! You obviously spent a fortune on your hair extensions, and everybody can tell you've had your lips injected—I don't know who you're trying to fool! You can do anything you want to try to improve your looks, but I'm not allowed to fix my facial deformity?"

"That's right," I said coolly.

"It's my face!"

"It'll be your face when you're eighteen. Legally, it's my face now and it's not finished growing. And you're right about my lips and hair. If I had it to do over, I wouldn't have done all this—"

Ruby stood up and started to leave the room.

"—*but* I'm a grown-up, and when you're grown-up, you can do anything you want to your face!"

"Uggggh!" Ruby shouted from the back hall before she slammed her door.

I went into the kitchen, where Catalina was tending to a roast pork tenderloin. A pot of potatoes was simmering on the stove. Joe was due home any minute and I suddenly wanted the kitchen to myself. I felt full of wifely goodness. Goodwife Ferraro, I was. In a few short hours, I had advocated for one child at his school and set limits with another. This was the best mothering I had done in weeks. Now I wanted my kitchen back.

"You don't have to stay, Catalina," I said with a smile.

"Oh . . ." she replied, confused.

"Just show me what to do and I'll finish making dinner. You can have the rest of the night off."

"Okay. Is almost ready. The roast needs to stay in the oven for another twenty minutes. Then it'll be finished. The potatoes are almost ready to be mashed. You're sure you no want me to stay and do that?"

"No, I remember how to mash potatoes."

"There is salad in the fridge, and a tofu stir-fry for Ruby. Just put it in the microwave for about a minute."

"That sounds good."

"And those green beans with garlic that Joe likes. They're on the stove. They're all done."

"Great," I said. "Thanks."

I said good-bye to Catalina and dumped the boiled potatoes into a bowl. I poured cream over the potatoes and dropped some butter in as well. "Plenty of salt," my mother used to tell me when I helped her make potatoes. Mashing potatoes was one of only a handful of things I clearly remembered doing with my mother. I'll have to show Ruby how to make mashed potatoes, I thought, and I'll say, "My mom always told me that the secret to her mashed potatoes was plenty of salt."

Ruby has a bit of a biased perspective on my mother. She thinks she was careless—even more careless than me. "Things were different then—we had more freedom," I had told her the day, two summers ago, when we visited my old neighborhood. Joe was shooting a film in D.C., so Ruby and I had taken a day trip to Annapolis, and after we went on a tour of the Naval Academy, we went to my old block. We gazed at the house—it had been a two-family home when we lived there but now it was a grander single-family home. I led her down to the old railroad tracks—now overgrown with weeds—and I told her about how Neil and I used to play down at the tracks in the late-summer afternoons, looking for snakes and bottles and treasure. I told her about the Confederate money that local kids believed had been buried in the woods behind the tracks. And about the house on the corner that was supposed to be haunted by a wife-murderer. It was hard to explain to literal-minded Ruby how the ghosts of murderers and witches and Confederate soldiers swam in our little minds. We didn't go to preschool, and we didn't need the constant supervision of our parents, the way kids do today. We were never expected to sit quietly in groups or develop sequencing skills. Our teachers were the six- and seven-year-olds in the neighborhood who told us that in elevators in skyscrapers there is no gravity, that dogs' mouths are cleaner than people's, and that cats can fall safely from a five-story building by landing on their feet.

"You were only five when you lived here, but you could run around the neighborhood without any grown-ups?" Ruby had asked.

"We weren't allowed past the railroad bridge," I told her, pointing to the stone structure ahead of us. It had seemed like the end of the world to us back then. "I can't believe it's really such a short distance from our house!"

The bridge looms large in my memories of that neighborhood because we were forbidden to cross it, but we had done so late one night, according to my father. He and my mother had left us alone in the house, Neil and me, because we were sound asleep. "You kids never woke up once you were asleep. Never!" my father said.

"Sometimes, not often, we'd sneak out after you puppies were asleep, just to run up the road to the neighbors for a beer," and the term *sneak* used here always amused me. The idea that my father—young, handsome, and strong—and my free-spirited mom had to "sneak" behind our backs to do anything was astonishing. Anyway, one night they returned from their drinks at the neighbors' and found Neil and me, frantic and hysterical, running across the railroad bridge in our pajamas in the dark. "Where were you two pups running off to?" my father used to laugh when he recounted the story, but I have no idea, because I think my only recollection of that night left for me is of his telling it.

I never share this story with Ruby—she wouldn't get it, just like she doesn't get the fun of "rounds." I had tried to get her and Joe, and later Sammy, to sing rounds in the car with me, but they all thought it was too tedious and kept muddling their parts. "You sing it yourself," Ruby said the last time we tried, and I had sung one verse, but it's no fun singing "Merrily, merrily, merrily, merrily, life is but a dream" when nobody's following you. When it ends, when you're alone—it's all at once. It's like hitting a wall.

When Joe arrived home half an hour later, the table was set. Ruby was in her room instant-messaging her friends, Sammy was watching Nick Jr. in our room, and I was in the kitchen opening a bottle of Chardonnay.

"Dinner smells good," said Joe. He walked up behind me and kissed the back of my neck. "And you do, too!"

I turned and kissed him on the lips.

"I know about Jenna," I whispered. I thought I'd take back my husband, while I was at it.

Joe stiffened, then pulled back a little. "Who?"

I grabbed the front of his shirt and remembered fighting with my brother as a child and the mistake of the shirt grab. Neil used to wriggle out of his shirt while I tugged on it, cursing and crying, trying to smack him on the head. He would squirm free of the shirt in the blink of an eye and then start shoving me, or worse.

I released Joe's shirt and he backed up a few steps.

"Jenna who?"

"Jenna! Your girlfriend. I've heard all her messages on your voice mail over the past two weeks. And, by the way, change your code. I can't get anything done because I'm wasting all my time listening to your simpering whore moaning about how horny she is. . . . Kids! Time to eat!"

The call to the children was issued in a singsong voice, but the preceding words had been said in the same quiet, controlled, but somehow ultra-menacing tone that my father used when he was really, really angry. His extensive military training always kicked in when he was emotional about something, and we knew that he was raging, fighting mad when his voice lowered to almost a whisper and he had to get real close to our faces so we could hear.

I lifted the platter of roast tenderloin from the counter and carried it into the dining room.

"What the fuck are you talking about? Wait a minute," Joe said, following me, but Sammy was running into the room and Joe picked him up for his hug.

"Wait," said Joe, "I think I know what this is about. . . ."

"We'll have to talk about it after dinner, won't we, honey?" I said, smiling and motioning toward Sammy.

Needless to say, Joe didn't eat a lot during dinner, but I finally had my appetite back.

"I've said it before, but I'll say it again: Catalina can really cook. This is delicious," I said, beaming. I took a small sip of my wine. I had to watch myself and not drink too much, but I wanted to drain the glass down my gullet and pour another. (I thought of my dad, in his current home at the VA hospital, cursing at nurses, his hands shaking and his mind sodden, and I left the rest of the wine in my glass.)

Ruby stared sullenly at her plate. Joe was in full spaniel mode, looking up at me imploringly and then looking away.

I don't know why I felt so good. Like I was in full charge, for the first time in weeks. Ruby brought up the chin surgery again and I thought Joe was going to break down and weep as he told her that she was perfect the way she was.

"You look like your mother. Like your beautiful mother, when we first met," he said, and I smiled as I cut into my meat.

After dinner, Ruby helped me with the dishes while Joe put Sammy to bed.

"I'm sorry about what happened last night. With Sammy," I said. "I've already told Sammy I'm sorry, but now I'm telling you."

Ruby moved about the kitchen quietly. She covered up the vegetables and placed them in the fridge, steering a wide path around the platter of meat.

"You're so . . . psycho lately."

"I know," I said. "I'm a little stressed."

"What do you have to be stressed about?" Ruby asked with a little laugh. "I'm the one who's taking too many honors classes. Daddy's the one who has to support us. You don't really have to do anything."

"I know. You have no idea how stressful that is," I said.

Eventually, Ruby went to bed and Joe and I were alone in our room. I was in bed, pretending to read, when he came in and shut the door quietly behind him.

"Jenna doesn't exist," he said.

I put my book down.

"It's Susanna."

"What?"

"Susanna has been cast in a film where she has to play an American. She's trying out this Southern accent—you know how British and Australian actors who can't really do American accents always do Southern accents?"

It's true about the Southern accent, I thought. *For some reason it's easy for foreigners.*

"She was just being silly and playful. You know she has no interest in me . . . and vice versa! I told her she could try out the accent on me, so she calls me sometimes after her sessions with her voice coach and she can never think of anything to say, so she just leaves those dirty messages."

I was looking right at him. He was looking right back.

"Call her," he said.

"What's the name of the film?" I asked.

Joe thought for a moment. "I don't know," he said.

I gave a short little laugh.

"Spike Jonze is directing it!" he announced.

Joe's laptop was next to the bed and I lifted it up, my eyes still fixed on his.

"Go ahead," he said. "Look it up."

I Googled Susanna. There were ten million Susanna Mercer links. Then I Googled Susanna Mercer and Spike Jonze and found a link to *Variety.* I clicked on the link.

Susanna Mercer is set to costar with Owen Wilson in You Rang?, *a new Spike Jonze film, DreamWorks producer Jeremy Winston announced today. . . .*

"I'm gonna have Susanna call you," Joe said. "She's going to feel horrible when she finds this out. I'm actually going to be a little embarrassed to tell her that my wife secretly listens to my voice-mail messages. . . ."

"It was an accident," I said. "We have the same code." And I told him the story of how I managed to get his voice mail instead of my own that night at Pastis.

"It was an *accident,*" I said.

[fifteen]

So you believe him?" Alison asked. We were in the Beverly Hills Vera Wang showroom. It was the following Friday, just two days before the Golden Globes. The dress I had chosen the week before had been flown to L.A. that morning, Joe and I had flown in that afternoon, and now I stood on a raised, carpeted pedestal while a seamstress carefully pinned my hem. Alison sat on a stool with her legs crossed and her ankle jiggling madly.

"Yes," I said. "I really do, Alison." I indicated with my eyes that I couldn't say more in front of the seamstress but Alison was determined.

"And how did he explain the . . . dirty talk?"

"The same as everything else. She was just working on the accent. Couldn't think of anything to say. Trying to be funny!"

"I see," said Alison, in a tone that implied she saw something I didn't.

"Turn, please," the seamstress said. I turned away from Alison and faced the three-way mirror, and there I was. My long, wavy blond hair was parted in the middle, looking, I thought, very seventies-chic. My skin glowed with yesterday's spray-on tan. My forehead was as smooth as a baby's, and when I smiled, no smile lines! The gown was simple but elegant, a satiny, steel-blue column that matched the color of my eyes and made me look tall and willowy. Behind me, through the floor-to-ceiling windows, clouds drifted by and palms swayed in the afternoon sun, and I thought, *I love California.*

We had thought of moving to L.A. when Ruby was younger. We looked at houses in Venice one winter, when Joe was shooting a film there. There were still some ramshackle bungalows right near the beach then, and Joe and I dreamed of buying one and fixing it up. A house was a very romantic notion in those days, when we were still renting and paying off debts. Now, when we go to L.A. and look at real-estate prices, Joe often says, "Why the hell didn't we scoop up one of those shitholes in Venice when we had the chance? Those places start at five million now." But what's the use of thinking like that? How could we have known then what we know today? It's like asking why we didn't look at ourselves then and see how precious everything about our marriage was. We should have poured ourselves into each other instead of miserly begrudging our time and energy, fighting over whose turn it was to get up with the baby and who got less sleep than the other. Everything appreciates over time. A long-term marriage is a rare and valuable thing, but fourteen years ago we weren't looking to nourish something that would someday be rare and valuable. We were just trying to claw Joe's way to the top. Now, standing proudly erect for the silent Filipino seamstress who crawled around my feet, I viewed myself as the steadfast guardian of our marriage. A weathered but still somehow beautiful figurehead proudly thrusting my protective bosom before the rising bow of a bountiful ship. My duty was to protect our marriage, not to dash it onto the rocks! I saw that now. That morning before we left for the airport, when I had guiltily tried Joe's voice mail one more time (just to be sure), I was met with a recording that informed me that his code had been changed. *Good!* I had thought. *I'm finished with all that witchery.*

"I'm sure she's going to the show on Sunday. Are you going to ask her about it?" asked Alison.

"Who?"

"You know," she said, and when I glanced at her, she mouthed the word, "Susanna."

"I doubt it."

"Julia! You have to!"

"It's too embarrassing! I'd have to admit to listening to . . . you know what, and she'd think I'm some hopelessly insecure shrew. . . ."

"No, she'd think you have her number, which you do."

"I'm just going to mind my own business. Joe and I are getting along great! It's like we're on a second honeymoon."

I hadn't told Alison or Beth about my Gawker postings. I couldn't. I could trust my two best friends with my life, but not with such a great bit of celebrity gossip as that. It would be too tempting at a party, after a few drinks, when the conversation switched over to celebrities, or the Internet, or to who's gay—there were many, many possible segues to the shameful "My friend is married to Joe Ferraro and she once, in a fit of anger, posted on the Internet that he's gay" story. Nothing had happened with the fake postings, anyway. Joe never followed up with his lawyers and there were no more blind items.

"So are you coming with us tomorrow night, or what?" I asked, changing the subject.

"Oh yeah, what is it again?"

"The *Entertainment Weekly* party." Alison knew that. And I knew she wouldn't miss it for the world, but she needed to pretend it was all too boring for her. Alison's career had sort of passed her by. Actually, in Alison's mind, it had not passed her by but had jumped ship and attached itself to Debra Messing when she barely beat out Alison for the part of Grace on *Will and Grace*. "Three callbacks," Alison still sometimes lamented when she'd had a few too many drinks. "And that bitch isn't even funny!"

"Okay, I guess I'll come." She sighed. "Maybe I'll buy something to wear. Can Joe get me on the list?"

"Yeah, I'll call his agent."

"Because I don't need him to. I'm sure I was already on the list, and when my assistant asked me about it, I said no, like I do to almost everything, but since you two are going, it might be fun."

"I'll make sure you're on the list," I said.

When the fitting was over, I made arrangements to have the gown sent to our suite at the Four Seasons. Alison gave me a kiss and dropped a small pill bottle into my purse.

"What's that?" I asked.

"Xanax. For the red carpet Sunday, in case I forget tomorrow. Just take half if you want. Me? I'd take two. Most people double their red-carpet dosage for the major awards shows."

"Well, thanks," I said.

Outside, I handed my parking stub to the young valet and he sprinted off, returning promptly with the black BMW Z4 rental convertible that Joe had surprised me with that afternoon. Joe had a meeting with his agent, but while I was unpacking, he left the keys to the car with a note that said, "In case you want to go to the beach. I've heard this is quicker than the bus! Love, J."

The first time Joe and I ever came to Los Angeles—for his first paying film job—we took a Metro bus from the Roosevelt Hotel in Hollywood to Santa Monica. It had looked like such an easy trip on the bus map. One bus would take us to Beverly Hills (Beverly Hills!) and we would switch to another that would take us to Santa Monica. To the beach!

My earliest impressions of Los Angeles had been largely formed by a handful of *I Love Lucy* reruns that I adored as a kid. The episodes where Ricky goes to Hollywood to sign a motion-picture deal and Ethel and Lucy go sightseeing in Beverly Hills. I felt, on that first L.A. trip, that Joe and I were a little like Ricky and Lucy, *sans* the Mertzes, but *avec* the wide-eyed, look-who's-hit-the-big-time attitude. It was pilot season and Joe's agent had arranged some meetings and auditions for him during the week we were in town, and when we flew into LAX, we felt as if we were being deposited on the very threshold of a bright, golden destiny.

We arrived on a Sunday and Joe wasn't scheduled to start shooting until that Tuesday. On Monday morning we woke up early, owing to the time change (this was before Ruby), and we decided to walk around the neighborhood. We strolled along the "Walk of Fame," and we studied the names on the stars with delight. Across the street was Grauman's Chinese Theatre and we meandered across Hollywood Boulevard, hand in hand, and just as we stepped onto the curb on the opposite side, a police officer on a moped pulled up next to us. The officer asked if we had a good reason for choosing not to cross at the light. We offered the lack of approaching automobiles as a good enough reason and were surprised to see the officer whip a citation pad from his breast pocket. He explained that there was a forty-dollar fine for jaywalking in the city of Los Angeles, and we honestly thought he was joking. Joe tried to explain that we had just arrived from New York City, where people are allowed to cross the street at will, but the cop would have none of it.

Anyway, that afternoon I wanted to go to the beach. Joe didn't particularly want to go, but he was willing, because I wanted so desperately to walk along a California beach. Somehow a rental car had not been part of Joe's deal (a teamster drove him and another actor to and from the set each day) and we couldn't really afford to rent a car, so we decided to take the bus. (I've told this story at a few Los Angeles cocktail parties and this is where people laugh uproariously.) Why bore you with the details of that epic journey? Short version: Long. Hot. Dehydrated and jet-lagged. Menacing Mexican gang behind us. Obvious TB victim catching sputum in hand, one row ahead. Otherwise empty bus that stops every few minutes even though there is nobody to discharge. Eyeing drivers in other cars, also stuck in traffic, we learn that even homeless people, even the blind, the limbless, the lepers, apparently even the children, DRIVE CARS in Los Angeles. Hours pass and finally it is time to switch buses in Beverly Hills! Hours later we arrive at the Santa Monica Pier and I have just enough time to sprint down to the surf and get my toes wet before we have to rush to make the last "express" bus back to Hollywood.

We had more or less wasted Joe's one free day in L.A., but he never blamed me or complained. That's one of Joe's pluses. He's really not a complainer. The first time my father went to a rehab for his drinking, my senior year in high school, he went to a good place—a real rehab with counselors and group sessions. When Neil and I went up for a family therapy weekend, one of our exercises was to list five positive things about each family member. It's hard to hold on to ill will and resentment toward somebody who has five good things about them, our counselor told us. And it turns out, we learned in that session, everybody has at least five things. One of Joe's is not being a complainer. Other things? He's generous. He has never begrudged me a thing—rather, he has told me that he wishes I would splurge on myself more. If I had driven straight over to Fred Segal that afternoon of the Golden Globe weekend and run up a ten-thousand-dollar bill, he would have been pleased for me. He's smart and intuitive. He can look at a situation and deconstruct it in a minute—for example, the time Sammy had the meltdown at his school interview—and know what to do next, while I'm more the type to panic and make things worse. *He's funny and loving and patient and . . . loyal,* I told myself that sunny Friday afternoon. *He's loyal.*

The valet pulled up with the black roadster and I tucked a twenty-dollar bill into his palm. I climbed inside and decided to put the top down. Why drive a convertible in Southern California with the top up? The valet saw me fumbling around with the roof latches and he leaned into the car.

"Like this," he said, reaching across me to unlatch one side, then the other. His arms were tanned and he smelled like shampoo and sweat and something else, some kind of musky aftershave, and this, combined with his youthful exuberance, made me smile.

"You have to put your foot on the brake. . . . That's it," he said, and he pushed a button on the center console. The roof retracted obediently and the young man stood back up and gave me a big grin.

"Thanks," I said, smiling back. I can't describe how long and blond I felt as I pulled away from the curb.

The car was equipped with a Global Positioning System that greeted me with a loud "Welcome!" and, to my surprise, announced that my destination was the Four Seasons hotel. Somebody at the rental agency must have programmed in the address of the hotel for us.

I started down Rodeo Drive. As always, I marveled at how immaculate the streets of Beverly Hills are. Joe says it's from the lack of snow and road salt and sand, but where is the detritus of man? The beer cans and chicken wings and pigeon shit and last night's vomit and spat-out gum that bejewel the sidewalks and streets of New York, London, Rome? Driving through Beverly Hills always makes me feel complicit in some kind of brilliant, but evil, urban-planning scheme. The garbage and dirt has to be *somewhere.* Now, though, driving a shiny black roadster down the pristine boulevard, I felt as if I was one of the chosen. The deserving. The breeze blew my hair extensions around my face and I flipped my head back like a teenager.

"In fifty feet, turn left," instructed my GPS guide.

Okay!

"At the next intersection, stay to the right."

Will do!

I followed the instructions of my electronic guide through several intersections and within minutes I was pulling up in front of the Four Seasons hotel.

"You have arrived!" announced the GPS.

You bet your ass I have!

I handed the car over to yet another valet and was welcomed into the lobby of the hotel by the doorman.

"Welcome back, Mrs. Ferraro. There's a FedEx package waiting for you."

"Thank you," I said, and I walked over to the desk to receive the package in all my blond loveliness.

"Mr. Ferraro left a message for you. He won't be back until six-thirty," said the concierge, handing me the package. We had decided to skip the various pre–Golden Globe parties that evening, to instead have a romantic dinner served to us in our suite. Now I had some extra time before Joe returned to the hotel. I would call the kids and then maybe take a nap.

As I headed for the elevators, I passed a door with a large Frédéric Fekkai sign above a photograph of a beautifully coiffed model. Two women were walking out of the door with bags full of hair products, and when they looked up, I saw that one was Teri Hatcher.

A hair salon. Perfect. I would get my hair extensions blown out while I was waiting for Joe. That way I wouldn't have to have it done before the *Entertainment Weekly* party tomorrow.

I smiled at Teri Hatcher, who smiled blankly back, and I pushed open the door of the salon. Inside, I waited behind two women who were checking in at the reception desk. When it was my turn, the perky young receptionist glanced down at a long list and asked, "Your name please?"

"I don't have an appointment, but is there any chance I can get a blow-dry?"

"Excuse me?" she said. The two women who had just checked in turned and stared at me.

"Just a shampoo and blow-dry," I said, smiling.

"Um, this isn't . . . a salon," said the receptionist.

I looked at her and then I looked around the salon, which, indeed, turned out not to be a salon at all. It was a conference room that had been turned into some kind of Frédéric Fekkai–sponsored, women-only cocktail party. Instead of hairstyling stations and blow-dryers and sinks, there were tables with white cloths and beautiful floral centerpieces, handsome waiters walking around with glasses of wine and trays of delicate hors d'oeuvres. There was Patricia Arquette and Claire Danes and . . . was it? Yes! It was Jessica Lange!

"What is this?" I asked the receptionist. I was whispering.

"It's a private party honoring Golden Globe nominees. I'm going to have to ask you to leave." She was braying.

My face turned crimson. "Oh," I said.

The two women were quietly cracking up next to me.

"Maybe I'm on the list. My husband . . . he's a nominee."

I had no interest in staying, but I knew that Joe and I were on a few party lists, and for some reason it was very important to me that the receptionist and the other two women knew this as well.

The receptionist looked me over and then said, "Your name?"

"Julia *Ferraro.* I'm *Joe Ferraro*'s wife."

She floated her pencil tip down the list of names. "No . . . no Ferraro."

"Oh," I said. "Okay."

I turned to leave and a woman handing out gift bags to departing guests absentmindedly started to hand one to me. When I reached for it, I heard the receptionist screech, "Tracy! She's not a guest!" and Tracy snatched back the bag and clutched it to her chest like a baby.

Later, as I was telling Joe about it, both of us weak with laughter, I described the way I then felt compelled to back out of the room, as if, had I turned my back on her, even for a moment, Tracy would have planted her boot in my ass and literally kicked me back out into the hotel lobby.

We ordered up grilled shrimp, haricot vert salad, and roasted rack of lamb that night, Joe and me, and we dined on our terrace, and the city of Los Angeles spread out below us like a sparkling kingdom. We sipped our champagne and we even smoked a little pot that Joe's driver had given him, and when I went inside to put on a CD, I saw that, in addition to the multitude of gift baskets that had been sent to Joe by various network executives, agents, and magazine editors, there was a new vase of large pink peonies that somebody had placed on the coffee table in our suite while we dined. Peonies are my favorite flowers, and when I pulled the card out from amid the blooms, I saw that it read: "To Julia, the love of my life, J." I carried the flowers back to the terrace and placed them on the table. The warm night air and the plaintive chorus of car horns and distant sirens reminded me of the summer nights of my youth, and I straddled Joe's lap like a showgirl and covered him with kisses.

[sixteen]

"Nobody carries their own children anymore," Karen whispered.

We were lounging by the Four Seasons pool, Karen Metzger and I, trying to get a little sun while Joe was in the gym. Karen was stirring her iced tea and peering over her sunglasses at a pair of twin babies being pushed past us in a double stroller.

"What do you mean?" I asked, blinking at the passing stroller. "What's wrong with carrying babies in a stroller? They're sleeping."

"No, I mean *carry to term.* Nobody carries her own babies anymore. Those babies had a surrogate mother."

I tried to catch another glimpse of the infants before they disappeared from view, but all I could see was the mother's back. The straps of her black bikini top and the back of her thong trisected her perfectly toned body.

"How can you tell they had a surrogate mother?"

"You can't tell! That was Brian Herriman's wife. You know, Brian Herriman from Paramount?"

"Oh, yeah!" I had met Brian Herriman and his wife (Jennifer? Gillian?) at a party once.

Karen was shoulder deep in her Marni tote. When she withdrew her phone, she said, "Gillian Herriman is in my friend Rita's book group. She tells everybody that she couldn't conceive and that's why she used a surrogate, but I think it was just to preserve that body."

She flipped open the phone. "I have to check my messages. I'm waiting for a call from Shane's play therapist." Karen touched the number 1 on her phone and that's how it dawned on me.

I didn't need Joe's code if I checked his messages using *his* phone.

Karen touched the number 1 just like I did when I checked my messages on my own phone. Apparently, 1 is the universal speed dial for voice messages. I hadn't known that. I could hear the staccato rhythm and varying tones of the different callers on Karen's voice mail as I pondered this new reality. It was still possible for me to check Joe's messages.

Why would I want to do that?

Karen snapped her phone shut.

"Yeah, so anyway, they were her eggs. She made sure everybody knew that, so I'm pretty sure she could have carried them herself. Katie Winston was the opposite . . ."

"Mmm-hmm," I said. *It's not okay. It's snooping.*

"They were somebody else's eggs, but she carried them herself so everybody would think they were hers. As if they could be at her age!"

I nodded. *He was telling me the truth.*

"That's why it kills me whenever I hear people say it's possible to get pregnant in your mid-forties. 'Look at Katie Winston!' people always say, and I say, 'Hello! Egg donor!' Katie Winston's eggs expired during the Clinton administration."

Joe's phone was attached to the charger in our room. I had nearly tripped over it on the way out. And he was in the gym.

No! Do not do it!

"Of course, who am I to talk? Everybody knows the twins were in vitro. But at least I had the decency to carry them!"

"I have to go to the bathroom," I said. "I'm just going to run up to the room."

"There's a bathroom down here!"

"I know, but I need to go up to the room. I'll be right back."

"Okay. Good, I'll call Shanie's therapist, then."

I pulled my jersey cover-up over my head, hastily pushed my feet into my flip-flops, and stumbled into the dark, cavernous hotel hallway, sun-blind and shaking. It was cool in the deserted corridor and I just stood there a moment, breathing in and out, heart racing. A long mirror ran along the wall opposite me, and when I glanced up at myself, I saw not the long-tressed beauty I had admired in our bathroom mirror just a few hours earlier, but an exhausted hag with near-jowls and dark circles under her eyes. The hair extensions seemed to actually age me in this shadowy light, and I was reminded of the "kitchen witches" sold in folksy New England shops in the 1980s with their dried-up, wrinkly apple heads and long, witch hair.

I'm just tired.

I had woken up the night before, actually in the very early morning hours, and had watched Joe sleeping and thought, *He's telling the truth. He's telling the truth.*

And yet . . .

The visit to the brownstone on a night I thought he was working. The sightings that were posted on Gawker. He had been seen making out at a bar with a blonde. Perhaps the reason he hadn't followed up with a suit against Gawker was because there were postings about him being in places he shouldn't have been, and he would be forced to prove he wasn't there.

It's easy to make up stuff and post it on those sites. Who would know that better than me?

She had said, "I love you, Joe." On his voice mail. Why would Susanna say that?

I brushed my hair away from my face and started down the long hallway to the gym. I pushed open the heavy glass door and discovered that the gym was the life of the hotel. While the pool area had been relatively empty, the gym was teeming with runners, elliptical climbers, ball squatters, and weight-machine crunchers. I scanned the robust, vigorously handsome crowd looking for Joe, and there he was, one of a long row of treadmill runners, neck and neck with the others. Joe wore headphones and was looking up at a bank of televisions—the electronic carrot that hung above all the runners, and toward which they all seemed to be pushing themselves, some sprinting madly, others slogging along at the end of a stationary marathon. I walked across the springy gym floor, and the relative quiet of the space seemed to belie the tremendous amount of human effort and energy that was being put forth. In another time and place, this amount of collective human sweat would be accompanied by the crack of a whip and the groan of oars or the resounding clang of metal upon stone. Here the only sounds were the quiet humming of the machines and the rhythmic breathing of Hollywood's glistening movers and shakers.

I padded over to Joe's treadmill, and when he saw me, he smiled and pulled off his headphones, still running, his shoulders rolling forward and back, his fists rising and falling.

"Hey," he said. His T-shirt was drenched.

"Hey," I said. "I have to go up to the room. Karen and I were going to order lunch in a little while. Do you want us to wait for you?"

Joe wiped his face with a towel that was draped around his neck and grimaced.

"I've . . . got . . . another ten minutes of cardio," he panted. "Then I want to steam."

"Okay . . ."

"Just order me a salad and . . . a banana."

"All rightie!"

I turned to leave and then looked back with a flirtatious smile. *Last night,* I thought, remembering, and I looked to see if he was remembering, too, turned to catch the old spaniel gaze, but he had his fingertips pressed to his jugular vein and his eye on his watch.

I unlocked the door to our room and saw that the housekeepers had already worked their magic. The carpet had rows of fresh vacuum-cleaner tracks, all the damp towels and dirty breakfast dishes were gone, and the gift baskets had been attractively arranged on the coffee table and bar. I had already pulled from the baskets the few items that I thought the kids would like—an iPod, some movie paraphernalia, lots of body products for Ruby—and I had meant to leave a note for the housekeepers telling them to help themselves to the rest.

The phone was on the floor where Joe had left it. He had plugged the charger into a wall outlet in the little entrance hall and left it there. It seemed like blasphemy the way he so carelessly left the phone lying there.

I picked it up and cradled it in my palm.

I would not listen to the messages, I had decided on my way up in the elevator. I would just have a peek at Joe's call log. I assured myself that the call log was basically public information. If I had come into the room and decided to use Joe's phone instead of my own—something I had done dozens of times—I might have just scanned down his call log to dial home. In fact, I was sure I had done exactly this many times. In fact, I *did* need to call the kids! I snapped open the phone and was greeted by a photo of Ruby and Sammy that Joe had stored as wallpaper. It was a close-up of the two of them, their cheeks pressed together, Sammy grinning a big cheesy grin and Ruby giving a funny little fake model smile. I slammed the phone shut and when I placed it back on the floor I felt exalted. Divine. It was what Goody Proctor would have done. It was a cold, conniving witch of a wife that spied on her husband, who had cast a wicked spell on the Internet. I wasn't that wretch anymore. I would call the kids on my own phone.

We had planned to go to the *Entertainment Weekly* party with the Metzgers that night, so Joe and I decided to drive to their house in Bel-Air and then ride with them to the party. There were a lot of paparazzi around the hotel, due to all the celebrities booked there for the awards show, and they caught us as we climbed into the tiny convertible roadster, my short skirt riding up on my thighs, my ridiculous long locks blowing wildly. A small crowd gathered around us and a woman pulled a beautiful silk scarf from around her neck and handed it to me. "Tie it around your hair," she said in some kind of elegant European accent. "I'm staying here at the hotel—you can just leave it at the front desk later." I tied the scarf around my head, and with my black sunglasses and all the makeup I had put on, I felt a little like Grace Kelly or Audrey Hepburn, so I gave the crowd a very dramatic wave. Joe also waved to the crowd. He put the car in gear, revved the engine, the crowd cheered . . . and then he popped the clutch and we stalled out violently, our upper bodies rocketing forward like a couple of test-drive dummies.

"*Ease* your foot off the clutch," I mumbled through my aching grin.

"I know, I know," Joe sputtered, starting the car again with a series of growling curses, and then we were off. The crowd cheered us on again, and as we pulled away from the curb, Joe reached for my hand and squeezed it tenderly. The afternoon sun cast a blaze of gold on the buildings around us, and we sailed down those gleaming, palm-lined avenues, Joe and me, smiling merrily, merrily, merrily. . . .

There was a red carpet and a long press line outside the *Entertainment Weekly* party. When we pulled up to the curb in the Metzgers' Town Car, we saw that a huge battalion of photographers had been stationed on one side of the roped-off red carpet, and on the other side were hordes of fans being carefully watched by large men wearing earpieces.

"You guys get out first," said Karen.

I was on the side of the car closest to the red carpet, which was unfortunate. It's better if the star gets out first. It always is.

The driver hopped out of his seat and opened my door. The fans pushed and shoved and craned their heads and cheered. The photographers cocked their cameras.

I placed one Jimmy Choo out on the sidewalk. Then the other.

The crowd roared with applause. Somebody yelled "Angelina!" and the whole street went berserk.

I stood up and turned toward the crowd. The screaming stopped and the clapping petered out like the sudden end to a much-needed summer rainstorm. The photographers lowered their cameras and resumed their conversations with one another, and then Joe stepped out of his side of the car and all hell broke loose. The crowd erupted in applause and cries of "Joe! Joey Ferraro!" rang out into the evening air.

The photographers were in full cry: "Joe, over here!" "Right here!" "Can you and the wife stand here?" "Here! Joe!" "Joey, over here!" "How about one alone, Joe?" "Without the wife!"

The first time I heard a photographer call Joe's name, I thought he must have been an old friend of his—perhaps somebody Joe knew from school. This was at the first L.A. film premier we ever attended. It was for *Siren Song,* the film Joe had done when we took the fateful bus ride across L.A. Joe only had a small part in the movie, but it turned out to be a breakthrough performance, with all the critics singling him out.

When the film came out, we were in L.A. again. Joe was working on his second mob film. He had a new agent by that time, a man named Scott Lendel, and we also had Ruby then, so Joe had told Scott that we wanted a car big enough to accommodate Ruby and her car seat. When we arrived in Los Angeles and were transported to the house that had been rented for us in Santa Monica, we were thrilled to find a gleaming black Lincoln Town Car parked in the driveway. When I told my dad that we were driving around L.A. in a Town Car, I think I heard him weep with joy for us. He drove a rusty pickup truck. Always had. We strapped Ruby's car seat into the back and we spent an entire weekend exploring Los Angeles in our luxurious chariot.

Soon after we arrived in L.A., we had dinner with the film's director, Jason Cummings, and his girlfriend the supermodel. They happened to arrive at the restaurant just as we did, and when we got out of the car to greet them, Jason burst out laughing. "That's too much," he said. "That's perfect."

We smiled stiffly. "What?" said Joe.

"The car," Jason said, and he laughed uproariously as he followed us into the restaurant.

We found that everyone we met in L.A. had one of two reactions to the car. Some, like Jason, would laugh conspiratorially as if they got the joke. Others would ask in all seriousness if we were driving my parents' car. One night we had dinner with Joe's agent, who, upon seeing the car, flew into a rage and started madly dialing numbers on his cell phone. "Don't worry," he said, "we'll sort this out."

We told Scott not to worry, that we loved the car. And then we drove it to the premier of *Siren Song.* When we pulled up to the red carpet that night, we were just following all the other Town Cars, not really cognizant of the fact that the passengers in the cars ahead of us were all being dropped off. When we arrived at the entrance, a uniformed man bent down and opened the door to the backseat of the car, which he found to be empty. He quickly recovered from the shock of seeing Joe and me in the front seat, all dressed up.

"What'd you do, rub out your driver?" he asked, laughing loudly. Then he directed us to a nearby parking lot. We parked the car and it was on the shameful walk back to the red carpet that a photographer stepped in front of us on the sidewalk and said, "Mind if I take a quick photo, Joe?" and started shooting away. We finally stepped onto the red carpet to flashes of lightbulbs and cries of "Joe! Joe!" from all directions.

"How do all these people know your name?" I asked. I still thought everyone knew him as "that guy."

This annoyed Joe. "I've told you again and again," he hissed, "I'm fucking famous, Julia!," which made me giggle, and Joe started laughing, too, at himself, at his *fucking famous* self, and we clasped hands and walked, blinking and dazzled, right into those blinding lights.

[seventeen]

It was on the red carpet in front of the *Entertainment Weekly* party that Joe's cover was blown. People wonder why actors are always hitting photographers. Here's why: As we walked along that red carpet, posing and smiling, a rogue photographer, somebody from the street who hadn't been allowed into the approved, cordoned-off press area, pushed himself into the crowd and yelled, "Joe, where's Jenna McIntyre tonight?"

Joe's head swiveled around and he glared at the photographer, who was rapidly snapping off shots. I saw Joe glance at me, saw him out of the corner of my eye, but I pretended I hadn't heard the guy. I just held Joe's hand and posed, waving gaily, blinking at all the flashing lights. They make your eyes tear after a while, those lights.

When we got inside, Alison was already there. She was with Richard, her husband, and Isaac Mizrahi, an old friend of hers from New York. We all sat at a table in a corner of the vast outdoor party space, and everybody gossiped about all the celebrities who walked by. I tried to join in the merriment but mostly I just sat there quietly.

I was thinking. I was calm. I realized that I had already known, that I had never believed Joe, really. We sat on one side of the table, on a bench covered with cushions, and several times I heard Joe's phone ringing in his jacket pocket. He didn't answer it. The third time it rang, he looked at the caller ID, then shut off the phone.

"Who was it?" I asked. Casually.

"Hmm?" Joe said. He was gazing off into the crowd. "Hey, isn't that Cloris Leachman over there?"

"Can I use your phone, honey?" I asked. So casually. I was squinting out at the crowd, acting as if I was trying to see Cloris Leachman. "I want to check on the kids."

"Sure," Joe said. He handed me the phone.

I touched the 1 key. Hers was the first message. And the second.

"Hi, baby. I miss you. Call me," was the first. The second said, *"When are you coming back? I just got a job in L.A. and might fly in on Tuesday! I know you said we shouldn't see each other for a while. I'm only going to be out there for a couple of days. . . ."*

"What's up? Nobody home?" Joe asked.

"No," I said, slamming shut his phone.

"C'mon. Let's get out of here," Joe said.

Outside, he put his hands into his pants pockets and his phone rang and made him jump.

"Maybe it's the driver," he said. "I just called him a minute ago to say we were on our way out."

"Well, answer it," I said.

Joe pretended he didn't hear me.

"Here's the driver," he said, and he opened the back door of the Town Car so that I could climb in.

I didn't sleep that night but Joe did, which is another of his pluses. He doesn't let anybody rain on his parade. You'd have thought he might feel a little guilty about the messages. Instead, he seemed almost jubilant on the ride home, and when we walked into the room, he leaned against the little bar in the living room and said, "C'mere."

I pretended I didn't hear him.

"Julia," he said, and then he stepped up behind me and pulled me close.

I turned and planted a brief kiss on his lips.

"Can you believe we're here?" he said, smiling. "Did you ever think, back when we were living in that dive in Alphabet City, that someday we'd be in a suite at the Four Seasons waiting to find out whether I would win a Golden Globe award?"

"No."

"Oh, thanks a lot," he laughed. He opened the mini-fridge and grabbed a beer. "You want anything, hon?" he asked.

"No thanks."

"So, you never thought I could do it?" he said, taking a swig off the beer.

"No, it's not that I doubted you'd succeed. . . . It's just that I don't remember this being the dream."

"It was mine, baby," Joe said, and he walked out onto the terrace and lit a cigarette. He leaned his back against the balcony rail and smiled at me. It was the old spaniel smile—and yet it wasn't. The old, heart-melting spaniel look had been replaced, over the years, by something more confident. More take-it-or-leave-it. His old expression said, *I can't bear to look at you for another second, I want you so badly,* and it was just for me. The new one was his "Yes, it's me" look. Joe shared it, generously, with everybody.

"My battery's dead. I want to see if Ruby or Catalina called," I said. "Can I use your phone?"

"Sure." He pulled it out of his jacket pocket and tossed it to me. Then he turned around and gazed across the city. I opened his phone and pressed the number 1.

Hours later as he slept, naked, curled up on his side, I marveled at the vulnerability of the human body. Devoid of fur, shell, claws, and quills, when our brains are at rest we are really as vulnerable as newborn babies. I was sitting on a chair next to the bed, smoking one of Joe's cigarettes, and I watched his eyebrows raise and lower and his lips quiver slightly in some kind of a dreamy soliloquy. Perhaps he was dreaming of his acceptance speech, or a scene he had been reading earlier for next week's show. Maybe he was having a conversation with a buddy or perhaps he was professing his love for Jenna. Maybe he loves her, I thought and watched, exhaling slowly, as Joe rolled from his side onto his back. His fingers were curled in toward his palms and his legs were splayed. I thought about a nature documentary that I had watched recently with Ruby, and how I learned that a wolf goes belly up when confronted by a more threatening member of the pack, exposing his throat, his soft belly, and his genitals to the menacing wolf. The narrator of the documentary commented on the effect this show of submission has on an aggressive wolf, who will sink his teeth into the throat of an upright, fangs-baring challenger, but will simply ignore the wolf who offers his gut, his balls, his soul. I stubbed out my cigarette and lit another. Joe sighed contentedly in his sleep. I watched him for some time. I sat in that chair, watching and smoking, until the silvery light of dawn crept over the City of Angels, under our drapes and into our suite, marking the dawn of Joe's big day. Then I pulled on a pair of jeans and a T-shirt and called down for the car.

I drove down La Cienega and took the 10 West toward the Pacific, my bare foot pushing the gas pedal to the floor at one point, just to see how fast I could really go on an almost deserted highway. I exited the freeway and drove west until I found the beach, and then I drove out onto the Santa Monica Pier and parked the car. Gulls dive-bombed the pier, snatching up stray french fries and pieces of hot-dog rolls, and as I walked along the splintery planks, I thought that it must be close to six in the morning. The sun was behind me, rising over the Malibu hills, and I walked down the stairs of the pier and onto the beach heading south. It was slow, heavy going in the deep sand, but when I got down below the tidemark, the footing was so delightfully firm and fast that I broke into a little jog. I followed the coastline, traveling just at the frothy hem of the surf, and when a rogue little wave suddenly wrapped itself around my knees, I found myself giggling helplessly. I remembered a game that Neil and I used to play in the surf and I made my way along the beach, running away from each wave and then following it as far back into the sea as I could without getting wet.

The early-morning crew was out, the beachcombing tractors making their way around me. Up on the wide-paved walkway there were garbage collectors and cops on bikes and fitness buffs getting in an early-morning run. I kept following the beach, in and out of the surf, past playgrounds and volleyball nets and homeless sleepers and dog walkers.

I walked and walked until I arrived at Venice Beach, and the sight of the boarded-up, surfer-inspired souvenir shops and tattoo parlors somehow eased this sense of doom that I had felt welling up inside me all night. I had seen these shops many times during the day, and the tattooed vendors and freaky locals and smell of marijuana and sounds of bongos and reggae music had all given it an authentically exotic air then, but now that the walkway was deserted, it seemed as if it had all been staged. As if nothing was real. I felt as if I was walking past an abandoned movie set. Even the hazy morning light seemed filtered and artificial and temporary.

I sat down on a bench. A woman wandered past me pulling a shopping cart that appeared to hold all her worldly possessions, and she stopped for a moment to search through its contents for something. She appeared to be in her sixties, and when she glanced up at me, I could see that her face had been cured to the color of an old paper bag, and was deeply creased and wrinkled from decades in the sun. The dark brown tones of her skin made her eyes appear to be an unnaturally pale shade of green. Her hair was caught up in a long braid, and while it was mostly gray now, there still remained a few yellowy blond streaks. She had the handsome bone structure of a Daughter of the Revolution, and I imagined her arriving here sometime in the 1960s from someplace like Boston or Greenwich and being absorbed into one long, wild night upon her arrival in California, only to find herself, one morning, living out of a cart. I wondered if her family missed her or whether she had children who spoke about her resignedly in crowded Al-Anon meetings. When I was a teenager, I sometimes tried to imagine that my mother wasn't really dead but that she had just run away. If she had, I could see her coming to a place like this and finding her tribe and never leaving.

I was tired. The bench was hard on my back and I decided to go rest on the sand for a few moments. I would just lie there for a little while and then drive back to the hotel to get dressed. I wasn't ready to make my morning call to the kids. It was Sunday, so I couldn't call Beth's lawyer to see about having separation papers drawn up. I had decided, while watching Joe sleep, that I would (a) let him live and (b) kick him out. But I decided to wait to tell him after the awards show. Maybe on the flight home. I had Googled Jenna McIntyre while he slept and learned that she was a young actress who had had small parts in a couple of television pilots, and a film here and there. Now I just wanted to rest. I stretched out on my side on the sand. My feet were cold and I grabbed a half-buried T-shirt that somebody had tossed on the beach. It was a large ripped yellow shirt with a faded portrait of Jimi Hendrix silk-screened on the front, and I wrapped it around my feet and placed my head back against the sand. The breeze was cool but I could feel the first rays of the morning sun on my face. The skin on my cheeks and forehead grew warm and then, gradually, hot and tight. I heard the sound of the waves slapping the shore. I heard the gentle chatter of a little girl playing on the sand nearby, and the lonely call of a gull. A plane droned overhead. The girl, the gull, the engine of the plane, and the foamy wash of the surf all began a staggered descent with me. I was falling asleep, leaving the waking world for just a little while, and the singsong voice of the little girl and the cry of the gull and the sound of the waves on the beach washed over me.

[eighteen]

The drone of airplane engines and the whisper of the distant surf were interrupted every few moments by the clear, earnest words spoken by a young man.

"Did you know that you have unlimited capabilities," he was saying, "and that your dreams and aspirations *can* be realized?"

There was a pause and I heard the clacking of skateboard wheels and the far-off pounding of some kind of drum-dominated world music. Then a girl's voice said, tentatively, "No?" as if she was afraid of getting the answer wrong.

"It's true. I'm only maybe one one-hundredth of the way to realizing all my capabilities, but the discoveries I've made so far about myself are fucking mind-blowing."

"Shit!" said the girl. "But what were you saying about a test? Do I have to take the test?"

"It's not like a test you take in school. It's a personality test. It's fun!"

"Oh. So it improves your personality?"

"The test itself won't improve it. But if you want to improve your personality, taking this test is the first step."

I sat up and blinked at the gawky, pimpled red-haired man—a boy, really—who stood over the teenaged girl sprawled out on the sand just a few feet away from me. *The girl is an easy mark,* I thought. It didn't take a Scientologist to see that her life could use a little changing. She was underweight and dirty. She looked like she had been "rode hard and put up wet," as my father had said once, much to Neil's and my great amusement, about a floozy in a bar.

"Where do I go?" she asked, and the boy kneeled down next to her and handed her a brochure.

The air smelled beautifully of the sea and of Coppertone, and every few moments the smoke from somebody's cigarette wafted past me in pungent, languid gusts. I just sat for a moment, blinking at the bright stillness of the sand all around me, and I breathed in the dissipating smoke, sucking it in through my parched nostrils. All that smoking last night had sparked up the old urge. My father is a smoker, so is Joe, and now the smell of tobacco filled me with a nostalgic sense of longing for men I have loved, and for my youth. The sun was high and I knew I shouldn't still be on the beach, but I sat there for another few minutes. Then I rose to my feet and kicked the soiled T-shirt onto the sand and began walking, sleepy and sluggish, back along the now-crowded beach to the Santa Monica Pier.

I arrived at the hotel almost an hour later, dizzy with hunger, and realized I had forgotten my key card. When I rang the doorbell to the room, I braced myself for Joe's enraged greeting. It was almost two o'clock and our car was picking us up at three-thirty. *He must be in a complete panic,* I thought, but when the door opened, it wasn't Joe but his agent, Scott Lendel, who greeted me.

"Hey! Julia!" he said exuberantly, and he pulled me into his arms for a rough hug. "It's the big day, huh? Where were you, at the pool?"

"Uh, no . . . Where's Joe?"

"He's in the shower, Julia," said a loud woman's voice. It was Joe's publicist, Laney, who was now pushing Scott aside to give me a hug. "Where have you been? Listen, I'm going to do the red carpet with you and Joe, hon. I've done the Golden Globes every year for the last ten years and it'll be a breeze."

"Okay."

I looked around the suite and saw that it was crowded with people: Joe's agent, business manager, publicist, network producer, and various wives and girlfriends. They were all dressed up already, and when I stepped into the room, they seemed to spontaneously form a sort of receiving line.

"Hi, Julia! Justin Fairlawn from NBC. You remember my wife, Helena? Just dropped by to wish you all luck!"

"Julia, so great to see you again. Love the hair! Love it!"

"I know Joe is going to win, Julia!"

"You must be so proud!"

Several room-service tables had been wheeled in, and a buffet of bagels, pastries, and salads had been set up and picked over.

"The groomers just got here," Laney said. "They were hoping to start on you, but since you weren't here, they're going to start on Joe first. Do you need to shower? You should jump in right after Joe."

I didn't have too many occasions where I had to interact with Laney, but I recalled now that all of her conversations were like this. More like monologues in which she rambled on and asked multiple questions and had no interest in the answers.

"I need coffee," I said, and Laney screamed, "Where's that girl that works for Joe? Kathleen! Julia needs a coffee!"

"Her name's Catherine," I said, wincing, as everybody in the room dove for the coffee table at once.

All the stares and smiles made me feel like a self-conscious bride, and I bit my lip and glanced at the closed bedroom door, and then down at the floor.

Laney clasped my wrist. "Uh, Julia, honey, you look a little burned."

"Yeah, I can feel it on my face," I said. "I fell asleep on the beach."

"You went to the beach? Today?"

"Yeah."

"Okay, well, you should have used a little sunscreen. Half of your face is really burned."

Somebody handed me a cup of watery-looking coffee, and I made my way through the crowd and into the bedroom, where I found Joe seated on the bed with a towel wrapped around his waist. Catherine was using a hand steamer on his tux and he was watching ESPN.

"Hey," he said, glancing up at me. Then something on the television screen caused him to cry out as if he had been stabbed.

"No! That's it!" he said. "I've had it with the fucking Knicks! Let's see some fucking defense, guys!"

"I'm gonna take a shower."

"Okay, hon. Where were you? Getting your nails done?"

"I went to the beach."

"No, no, no, NO!" Joe hollered at the television, leaping to his feet and almost losing his towel.

"Joe, do you know that there's a roomful of people out there?"

"Yeah."

"Oh," I said, and I went in to the bathroom to take my shower.

When I came out, Joe and Catherine had left the room and there was a petite "groomer" named Annette seated on our bed. She wore black jeans and her blond hair was pulled loosely back into a ponytail. "I'm doing your makeup," she said, standing up, and she studied my face carefully. She pointed to a stool that she had set up next to the window, and when I sat down, she pulled the heavy bedroom drapes open as far as they would go, allowing the midday sun into the dark room.

"Laney warned me about the burn. You're swelling up already," she said with a sympathetic pout. "Let's put something on that. . . ."

Annette applied creams and then a foundation to my face. I closed my eyes and felt the light, upward stroke of her delicate fingers against my tired, sun-ravaged skin, and I breathed deeply, relaxing for the first time since I left the beach.

"I shouldn't have taken the 10," she said, and I thought that I had never heard anyone speak with a voice so sweet and whimsical. "The local roads would have been the faster way." My eyes were shut tight. I heard the clean sound of a lid joining a porcelain jar. I had a sudden memory of my mother's nightly cold-cream ritual—her long fingers sweeping rapid white circles all over her face as she glanced at herself in the mirror, first from the outer corner of her left eye, then from the right. She smoothed the cream into her forehead and cheeks and down her throat before she plucked a tissue from a box next to the sink and wiped her face clean with quick swiping motions, her lips pursed, her eyes open wide. Sometimes, without taking her eyes off herself in the mirror, she managed to dip one of her fingers into the tub of cool, slippery cream and plop a dollop right onto the tip of my nose to my delighted squeals.

Did it happen once? Every night? Ever?

Once, when I was pregnant with Ruby, I opened a jar of cold cream in a Duane Reade. I had to smell it. I intended to buy it and start using it, but when I found that there was no smell, I slid it back onto the shelf next to the other cold-cream jars. I had thought there would be a fragrance, that I'd remember my mother clearly when I inhaled it, but there was nothing.

When I left Dr. James's office—was it just a week ago? It felt like years since I had slapped poor Sammy—he had shaken my hand as usual on my way out.

"I wish I could kiss you," I said, and then I had blushed and bit my lip, because I had really meant to say *hug.* Really. I meant to ask him for a hug.

He loosened his grip on my hand. "That's probably not a good idea," he said.

"I know, I know, it's not you I want. It's my father . . . blah, blah, blah."

"No, it's because it's me," he had said. Then: "Did it ever occur to you that you've created this idealized persona and assigned it to me?"

I squinted at him through my puffy eyes.

"And that these traits—honesty, reliability, genuine caring—might be what you're looking for in a partner and that you might find them someday, either in Joe or in somebody else?"

"I don't think genuine honesty will ever be one of Joe's pluses."

"People change. Act as if you believe he's capable of changing. He might surprise you."

Act as if. Two hundred dollars an hour and that's what I get.

I opened my eyes. Annette was removing compacts and brushes from a makeup box and I realized that I was starving. I hadn't eaten all day.

"Can I get up for a minute?" I asked.

"Sure!"

I walked to the door, but when I opened it, I saw all of Joe's people again. They were still there and Joe was with them now, in his tuxedo trousers and a wife beater, smoking a cigarette and taking a sip of coffee. Somebody had turned some music on, so I couldn't hear what Joe was saying, but I didn't need to. I could see by the glimmer in his eye and by his smirk that he was trying to be amusing, and he had a great audience—most of them were on commission and the laughs came easily, the adoration already bought and paid for. I returned to Annette's stool.

"How do you feel about eyelashes?" she said.

"Hmm," I said. I supposed that I liked eyelashes.

"I think we should do eyelashes. Definitely," she said, and I watched her remove a delicate curving wisp of black lashes from a case.

She smiled and slowly lowered her eyelids for me, then opened them. "Close," she said, and I closed my eyes, just as she had shown me. I felt the lovely tickle of lashes against my eyelid and I thought of butterfly kisses and the tender touch of my children.

"What the hell is all this grit in your hair? Is that . . . sand?"

My blowsy hairstylist's name was Lana. Annette was packing up her case and I had just nodded off for a moment.

"Yeah," I said, stretching my cramped legs out in front of my stool. "I fell asleep on the beach."

"You went all the way to the beach? This morning?"

I didn't answer. I just looked at my reflection—at the thick matte complexion, the smoky eyes with the heavy cow lashes, the bronzed cheeks and the glossed lips.

Who?

"It seems like the bonding agent on your extensions kind of melted and then hardened again with sand attached. It's like your head is covered with . . . spackle."

"Oh," I said. "Oops!" It was like I was drugged. I was almost giddy with exhaustion.

I dozed off once or twice while Lana chiseled away at my hair. At some point I dreamed that I was a Persian princess being attended by beautiful handmaids. Their faces were veiled with brilliantly colored scarves, and all I could see were their dark, almond-shaped eyes, heavily lashed. I lay on my back and they rubbed scented oils into my scalp, and instead of dressing me, they placed delicate silk panels across my body, one on top of the other. The silk swatches formed a paper-thin gown that accented my breasts and youthful, tanned skin and made my lower body look long and lean, but if I moved, the swatches would drift off to the side, revealing a lumpy, shaggy, wrinkled body underneath. I asked my handmaids to help me sew the panels together, but they couldn't understand me. They just continued laying the silk panels across my skin.

The phone rang. Lana answered it and said, "Just a minute, sweetie!" Then she handed me the phone. "It's a little one!"

"Sammy?" I said, my voice hoarse. I had to hold the phone away from my just hair-sprayed coif.

"Hi, Mommy!" he said, and I could see his sparkly face.

"Hi, baby," I said.

"Come home, Mommy," Sammy said.

"I will, baby. Tomorrow."

"Is Daddy coming home tomorrow?" he asked.

"No," I said. Almost cheerfully. "I love you, baby! Now can I speak with Ruby?"

I could hear Sammy drop the phone, and then, after a lot of calling back and forth between the two kids, I heard Ruby pick up.

"Hi, Rubes!"

"Hi, Mommy!" She missed me. She only called me Mommy when she really needed me.

"What're you up to?"

"We're watching the pre-preshow. I can't wait to see you and Daddy."

"I'll tell Daddy to say hello to you when he's on camera."

"No! Mom! Do *not*!"

"Okay." I laughed. "Let me speak with Catalina."

"I miss you, Mommy."

"I miss you, too, sweetness. See you tomorrow."

There was a pause, then some mumbling in Spanish and then Catalina said, "Hello, Julia!"

We spoke about Sammy and Ruby for a few moments and then Catalina said, "You sound tired, Julia."

"I am a little tired."

"Eat," she said.

"Okay."

"No, really. Eat, Julia. *Barriga llena . . .*

"Corazón contento," I finished with her. "I know. Thanks, Catalina."

"We'll be watching you and Joe!"

Annette and Lana had gone. Back in New York, I'd bought a

padded bra to wear with my strapless gown, but now, wandering aimlessly around our room in a pair of Spanx (it's a sort of . . . girdle) and heels, I couldn't find it anywhere. It wasn't in my bag or in any of our drawers or in with the dirty laundry. I could go braless, of course, but the dress had been fitted with me wearing that padded, strapless bra. Without it, it was possible that my deflated breasts wouldn't even keep my dress up. And those Spanx! I couldn't breathe. I pulled them off.

Laney stuck her head into the bedroom.

"Oh, sorry, hon. I thought you'd be dressed. The car's here!"

"Okay," I said, "I'll be ready in a minute."

She left.

Then I forgot what I was looking for, so when Joe walked in a minute later, I was just staring at the ceiling.

"Why aren't you dressed? We're supposed to be on our way there now," he said, and then I remembered and explained to him about the bra. He went into the closet and threw a few things around. Then he reemerged with the bra in his hand and I smiled gratefully up at him from where I lay across the foot of the bed.

"Julia, what're you doing?"

"I'm hungry," I said. "And I'm tired."

"Well, grab some candy out of the minibar. We're late. Here, put these on," Joe said.

He helped me put on the bra and then he started examining the Spanx.

"What the . . ."

"Give me those," I said. I peeled them on.

"Okay, for some reason, the sight of you in these . . . granny pants . . . now I've got a fuckin' hard-on. Shit," Joe said. Then he said, "Didja ever do it on the way to the Golden Globes?"

"Joe . . ."

"C'mon," he said, and started kissing me, and before I knew it, we were all sprawled out across the bed.

"Wait," I said. "I think we should stop." But I was getting a little turned on, too. What would it hurt? Once more for old times' sake?

"Hmm?" Joe whispered, kissing my neck. Then I thought about Jenna.

"You know what?" I said.

"What, baby?"

"I think I'm gonna stay here."

"When?" he murmured in my ear.

"Tonight. The awards. I don't feel like going."

Joe sat up. "WHAT?"

"Actually, I might see if I can get on the red-eye. I miss the kids. And I want to see my dad."

Joe stared at me. "You're joking, right?"

"No, I really don't want to go."

"Why?"

"Why do you think?" I said.

"Listen, Julia . . ."

I stood up and reached for the gown, which was draped across the bed. I wanted to be sure that it went back in the same condition it came in. I didn't want to have to pay for it. Then I wondered if the Vera Wang people would make me buy it since I had reneged on our agreement that I'd wear it on national TV.

"Julia . . . listen. Listen to me," Joe said.

I started to gather up the fabric.

"Look, I was going to tell you. I . . . just wanted to figure out how we could discuss this. We need to talk . . . about things. I haven't been as honest as I could have been and I hate myself for it. . . ."

I folded the silk panels into one another.

Joe whispered, "Please, Julia. Look at me."

After a moment I peered through my heavy lashes into those puppy-dog eyes. Ugh, he was tearing up. Crying is like yawning, easily faked by some but also hopelessly contagious, so I grabbed a tissue from the bedside table and dabbed like crazy. Any moisture on those lashes would be a disaster—I imagined a tar-black tsunami crashing down my cheeks and over the gown, false-eyelash flotsam everywhere. So in order not to cry, I thought of one of my favorite memories: a video we have of baby Ruby running down a hill in Ireland. It begins with her at the top, the tall grasses tickling her chubby thighs. She performs her adorable new wave for the camera, her fat hand flopping back and forth on the end of her wrist, and then she starts to gambol down the hill toward us.

"Careful, Ruby. Careful," is my off-camera warning, but on she comes, running now, and as she gains momentum with the steep decline of the hill and her little legs start to pump faster and faster, we realize that she's wide-eyed and panicked. She can't stop. The video becomes shaky and blurry here because Joe, who is working the camera, is panicking, too. "Whoa, slow down, Ruby, Jesus Christ . . . SLOW DOWN!" he says, but she has no choice but to ride those runaway legs all the way to the bottom of the hill, where she finally tumbles over, pausing for a moment to assess the damage, then bursting into tears.

She was fine, just scared. Now whenever we watch the video, Ruby laughs until she cries every time. We all do.

"You're the one I love. You're the first woman I ever really loved and you'll be the last, Julia. I swear. She was an extra. She was always hanging around the set. Always paying all this attention to me. One night we got drunk . . . it was after the wrap party . . ."

I didn't go to the wrap party at the end of last season. Those parties are like a company picnic—only fun for the employees, really. And Ruby had something going on that night, somebody's bat mitzvah, and I had wanted to stay home to help her get ready. Joe went alone. I forced myself to think again about Ruby running down that hill. It really is impossible not to laugh when you see that video, because in its brief course lie all the elements of a great drama. The expectant joy on her face as she begins her spirited descent, then the dawning realization that she doesn't yet have the skills necessary to control the situation. The moments of unbridled panic—little white shoes a bionic blur—Joe bellowing, me screaming, and then . . . it's over. The child is in one piece.

"Change is difficult but not impossible," Dr. James said to me once. It's probably what he would say to me now, if he were here.

"Don't be a crybaby," is what my father would have said.

"Where's Mom?" I imagined Ruby asking Catalina when they saw Joe on TV later, and I thought of Catalina crossing herself, imagining the worst.

"Okay, Joe," I said. "I'll go. Let's just go to the show. But let's not talk about the rest of it tonight."

"The rest of what?"

"The details."

"Details? What— Are you thinking of leaving? We have to talk about this, I want to explain. . . ."

"Explain, then."

"Julia. We need time. To talk. Stay tomorrow, let's talk in the morning. . . ."

"How much time does it take to tell the truth?" I asked. "It's quick. I'm the one who planted those gay rumors about you on the Internet! See? See how quick that is?"

Joe laughed nervously. "Right," he said. Then he said, "You just made that up, right?"

"Let's just go to the show so the kids don't think something happened. Then I'm taking the first flight to New York in the morning. I'm gonna pick up the kids and drive to Bedford. Today's my dad's birthday. I want to go see him."

There was a loud knock on the door. "It's getting really late, kids. You do *not* want to be walking down the red carpet behind Brad and Angelina!"

"Okay! Okay!" Joe shouted. Then he said, "Julia, let's not fuck everything up over this. . . ."

"I'm not talking to you about it now," I said quietly. "Should I put the dress on or not?"

"Yes," Joe said. Then he said, "Please tell me you were joking about the Internet thing. . . ."

"No. C'mon, let's go, it's late."

"Okay . . . so no, you won't tell me you were joking, or no you weren't joking?"

"Believe whatever you want," I said. "Let's go."

And so we went to the Golden Globes, Joe and me. We really were late, and the line of limos and Town Cars leading to the Beverly Hilton seemed to stretch for miles. We were in the backseat of the Town Car this time. We knew not to drive it to an event like this ourselves. We had a driver and a publicist sitting next to him, madly barking at some assistant on her BlackBerry. We had two kids, two cars, a Manhattan apartment, and a beach house in Amagansett. We had stocks and mutual funds, hard cash, liquid assets, and various trusts. We rode in silence. When we arrived at the Beverly Hilton, Joe was on the right side. He knew to get out first, and the crowd showed its appreciation with a triumphant roar. If you saw us on one of the preshows, you might have thought, *There's Joe Ferraro. That must be his wife. Look how she holds his arm so lovingly, how she gazes up at him. . . .*

Because I did hold on to Joe's arm that night on the red carpet. I actually clung to it during the long series of interviews, the California sun scorching into me, melting me beneath my borrowed finery. Cameras were flashing and people were nudging us from all directions. I feared that if I let go, I would lose him forever to the crowd and I would be forced to make my way back, upstream, through the pressing throngs to where our empty car awaited. I clutched his tuxedoed arm—the same strong arm that had held me so tight when we made love, that I had seized like a vise during childbirth, that had cradled our babies so tenderly, their plump bodies fitting perfectly into its crook. We followed Laney through the thick, antsy flock of celebrities, stepping over the long trains of flighty young starlets and bumping up against the gentle giants—great legends of television and film who smiled patiently and waited their turn to be interviewed. We stopped and smiled and posed for photographers and later, after Joe won, we had to go to the outdoor press area, where Joe posed again and again with his gleaming Golden Globe award held triumphantly above his head. Somebody asked us to kiss. For the cameras. And of course we did. Joe pulled me into his arms and we kissed giddily, and the cameras shot us just like that.

Joe and me kissing, the trophy pressed into my back.

The photo ended up in *People.* It looked like we were madly in love again, like we were starting anew.

"What's it like being married to Mitch Hollister?" a reporter called out to us.

I never know what to say in situations like that, so I mumbled, blushing and stammering like an idiot, "He's just . . . Joe to me . . . I guess."

"Yup, he's a Joe, all right," my dad would have said if he was there.

The next award recipient, a shaken and hysterical best actress, was led onto the platform and Joe's moment was over. We stepped out of the bright gaze of the hundreds of cameras and into the blackness of the night. I was still holding Joe's arm and he pulled me close, and we walked tentatively together like that, like two uncertain children, taking one little step and then the next.

"Watch it," Joe said, helping me lift the train of my dress. "Watch your step."

"Okay," I said, holding his arm tight. "Okay."

And we walked on like that a little longer. We were being careful. It was so dark. Phantom auras of flashing lights still swam before us, so we went along slowly, helping each other find the way, one step . . . and then the next . . . until our eyes grew accustomed to the dark.

Acknowledgments

Many thanks to Sally Kim, my gifted editor; to all the great people at Shaye Areheart Books; and to the smart Davids: Black and Larabelle at the David Black Literary Agency. Also to my friends Dani Shapiro and Heather King for their generous advice, wisdom, and support. Thank you to my beloved sister, Meg Seminara, and my sainted mother, Judy Howe, who read the book and said only nice things about it. Warmest thanks to another smart David, who suggested I write something, and finally, my deepest love and gratitude to Denis, Jack, and Devin for bearing with me while I did.

About the Author

Ann Leary was born in Syracuse, New York, in 1962. Her father's jobs and his natural wanderlust moved the family to various parts of Pennsylvania, Maryland, Michigan, and Wisconsin before they settled in Marblehead, Massachusetts, during her fourteenth year. Ann attended Bennington College from 1980 to 1982. In 1982 she transferred to Emerson College in Boston and there she met Denis Leary, a stand-up comic who was teaching a comedy writing class. She took his class and received one of the few *A*s in her academic career. At the end of the semester-long course, she agreed to go on a date with him. It ended up being a very late night, that date, and she invited him to stay in her studio apartment in Boston instead of trying to get back to his place in Cambridge, and he did stay that night—and every night after that for the next twenty-five years, and still they are together. They were married in 1989. In 1990 their son, Jack, was born prematurely during what was supposed to be a weekend-long stay in London and they remained in England for the next six months, as uninvited guests of Britain's national health care system. Ann's memoir about the experience, *An Innocent, a Broad* (William Morrow), was published in 2004. Jack is now eighteen and his sister, Devin, is sixteen. The Learys live on a small farm in Connecticut with their four dogs and four horses. When not writing books, Ann is a hockey mom who is involved in fund-raising for several local charities. She also trains and has competed in eventing, an equestrian sport, and has recently taken up tennis.